D1212396

The Secret Diary of Dr Watson:

Death at the Reichenbach Fall

The Secret Diary of Dr Watson:
Death at the Reichenbach Fall

ANITA JANDA

First published in Great Britain in 2001 by
Allison & Busby Limited
Suite 111, Bon Marche Centre
241-251 Ferndale Road
Brixton, London SW9 8BJ
http://www.allisonandbusby.ltd.uk

A catalogue record for this book is available from the British Library

ISBN 0 7490 0510 X

Printed and bound in Spain by
Liberdúplex, s. l. Barcelona

ANITA JANDA lives in New York City, where she earns her living writing about wireless software applications. She earned her PhD in linguistics with a grammatical analysis of the dance language of the honey bee.

To my sister, Joan Janda,
which should surprise no one

In compiling a book of this Sort, a great deal consists in the knack of not saying too much, nor by saying too little leaving any doubt as to the point, tho' in some cases the point is best gained by raising a doubt—Nor is it only in this Book that such is the case...

—CHARLES ALTAMONT DOYLE

1888

Chapter 1

As Sherlock Holmes remains the only one of our immediate acquaintance whose news cannot wait upon the pleasure of the post, so my first reaction upon perceiving the telegram on the sideboard was to wonder whether I would have time for breakfast. It was singularly cold for mid-October and I did not relish the thought of a long train or hansom ride without so much as a cup of coffee to fortify me. In the event, however, my anxiety (if anxiety is not too strong a word for it) proved unfounded.

The telegram was from a Miss Hermia Marie Cathcart, evidently prey to the fixed delusion that she was a patient of mine. There was a note of desperation there that I did not like to see in a request for help which I was bound to refuse.

> With the return of the cold weather, I find I am as great a prisoner of my diabetes as I was before your excellent course of etheric manipulations at Pondicherry Lodge this summer. I trust this summons does not find you unprepared, and that you and your associate will attend me with all speed. Do not fail me.
>
> HERMIA MARIE CATHCART

There followed her address, in a fairly select area of town, as I could not help noticing. The idea that I might have a patient at such an address and not recognize her name was patently absurd. Quite apart from this, I resented being confused with whatever medical charlatan had deluded her with "etheric manipulations" as a specific for diabetes, which requires the utmost care and attention if it is not to advance at a menacing pace. At the same time, I found the reference to Pondicherry Lodge disturbing

15

inasmuch as a residence of that name had figured promi-
nently in the adventure I had chronicled (chronicled, but
not alas, published) under the title 'The Sign of Four'—
the adventure that had brought me my Mary, née
Morstan. I have it on the best authority that 'The Sign of
Four' is not publishable.

I had just reached this stage in my cogitations when my
wife broke in upon my thoughts, inquiring as to what Mr
Holmes might have to say in his wire. The coincidence of
our reasoning was amusing and the rest of the meal
passed in a concerted effort to apply Holmes's methods
to our domestic puzzle. Eventually, we succeeded in
reducing the question to its simplest form: assuming, for
the moment, that I was the intended recipient of this message, what then was I meant to do? This at least was clear:
I was to rush to Miss Cathcart's side with my associate to
apply a course of etheric manipulations to mitigate the
effects of her diabetes. My associate? Of course, Sherlock
Holmes! Reading the telegram again, I was struck anew
by the sound of desperation, in particular the closing
words, "Do not fail me." Surely this was a message for
Holmes. We could not be mistaken.

Leaving my wife to arrange for the neighbouring Dr
Anstruther to handle such of my patients as might chance
to call in my absence, I hurried out into the thin sunshine,
stopping only long enough to gather up my bag of medical instruments. I believe I had some confused idea that
they might be needed to treat a diabetic. As I hailed a
hansom cab and rode to Baker Street, I had to confess
myself hard put to imagine what Miss Cathcart might
mean by etheric manipulations, particularly etheric
manipulations as supplied by a consulting detective.
Perhaps Holmes would be able to unravel that part of her
message, or her quaint reference to Pondicherry Lodge. I
could make nothing of it.

Happily, I found my friend at home, with no very

pressing occupation to hand and every interest in Miss Cathcart's case. He was in one of his lethargies, which as I well knew signified a dearth of intellectual stimulation. He read the telegram once, twice, and then welcomed this new mystery with open arms, springing to his feet to clap me on the back.

"Well done, Watson! At last, a case that presents some features of interest. I had begun to fear that there would be nothing left for me but long-lost lovers, errant wives, and suspicious employees. Indeed, I venture to say that this case will draw upon all our talents. But Watson, you aren't dressed properly."

I looked down at my plain dark trousers, black frock coat, and simple necktie, and compared myself to Holmes, still in his disreputable violet dressing gown with the dull gold lining. I maintained a dignified silence, but to no avail. In a twinkling, Holmes had replaced my sober necktie with a soft neckerchief of startling dimensions and even more startling pattern, and had handed me a walking stick shod with some copper-coloured metal worked in a cheap imitation of Egyptian hieroglyphics. "There, now you look less like an Army surgeon and more like an etheric manipulator. The medical bag is a nice touch, Watson, you may keep it." For all the world as if I were not entitled to my medical bag, had not in fact earned it over eight long years of study and practice!

Holmes drew a large and battered trunk out from under a great stack of newspaper clippings, as heedless of the clouds of dust that filled the air as he was oblivious to my sentiments. "I will be with you in a moment, Watson. Perhaps you would be good enough to flag down a cab?"

During the twenty minutes I spent cooling my heels in front of 221B, I had ample leisure to worry that I might encounter my former landlady, Mrs Hudson, or one of my patients. It is all very well for Holmes to engage in these dress-up affairs. When he is in costume, he is completely

17

transformed, whereas I am always John H. Watson, regardless of my dress. When Holmes finally emerged, hauling the trunk down the front steps, he was every inch the harried assistant of the etheric manipulator. My misgivings grew.

We excited some little attention trying to make the turn onto Park Lane and between that and the inevitable difficulties attached to managing an unwieldy trunk, we arrived at Miss Cathcart's residence without my having any very clear idea of the part I was to play. There was no help for it, I would have to be myself and trust to my costume for the rest. I comforted myself with the thought that the scarf and walking stick had made a considerable impression so far—I had had the devil of a time first in inducing a cab to stop for me in Baker Street and then in persuading the driver I was not a flat, to be cheated over the fare. Clearly, it was to be a day of new experiences, I thought as I mounted the steps. I hoped the new experiences would not include that of being sent round to use the tradesmen's entrance. It was an exceptionally beautiful townhouse.

I reached the head of the stairs and watched the door swing open on its well-oiled hinges, revealing that we were expected by the servants as well as their mistress. I announced myself to the half-hidden manservant as Dr John H. Watson, surrendered my card with a rather theatrical flourish (I have my moments), and resolved then and there to let Holmes struggle with the trunk unaided, as befitted my hard-working assistant. For some reason, that decision gave me the confidence I needed to go on. I began to enjoy myself.

The manservant, like many another servant in this well-to-do area, was more than a little inclined to corpulence, so that it was a stately procession that passed along the corridors with measured tread to the sick-room. Holmes had no difficulty matching our pace with his trunk.

"Dr, ah, Watson, Ma'am," the servant wheezed.

"Miss Cathcart," I greeted her, remembering just in time that we were supposed to be acquainted. I gave her my most judicious medical nod. "You remember my assistant, Holmes? Of course. Now if your maid will be so good as to draw the curtains against the magnetic influences, we may begin."

I had no idea what magnetic influences might be lurking beyond the windows, but I thought it as well to secure our consultation against onlookers and spies. I was gratified to see Holmes dart me a glance of approval.

As the maid moved to do my bidding, Holmes proceeded to open the battered trunk, unpacking vast quantities of perfectly ordinary chemical equipment, such as had frequently rendered our rooms at Baker Street full of noxious fumes. I had no doubt that we would be able to create "etheric manipulations" of magnificent proportions at the appropriate moment. Meanwhile, I occupied myself with the usual medical preliminaries of taking her pulse, asking irrelevant questions, nodding thoughtfully at regular intervals, and generally commanding the entire operation with a few well-chosen words ("My dear Holmes, NOT the mantelpiece!"). Miss Cathcart harassed the maid, responded to my queries, and kept a sharp eye on the machinations of my clumsy assistant.

Afterwards, Holmes and I were to agree that her most striking feature was her remarkable composure, her sheer presence of mind. At the time, however, the word that sprang most forcibly to mind was not composure, but arrogance. From first to last, it was clear that the Hermia Marie Cathcart who had sent that telegram did not normally condescend to apply for help from strangers. The mixture of gratitude and resentment that greeted us on our arrival was absolutely unique in my experience. Propped up by an enormous mass of hard little cushions and fringed pillows, she reclined on the low divan with much the same attitude Nero must have displayed to Rome on the occasion of the great conflagration.

I must confess that this, my first glimpse of our client, came as a great relief to me; it would be difficult to imagine anything less like a diabetic *in extremis*. Whatever else Miss Cathcart might require of her etheric manipulators, it would not be a diabetic cure. My worst fears were over. I felt justified, finally, in lending myself and my reputation to this medical charade. I am afraid that Sherlock Holmes does not always appreciate what he is asking of me, a physician.

Although well past the first flush of youth, Miss Cathcart remained an extremely handsome woman. Her eyes were a clear blue that time could not dull, her habit neat and stylish, her voice an unusually pleasant contralto. Since I had no need of her answers, my questions being by way of a distraction, I was free to enjoy the sound and ignore the fury. Her maid, however, had all my sympathy, especially when we were treated to a detailed description of the right way and the wrong way to draw the curtains in the Yellow Salon.

Under Miss Cathcart's supervision, the drawing of the single remaining curtain took all of ten minutes—and most of my patience. Now that I knew I would not have a desperate diabetic on my hands, I was all curiosity. What could have precipitated this morning's tortured telegram, this afternoon's strange charade? Watching my assistant shrink behind his trunk, to all intents and purposes taking today's curtain-drawing lesson very much to heart, I was struck again by his artistry. In his natural state, my friend Holmes is no shrinking violet.

At last the parlourmaid was graciously permitted to withdraw (in tears, poor girl), leaving her mistress in possession of the field, a temporary state given Holmes's presence, I felt sure. And so it proved. The maid wasn't gone from the room for fifteen seconds before Holmes was on his feet, striding neatly across the rich figured carpet, listening at the keyhole, checking the corridor and in one liquid movement, edging that ubiquitous trunk against the complications of an untimely interruption. I don't know how he does it, but when he turned to face us, Holmes the consulting detective was some six inches taller than Holmes the etheric manipulator's assistant.

He introduced himself, "Sherlock Holmes, at your service, Ma'am," and added, "You have already met Dr Watson."

I was not amused. What was more to the point, his prospective client was not impressed. To put it as charitably as possible, Holmes's pronouncement did not appear to afford Miss Cathcart as much satisfaction as he had anticipated.

"Indeed, Mr Holmes. You seem very young for the present case," she snapped. "Just how old are you?"

"Young enough," he answered evenly, "but not, I think, inexperienced. What reason do you have for suspecting your maid of complicity in this unsavoury business?"

This conversational gambit effectively silenced Miss Cathcart, who found herself unexpectedly on the defensive. Holmes often has that effect on people. This time, however, it did not serve as well as it usually does. Miss Cathcart was made of sterner stuff than most and as she rose gracefully to her feet, her reply was brusque to the point of rudeness.

"My maid, incompetent as she is, is not to the purpose. I did not seek your help in this roundabout way," here she eyed my scarf with marked distaste, "in response to a domestic quandary, Mr Holmes, but because there is a life in danger."

I must have made some sort of move to protect her, for she halted me with an abrupt gesture. "No, not my life," she said, "but a life nonetheless, presumably of some value to its owner. At least we must assume so for the present."

She crossed the room and looked Holmes full in the face. "Mr Holmes, I demand to know how many times you have been approached by a client seeking protection that you later found yourself unable to provide. It is a reasonable question, surely?"

"So, it was not just the maid, but that window as well," Holmes mused in his irritating way.

I had no idea what he was talking about, although it was clear from her reaction that Miss Cathcart did. It was an interesting conversation, taking it all in all, with distinct similarities to lawn tennis. She returned his serve with a crushing backhand.

"I have no particular desire to see you solve the puzzle if you once manage to forfeit its human pledge. As the years go by, I find myself less and less in sympathy with the medical point of view that can label a surgical procedure a success when it takes a sick patient and makes a cadaver of him. So, Mr Holmes, I ask you again, how many of those under your protection have died?"

The medical allusion restored Holmes's good humour, as no doubt she knew it would. As for me, I was past wondering whether she had taken me in dislike or was just naturally disagreeable. I looked forward to Holmes's rejoinder, but resolved not to enter the fray. She was his client after all, not mine. The saving grace of the entire experience was of course the pleasure of seeing that today held some new experiences for Holmes as well as myself. He would not have it all his own way today; that much seemed clear. I cannot recall anyone else who displayed quite this much tenacity or who interviewed him in quite this way. His capitulation came as a complete surprise to me.

"Four," he said.

"Four?" she repeated. She seemed to be as confused as I was.

"Yes, four. Four clients who sought protection I was

unable to supply. One you already know about, Watson: Mr John Openshaw of the five orange pips, whose story you have chronicled as, let me see, 'The Five Orange Pips.' Yes. He waited two full days before consulting me and was struck down before he could act on my advice—sound advice, I might add. Then there was the case of the false mutiny; remind me to tell you about that one someday, Watson, it presents some features that might interest your readers. I haven't thought of the case for years. Finally, there were the two Vandek brothers. Had their English (or my Dutch) been better, they might be alive today.

"That was an unfortunate case, Ma'am. Indeed, they were all four unfortunate, but I hardly think that yours can be a parallel case. Not a military mutiny, no, nor a language barrier. Not even an unnecessary delay. You clearly are a lady who acts with some dispatch. I should be surprised to find that your problem had been known to you for more than a few hours before you had devised your telegram..."

I had rarely heard Holmes more persuasive. Or more loquacious. I began to think this case would prove to be something quite out of the ordinary, even measured against the usual extraordinary demands on Holmes's time. I was much moved. Miss Cathcart was not.

"You flatter me, Mr Holmes," she interrupted. "I lay awake far into the night before I hit upon that ruse. The telegram then could not go out until the morning. And what do I find? A delay on your part of almost two hours. And Dr Watson here, telling all and sundry that his assistant's name is 'Holmes.' After all my work to bring you here anonymously! I could scarcely believe my ears when he made my maid a present of your name. Is it any wonder I tried to give her something else to think about?"

Holmes is nothing if not fair. He let me apologize profusely for what felt like hours before he put an end to the interchange with a few well-chosen words.

"Miss Cathcart, we are wasting valuable time. Watson has apologized for his momentary lapse of attention; it is enough. You ask me for a list of my failures and I oblige you. We can do no more." His voice was riveting in its softness, mesmerizing in its intensity. "You complain of a two hour delay on our part. I tell you, you are fortunate that your telegram did not arrive when I was from home or committed to some other, even more pressing investigation. It is past time for you to tell us why we are here. What happened yesterday to stimulate your powers of invention to the heights of that telegram? What lies concealed on that window ledge? And what does your maid have to do with it?"

He might have elaborated on this general theme for some time had Miss Cathcart not abruptly turned away, admitting defeat with a graceful wave of her hand as she disposed herself on a nearby loveseat. I was glad to see it, not least because I had been on my feet all morning. I seized my opportunity and selected a substantial-looking armchair placed well back in the shadows. Holmes checked the corridor once more, propped his lean form against the door, and in his own inimitable fashion, indicated that the subject was officially open for discussion.

"Very well, Mr Holmes, we will do this your way. I owe you that much for your performance this afternoon. When you have seen and heard the whole, perhaps you will be good enough to tell me what you make of it. I warn you, there is very little for you to go on."

This was apparently supposed to be my cue, but I make no apology for having missed it. The role of the participant/observer is a difficult one at the best of times and Holmes himself would not have called these the best of times.

"Perhaps, Watson, you would be good enough to retrieve the evidence. The third window, I think."

Remembering the general import of the lecture on the

right way to draw the curtains in the Yellow Salon, I managed the first part of the business without exciting undue comment and after a brief struggle with the sash, retrieved a small and rather sooty parcel, which very nearly came undone in my hands. I observed that the twine securing the brown wrapping paper had been cut and felt sure that this would prove to be of major significance. I deposited the whole on top of the trunk, this being the only horizontal surface in the room that was not festooned with family portraits, bits of needlework or chemical apparatus.

As always, Holmes's inspection was minute. The tarred twine, the knot in the tarred twine, the quality of the wrapping paper, the blurring of the Belfast postmark, the peculiarities of the handwriting, the smudgy thumb marks in one corner, the pigeon droppings in the other, all received his careful attention. I listened to his discourse with half an ear, secure in the knowledge that he would be only too glad to explain to me later just which aspects of the packaging or the clumsy uneducated script decorating it had enabled him to deduce the writer's sex, occupation, probable height, and habit of smoking cigarillos. I had no patience for this exercise today, being fully occupied trying to place the slight but sickly odor of it, a scent that took me back to my military days in Afghanistan in the most extraordinary way. Not a spice, no, the odor was both more and less than that. More immediate and less pungent perhaps. Or more obtrusive and less foreign.

So it was that Sherlock Holmes opened a half-pound honeydew tobacco box made of yellow cardboard to reveal two severed ears nestled in a quantity of salt without surprising anyone but himself.

Chapter 2

What to say? What to write? It is difficult to decide how to continue a task you had no great wish to begin.

Mary smiles at me over her mending. Her little stratagem has worked: John is writing again. She was so wise to give me this journal, "Bound in real morocco leather, John!" (as though that could make a difference), so wise to refuse to hear a word about the day's adventure with Holmes.

"You have your diary now, John. Please to write it down! I am sure you have a great deal to say about your Miss Cartwright,"—Mary has no head for names—"but you must not say it at the expense of your readers. I married a Writer," she concluded, with a kiss on my brow.

I have been at this journal for over a week now and she has yet to read a word of it. Marriage is a complicated business.

* * *

"Perhaps, Mr Holmes, you would be kind enough to tell me what you make of my cardboard box?"

No tremor in her voice, no hesitation over her words. Then as now I find myself fairly overwhelmed by Miss Cathcart. When she said, "I warn you, Mr Holmes, there is very little for you to go on," something almost everyone said to Holmes eventually (or why should they have gone to the trouble and expense of consulting him in the first place?), she said it with such an air.

"The box, Mr Holmes?"

"I had not forgotten it," he assured her. "Or its contents. You called on me because you knew of my monograph, 'A Practical Typology of the Human Ear'?"

"Certainly not. I called on you because I did not like to

trust what I am persuaded is a delicate matter to the tactless incompetence of Scotland Yard. My conscience would not permit me to ignore the incident as I should have preferred to do."

The thought of a woman with sufficient aplomb to be able to ignore the receipt of such a parcel was alarming at best. There was an awkward silence. Perhaps I should say that there was a silence which felt exceedingly awkward to me, for I am bound to admit, neither Holmes nor Miss Cathcart appeared to notice it. At last I could stand it no longer. I hurled myself into the breach, saying the first thing that came into my head.

"A medical student, do you think, Holmes? Some sort of prank? The Ripper has gotten an extraordinary amount of publicity with his threats to clip the lady's ears and send them to the police."

It was the right thing to say.

"I think not, Watson. You cannot have been listening to my description of the man who addressed this package: a probable seaman, left-handed and semi-literate or clever enough to pretend to be so. I see no sign of the dissecting room. No special surgical skill or knowledge of anatomy was required to make *these* incisions."

I winced at this off-hand reference to the Ripper's dexterity in disembowelling his victims, and his client winced with me. I knew, of course, that Holmes disagreed with the official view of the Ripper's surgical expertise (as I do myself), but I hoped he would not feel obliged to go into it here. No one was suggesting that this crime had been perpetrated by a physician, and that was good enough for me. It is as much as a medical man's life is worth to be caught at dusk in Whitechapel now, carrying a black bag. I hear they nearly lynched poor Hartrey last week and Hartrey has been a fixture in the East End for years.

Holmes was oblivious to our discomfort, intent on his analysis. "Any moderately sharp knife would do. A herring

27

knife, for example. The specimens are relatively fresh and have not been treated with an embalming or preserving fluid. They are most assuredly not 'a lady's ears,' Watson. The larger one is almost certainly a man's, possibly belonging originally to another (or the same) seaman. The earring suggests the sea. They have not been sent to the police or to any official or quasi-official body. Finally, I do not suppose Miss Cathcart to be acquainted with very many medical students." He turned to his client. "You are not, I think, in the habit of renting rooms to medical students? I thought not."

I didn't think she was in the habit of receiving parcels from illiterate sailors, either, but I kept the observation to myself. If Holmes has told me once he's told me a thousand times that once you have eliminated the impossible, whatever remains, however improbable, must be the truth. I did not need to hear it again. In my experience, the impossible, like beauty, is commonly in the eye of the beholder.

"The Ripper himself, then, Holmes?"

I spoke idly, but it was no idle matter to Miss Cathcart. She leaned forward in her seat, her hands clasped convulsively. This must have been her fear from the beginning. It only remained for Holmes to pronounce upon the foundation of that fear in reality. It did not take long.

"Unlikely, Watson, and for much the same reasons as ruled out the possibility of a prank by a medical student. There is also the matter of the earrings. No Whitechapel drab," he caught himself just in time, I think, from saying something worse, "can afford jewellery of any description. They sell themselves, as you know, for the price of a doss or a tumbler of gin. There are no earrings even of this paltry quality in Whitechapel."

He paused thoughtfully and then, removing each earring in turn, examined it with his glass. First the earring, then the lobe. The other earring, the other lobe. The sight appeared to afford him gratification.

"Some dust, yes. Not conclusive, but suggestive certainly.

And the ears themselves, not newly pierced. The wounds are thoroughly healed. Yes, well, it is of course impossible to be sure, but all of the available evidence supports the hypothesis that the earrings were worn by the victims in life and not supplied afterwards by their assailant for artistic reasons of his own. Greater wear on the post of the earring worn by the lady than that of her weatherbeaten counterpart, contrary to what one would expect had the idea of the ornament been original with him and copied by her. I surprise you, Watson? You are easily surprised. The criminal mind is as inventive as our own; I have often observed it. Indeed, when Scotland Yard handles a matter, it is frequently the case that the criminal mind is significantly more inventive than our own. Well, well, enough of that."

Holmes brought the full force of his attention to bear on his client. More precisely, as he would say himself, he brought the full force of his attention to bear on his client's left ear. Absently, he patted his pockets. Absently, I stepped in front of the little table where he had laid his calipers. (The spectacle of Holmes bearing down on Miss Cathcart in order to measure a characteristic feature of her shell-like ears was one I knew instinctively I was prepared to forego.) "My calipers, Watson."

I passed them to him.

At no point had he taken his eyes off her ear. It was another, superior demonstration of the right way to draw the curtains in the Yellow Salon. Miss Cathcart was flushed to the roots of her hair by the time he turned to me across the cardboard box and said in a low voice, "You might ask yourself, Watson, under what circumstances a man other than the Ripper might elect to 'do a Whitechapel,' that is, to treat a man and a woman in the advertised Whitechapel manner, at least to the extent that we see here. If a-whoring she will go…"

Humming under his breath, Holmes pocketed his calipers, eliminated the larger ear from consideration and fell to a detailed analysis of the feminine specimen. "The conformation of the cartilage, Type E, yes. The most common type, Watson." (I should have thought Type A would be the most common type.) "Overall shape, the common oval; nothing distinctive there. No evidence of the subject's hair colour. Pinna neither unduly long nor unduly short. No tell-tale fatty deposits, no bumpy ridge, no pockmarks, no freckles. In short, all heritable characteristics in their least distinctive, most prevalent Anglo-Saxon form. The genetic patterning is not clear. The other specimen is Type B Prime: unusual without being remarkable."

My disappointment echoed his own and I found myself silently vowing to make it up to him in the published version, a spectacular piece of illogic I am very glad I shall never have to explain to him. To be sure, I had hoped that my inclusion in the day's adventure, secured as it was by the client's own telegram to Holmes's biographer, might have signified more than this passion for secrecy that thwarts me at every turn. I had hoped it at home when I first discovered it to be a message for Holmes, and I had hoped it again in Baker Street when I found myself decked out as an Egyptian horse doctor, the worst kind of medicine monger. Then we went to Kensington. And what did we find waiting for us in Kensington? Two ears neatly severed from their owners' faces, no sign of Scotland Yard, and Hermia Marie Cathcart. It is getting so that every times Holmes says to me, "Come, Watson, this sounds promising, there may be something in it or there may be nothing at all," my heart quails within me. So often, there is nothing at all, at least for me.

Still, in spite of that, there I was, awash in righteous indignation over the injustice of a world that could give Holmes an ordinary Type E ear after he had contributed not one but two scientific articles that I know of to *The Journal of Scientific Anthropology* on the neglected topic of the taxonomic classification of the human ear. France has her Bertillon and he has his measurements, but we have our Holmes and he has his ears, and who can say which will ultimately be of greater service to the science of detection? Holmes should have every advantage his biographer could give him, I vowed. He should have an ear that resembled Queen Victoria's if he wanted one.

Why he should have wanted an ear that resembled Queen Victoria's is more than I can say. I must have been more impressed with our client than I knew. It was, of course, an unpardonable liberty for me to have stared at Miss Cathcart like that. More than an unpardonable liberty, however, it was a mistake.

"You have not asked me why I sent for you, Doctor."

"I assumed you had sent for Holmes," I babbled.

"I sent for you because I wished to know what if anything can be medically established about the two victims."

"You mean…"

"I mean," she snapped, "are they alive or are they dead?"

This could not be happening to me, I thought, as I turned the two ears over and pretended to examine the backs. In the stress of the moment, I could not imagine how one might determine from a severed ear when the heart last beat its bloody tattoo. The ear is such a minor appendage. A leg, yes, a leg or an arm will testify to the victim's state by the degree of contraction in the musculature, although even then I had known exceptions. If death was due to exposure and the subject was in a state of muscular degeneration, even a leg might not… but an ear?

Holmes had his back to me and was serenely unconcerned, deep in the contemplation of some family photographs in heavy silver frames. I know how interested Holmes is in things of that nature: not at all interested. If he has as much as a single photograph of his own family, I have not seen it. This was a fine time for him to discover an interest in photography.

"Yes, Dr Watson?" she purred.

It was impossible to determine from the set of Holmes's

shoulders what he would wish me to say. With great presence of mind, I resisted the impulse to announce that I should know more after I had examined the specimens in my laboratory. We had brought an entire trunkful of laboratory equipment with us when we arrived and it was everywhere I looked: on the mantelpiece, along the far wall, among the photographs Holmes found so absorbing, beside the vase, below the portrait, against the bookcase. Everywhere. I had only to decide whether it was likelier for two maimed people to languish *in durance vile* in England, for, say, three days, or two bodies to remain undiscovered for the same length of time. Which?

Holmes abhors guesswork. "The answer she is looking for, Watson, is that at the time these trophies were taken, one of the victims was alive and one was dead. Is that not so, Miss Cathcart? Where is she? Come, come, I have no time for games. What is her name—Harriet, Helen, Heloise, Henrietta, Hilary, Hope, Hortense?"

He reeled off half a dozen names. If pressed for a list of women's names beginning with the letter "H," I might have thought of three. And they wouldn't have been in alphabetical order, either.

"Your sister, of course. Half-sister, then. The Miss H. Cathcart that this parcel was meant for. Is she here? Upstairs, perhaps?"

His stroll through the Cathcart family photographs had told him everything he needed to know. Afterwards, as we made our way back to Baker Street, he told me candidly that he was doing ear research at the time.

"You know, Watson, that I am ever on the alert for data that will confirm or disprove one of my theories. A well-photographed family with Type E ears offered a rare opportunity for me to study the systematic genetic suppression of the idiosyncratic, an aspect of the problem I had hitherto ignored. It is very odd, Watson. The ear must be one of the least well-documented features of the human face. Do you know, nine times out of ten I found the sitter staring straight into the camera? I was about to give it up in disgust when I came across a wedding photograph, circa 1880, where the husband had been so distracted by the charms of his young bride as to appear very nearly in profile. It was a textbook example of a Type B Prime ear, attached, as I had predicted, to a sailor. Once I stopped focusing on the family ears and looked instead at the family, it was perfectly obvious what had happened."

That Holmes was able to identify the victims from their wedding photograph is remarkable, yes, but that his mind could leap from there to the "Miss H. Cathcart" scrawled on the packet to the awful truth, as I know it did, that is uncanny. A man's wife maimed at his hands, he dead and mutilated in his turn, and the evidence sent to the widow under her maiden name as a tactful way of informing her of her sudden return to the single state. It is incredible. Holmes must be the only man on earth who could find this particular scenario "perfectly obvious."

Her miserable brute of a husband was to be expunged from her memory. Life was to go on as though he had never been. She was to be Miss H. Cathcart again.

I find myself shuddering as I write this. *He had loved her.* I had seen it in their wedding photograph, the one Holmes thought of as a beautiful example of a Type B Prime ear.

"*Lex talionis*, Watson: an eye for an eye and a tooth for a tooth. Or, in this case, an ear for an ear." I know what *lex talionis* means. And to my mind, it doesn't include slicing the ear off the man you've killed, in order to send it to his widow.

We left Kensington on a tide of goodwill, Holmes well pleased with the results of his exertions (and his fee), Lestrade loud in his assurances that he would keep Holmes apprised of the progress of his investigation. I felt exhausted, drained in mind and body. Unlike Holmes, I had not been paid for my professional services. Our hansom slowed to a walk; the press of traffic was severe. We were still some distance from Oxford Street.

"Is there any aspect of the case that is still unclear to you, Watson?"

I roused myself with an effort. "I don't think—no, you are right, I do have a question for you. How in the name of all that's wonderful did you know that she was alive and he was dead? I examined those ears myself and they said nothing to me about the condition of their former owners. There's not a pathologist in the City who could have done what you did. It was the first solid link in the chain. How did you do it?"

He sighed. "It wasn't wonderful at all, Watson. It was common sense. The client tells us that there is a life in danger—one life. Ergo, she knows the fate of the other victim. I knew no more than you did, Watson, what that fate might be, but he (or she, Watson, or she!) was bound to be alive or dead, one or the other. The only safe response then to a question regarding the victims' combined fates was that they were different: one was alive and one was dead. Had we made any other response to that very inconvenient question, we should have run the risk of being shown the door. It was a risk I did not care to take. The case interested me; I might even say it intrigued me. Grasping the conversational nettle with both hands was enough to render it harmless. Once I realized that the essential feature of the case was the form of address employed on the wrapping paper that had secured the cardboard box, I realized that the judicious response would in all likelihood turn out to be the literal truth."

I left him at the corner of Oxford and the Edgware Road and made my way slowly home. Let him unpack his trunk himself, he could have replaced every last piece of equipment twice over with what he charged her.

It was good to leave the hansom behind, to feel the pavement beneath my feet, to breathe the somewhat fresher air of the open street. It was turning colder, I noticed. There would be frost by morning. Mary would be waiting to hear about the day's events, everything that had happened since our breakfast was interrupted by the telegraphic appeal of an unknown diabetic familiar with Pondicherry Lodge. I don't suppose Miss Cathcart realized that in sending that wire she was exchanging the "tactless incompetence of Scotland Yard" for the equally tactless competence of Sherlock Holmes, but she knows it now. And Lestrade is on the case. I was grinning as I rounded the corner and waved my Egyptian walking stick at my wife. Who did not recognize me.

"Oh, John! Don't tell me you have been walking the streets like that, John! Have you met any of your patients? Our friends? Think, John! Oh, it is too bad of Mr Holmes!"

Chapter 3

Mary is beating the carpets and I am bid to keep writing, quite as though there were some point to this activity, which she assures me there is not.

"I can't read your journal, John!" She was horrified at the prospect. "No, not even at your express invitation. Not though you should *command* me, John. I couldn't. This is your diary, John, your private narrative journal. Don't you understand? There are only two rules for keeping a journal: the entries must be dated and they must be safe from prying eyes—from my eyes, John. How would it be if after going to all this trouble to give you back the writing habit I were to interpose myself between you and the printed page, a self-appointed editor? You don't need my approval, John. You never did. There are no wrong ways to keep a diary."

* * *

I wish she had seen fit to tell me that when she gave me the blessed thing! Forbidden to speak of Holmes, my new diary thrust into my hands on every conceivable occasion, I have been laboring over this account of the Cathcart case for over a week. There are only two rules for keeping a diary and so far, I have broken them both. What can I possibly do for an encore?

Very well. If there are no wrong ways to keep a diary, then there is no reason for me to date my entries. I think in chapters, not the ordinary verse of everyday life. The calendar has no place here. "Once upon a time in Paddington" will do nicely, thank you. All great writing is timeless, anyway.

Mary's other ruling has more weight. Apparently, I am to be encouraged to pursue the narrative activity by being relieved of the possibility of having any audience whatsoever for my narrative product. She will not read my journal and there's an end to it. You can tell she used to be a governess.

Had I known that I was writing up the Cathcart case for my own amusement, I could have finished it in a matter of minutes. "HERMIA MARIE CATHCART: two ears, one box, tarred twine, one knot, sturdy wrapping paper disfigured by a heavy-handed scrawl and a Belfast postmark, plus an 1882 wedding photograph." Oh yes, and Inspector Lestrade.

Holmes would dispute the point, I know, but Lestrade's presence ("Lestrade? Guardian of the physical evidence for a murder he does not believe in, source of doubtful remarks, misleading conclusions, and erroneous theories— that Lestrade?") is crucial. There is no doubt that Lestrade complicated things for Holmes, but that doesn't mean I can leave him out any more than Holmes could. Scotland Yard must be notified in a case of murder.

Of course, I could arrange for Lestrade to be the one to contact Holmes instead of the other way around. That would help. That way, Lestrade could be baffled at the beginning of the investigation, where it would do no harm, instead of at the end, where he functions as an obstruction to justice.

"Murder, Mr Holmes? I doubt that. Why, the doctor will tell you that barring infection, an injury of this kind is the merest scratch."

Neither was Lestrade impressed by the startling coincidence attached to the delivery of a package, however loathsome, to the very lady whose name and address were inscribed on its exterior.

"Let me understand you, Mr Holmes. The package that we see before us, bearing the inscription 'Miss H. Cathcart' and directed to this address, where your client, Miss Hermia Cathcart—I beg your pardon, Ma'am, Miss Hermia *Marie* Cathcart—has been the sole resident since her sister became Mrs Smith some six years ago and removed to Bristol, was actually intended for this Mrs Smith, is that right? And you dedooced this because Mrs Smith's given name is

Henrietta—excuse me, Henrietta *Marie*—and because she is the, ah, younger of the two ladies?"

It wasn't until I stepped in to deny Lestrade all access to my patient that he began to comprehend the situation.

"You mean Mrs Smith is here? It is her ear? Why didn't you say so?"

Lestrade is an impatient fellow. Personally, I had enjoyed Holmes's exegesis. I always do.

* * *

Moving Lestrade to the introduction patches one tiny pinhole in a narrative fabric that is about as watertight as a piece of cheesecloth. What I need is a situation where Scotland Yard is baffled, Holmes makes himself useful, the mystery is solved, and justice, mercy and repentance prevail, with all parties concerned willing to see some version of the truth in print, disguised as fiction.

I can't do anything with this. This is a situation where Holmes makes himself useful, the mystery is solved, Scotland Yard is baffled, and justice has very little to do with it. A case of adultery (suspected adultery, I should say) is no fit topic all by itself, and the addition of a couple of ears travelling by parcel post from Belfast to London only makes it worse. This is hardly the kind of thing I would care to set before my readers in the name of entertainment. I am no Fleet Street hyena. The madman who calls himself Jack the Ripper will get no encouragement from my pen. I can keep a secret.

I wish Mary would read this.

This morning's *Daily Telegraph* included a small article, buried (as Holmes would put it) on an inside page, announcing that Alec Brownley, able-bodied seaman on the cargo ship *Dainty Mary*, has confessed to the brutal slaying of Stephen Smith, late of Bristol, whose dismembered body has been recovered from a shallow grave in Belfast. He was apprehended in Waterford by Scotland Yard's own Inspector Lestrade, "acting on information received." Mrs Smith, who was injured in the murderous attack that claimed her husband's life, remains in seclusion with her family.

The information received was of course received from Sherlock Holmes, but it was not until I spoke to Holmes that I was able to appreciate how much error was contained in those few lines. His theory of the case had been proved in every particular. Far from having been acquired during the attack on her husband, Hettie Smith's injuries had been its motivating force. In the light of Alec Brownley's confession (and the continuing furor over the Ripper, which has driven almost every other item of public interest out of the papers), there was every reason to expect that Stephen Smith's brutality to his wife would remain a Cathcart family secret.

According to Holmes, Brownley seemed glad of the opportunity to tell his story. The only difficulty they had lay in persuading him to keep to what they considered to be the topic. He wasn't very interested in the murder, but kept coming back to the question of Hettie Smith. Why hadn't she come? She knew he was on the *Dainty Mary*. Didn't she know that he loved her? What must a man do to prove his devotion?

I am glad I didn't see it. I shall have enough to do, living with the memory of Hettie's anxious ramblings. "Brownley? Have you seen Brownley? Where is Brownley?" I don't know when she will be well enough to be told about Alec Brownley and the cardboard box. Not for some time, certainly.

Holmes returned from events in Waterford, saying darkly, "I hope Hettie Smith has deserved to be loved like that."

I had no answer for him then, but I remember a wedding photograph of a beloved bride and her young husband, and I remember my one-time patient, wounded in mind and body, and I do not believe that anyone has deserved to be loved like that.

Not like that.

Chapter 4

No one reading 'A Study in Scarlet' or 'The Sign of Four' would believe how difficult it can be to set such a tale to paper. They seem simple enough, plain round tales that begin at the beginning, muddle along when Holmes and I were muddled, and draw to a neat and tidy close in their own good time. I know, I've read them. I've read them so many times that I have lost all sense that I wrote them. I have read them so many times that the mere sight of me with the final versions in my hands is enough to set Mary fluttering about me. I have had to take them down to my surgery and content myself at home with studying my old notes for some clue as to the method I employed to arrive at those narratives. There must be a method, I tell myself, in defiance of my own memories.

It began innocently enough, I recall, as an attempt to make some return to Holmes for the interest, not to say the adventure, he had brought into my life. It seemed the least I could do and, as the least I could do, it provided steady occupation for a good many afternoons and evenings. Holmes grew quite used to the sight of me scribbling before the fire and proved remarkably patient in the matter of explaining how it was we happened to go here rather than there, to pursue this rather than that, to talk to this one rather than that one.

It was an occupation admirably suited to my condition and I was rather proud of myself for thinking to prescribe it. Physically, I was over the worst of it and if the slight stiffness on my left proved to be a fixture, it was still less noticeable an infirmity than many others created by the Jezail bullets of the Second Afghan war. For me, as for many people, however, the obstacle to full recovery was the convalescent idea. After a bout of enteric fever so severe as to leave my health as I thought permanently impaired, I found it all but impossible to imagine myself out and about as a matter of course, to be taken for granted by the world at large. Only a few short months ago, rising from my bed had been an act of heroism, worthy of applause. It felt that way still.

Holmes himself worked by fits and starts, often spending weeks at a time lying on the sofa, rising only to make an indifferent meal or to spend an hour or so scratching tuneless airs on his violin, a practice all the more infuriating once I learned what music he was capable of coaxing from it under other circumstances. How someone who can play so beautifully can endure such caterwauling!

I know now that these periods of apparent inertia are punctuated by the most intense mental exertion as he wrestles with possibilities to arrive at hidden truths. At the time, however, all I could think was that here was this perfectly healthy specimen who had never seen military service in his life and if he could spend the day on the sofa, staring into space and ruining his health with cocaine, then I could have another whisky and soda and write that letter, take that walk, read that book, visit that old friend, tomorrow. Or better yet, next week. I was restless, but not yet restless enough, and I felt no closer to resuming the practice of medicine then than I had been on the ship back from Peshawur, a prey to seasickness all the way.

I was more of an invalid than I knew in those early days, and very glad to find lodgings that were within the reach of my Army pension, roommate or no roommate. Having Sherlock Holmes as a roommate was in any event quite similar to having no roommate at all. To surrender the sitting room to Mr Holmes when he should chance to have a visitor proved to be no greater hardship in practice than it had seemed in theory, if only because there were so few visitors. I can honestly say that it was a good six months before it even occurred to me to wonder what service he might be rendering his clients, for such they clearly were. There was no discernible pattern that I could see—old or young, male or female, well to do or down and out, some in sickness, some in health, they came to him as if to their confessor and would be gone after an interview that often lasted only a quarter of an hour. If any came a second time I did not observe it, and that in itself was strange, for how did they come to hear of him when they needed him, or, more sinister still, when he needed them? How could a professional practice of any kind come to flourish if it satisfied a client in a single visit? What would become of medicine as a profession if the physician could arrest the course of an illness after one examination?

I am not a curious man but Holmes is, and it occurs to me now that whatever minor observations I was able to make about him in those days—and they are catalogued for the curious in 'A Study in Scarlet'—must be as nothing compared to the observations he was able to make about me during those first crucial months in Baker Street. I can see now, as I could not see then, that he deliberately drew my attention to that magazine article of his, 'The Book of Life', and let me pronounce on the impossibility of the thing in order to be able to announce that he was its much misunderstood author, willing to demonstrate the truth of his preposterous claims to me, very nearly at my convenience, although my convenience hasn't come into it much since then.

I do not know how many men, bored, restless, and with no immediate occupation to hand, could have resisted such an invitation, but I do know that I am not one of them. It has only just occurred to me that Holmes may have known as much about me himself. It would be very like him.

That first adventure, now famous as 'A Study in Scarlet', tested my physical and intellectual mettle in a way that made me glad my convalescence was behind me. In a way that let me see that my convalescence *was* in fact behind me. Afterwards, Holmes returned to Baker Street and retired to the sofa with his shag and his violin. I returned to Baker Street resolved to do no such thing.

While Holmes stretched before the fire in an apparent stupor, my mind was working furiously. I knew that my reaction to his article had not been founded in spleen, but rather was the reaction of any rational man confronted by an unknown caught boasting that he could do the impossible. It came to me in a moment of inspiration. Now that I had seen him do the impossible with my own eyes, I was in a position to contain that reaction by telling his story myself, as one might give evidence in a court of law. With that analogy firmly in view, I began to write. I identified myself, gave a quick synopsis of my background in witness of my probity, and was careful to mention our 221B Baker Street address often enough (I hoped) to catch the eye and ear of anyone who might need the services of a consulting detective. Holmes should not have to rely on cases that Scotland Yard had first been honest enough to give up as beyond their powers. There, at any rate, my opinion had not changed: it would be difficult, I thought, to sustain a professional practice of this kind, no matter how needed, unless it were at least known to those people who might in the course of time become paying clients.

There is a deal of difference between writing a letter and writing a story but for some reason, I did not realize that then and 'A Study in Scarlet' took shape steadily, giving me no serious difficulty and whiling away many a dreary hour. During this period, Holmes had several calls upon his time that he chose to pursue alone. Trivial matters, he called them, and perhaps they were, but they were not trivial to me. I redoubled my efforts on the manuscript.

Finally, the thing was done. I began to think that we would do very well together, he and I. Perhaps I was meant to be a Writer.

I read it through, weeding out the parenthetical material (Holmes brings out the parentheses in me, I'm afraid) and admiring the structure of it: its two Parts, with seven Chapters in each Part, had a certain military neatness that appealed to me. Then I read it through again, this time pretending to be Holmes, and found the difference disconcerting. The title, for example, would surely strike him as pompous or even overly sensational. Then again, a man who could call a magazine article 'The Book of Life' was in no position to...

It was my first experience of The Editorial Shift.

In the event, Holmes bore the ordeal rather better than I did, commenting only that I should have to change the names of Inspectors Tobler and Lombard, "or there will be even less trade through here than there was formerly." Thus did Inspector Lombard become Inspector Lestrade. As for Inspector Gregory Tobler, it was the work of an instant to make him Tobias Gregson. Such reasonable criticisms I was bound to respect. If, however, I had anticipated any words of praise or encouragement, any least hint of gratitude, I was doomed to disappointment. I reached for my manuscript, he reached for his violin, and the subject was dropped.

I was months in finding the energy to offer it for publication and almost two years in developing the kind of resolution that would let me return from my morning constitutional, find the manuscript back on the mantelpiece, and wrap it up for the next editor on my list without so much as removing my hat. Holmes would watch me with narrowed gaze, his lids lowered against the effects of the tobacco smoke. Once or twice at this time, he tried to include me in one of his cases but I was generally proof against the temptation. My experiences over the adventure I later (much later) described as 'The Adventure of the Speckled Band' had persuaded me that it was better not to indulge him in that way until such time as 'A Study in

44

Scarlet' might burst upon the British public and exert its effect. I had no doubt that the effect would be a profound one, probably because I hadn't looked at the story since Holmes had had me change the names of the two Inspectors.

My bulldog, now gone grey about the muzzle, learned to associate the presence of the package on the mantelpiece with an extra outing. Mrs Hudson learned to boil a three-minute egg for three minutes. Holmes learned to abuse his health alternately with morphine and cocaine. I learned to simply tear off the old wrapping, pack the thing up again, and write the new address as neatly as I could.

Then came the day I acted on a stock tip from my old friend Stamford, more than tripling my unfortunately sensible investment. I got out just in time and exhilarated by the experience, decided I could not do better than to gamble the whole of it on one John H. Watson. Somehow, on John H. Watson. I had had my eye on a Mr Farquhar's practice for some time, but my speculation in Stamford's wake had been too modest by far to permit me to buy the old gentleman out just yet, so I resigned myself to doing his rounds for him on Tuesdays and Saturdays a while longer, and quietly sunk the whole of my profit into a private printing of 'A Study in Scarlet'. It should have been handsomely illustrated had I not decided in a moment of inspiration that double the quantity on poorer paper was the wiser move. This was to be an investment, not an epitaph: Dr Watson had survived it all and was lodging in Baker Street with the world's only consulting detective, Mr Sherlock Holmes. What was needed was 2,000 brochures to that effect, hawked by enterprising urchins at all the major stations in the vicinity of Baker Street: Waterloo, Victoria, Charing Cross, etc.

Seldom do yesterday's tactics impress the armchair strategist as being beyond all possibility of improvement. Equally seldom, however, do they fail to survive a ten minute hansom ride. I arrived at the doors of No. 221B

Baker Street, footsore and weary, after delivering the last consignment of brochures to the urchin who worked the Jermyn Street station, to find Holmes expostulating with some fifteen journalists.

'A Study in Scarlet' had found its audience.

Chapter 5

I am sorry I ever mentioned the giant rat of Sumatra! Or the peculiar affair of the aluminium crutch. And I rue the day I met the glory-grabbing Grice Patersons and so, heard the story of their ill-fated expedition to the miserable island of Uffa. No wonder the place is uninhabited. No wonder Mary thinks I have an inexhaustible supply of these stories. No wonder I am condemned to the task of keeping this journal.

I might at least have had the sense to tell her these stories privately. But no, I had to wait until I had an audience.

In my own defense, I may say that I was young and in love and not thinking altogether clearly at the time. That was it. That and the inevitable shock of discovering that my bride-to-be, orphan though she was, nevertheless possessed a secret horde of relatives: aunts, uncles, great-aunts, relatives on her mother's side, relatives on her father's side, first cousins, second cousins, third cousins once removed (but still present), and nieces and nephews of all ages. There they were, all of them (at least I hoped that was all of them), and all of them wanting to ask Mary's young man just how he was proposing to support her, as a medical doctor without a medical practice. It was a nightmare. And how long had it been since I left the Army? Seven *years*? Seven years is a long time.

"I'll drink to that," I remember thinking.

Maybe it was the wine. Bad sherry is a great provocation and this was very bad sherry. As I made my way from Great-Aunt Gertrude to Uncle Ned, I was acutely conscious of the slight drag of my bad leg and full of sudden resolution. *They should at least find me good company*, I told myself. With that, I dropped the aluminium crutch on Uncle Ned, brought out the giant rat of Sumatra for the sake of the women and children, and launched the Grice Patersons on their way.

The Morstan family was spellbound. I know—I was spell-bound with them.

How I was to know that Mary's "favourite relative," intro-duced to me as Cousin Nat Fitscherton, was also Nathaniel Fitsch, editor of the *Strand Magazine*? He didn't look like an editor. Before I well knew what was happening, I was giving Cousin Nat "first refusal rights" for my forthcoming adven-ture, 'The Sign of Four'. I should have known then how it would be: I hadn't even written it yet and already he was refusing it. Youth doesn't excuse everything. And yet, all I could think about was how to manage the writing of it now that I had an Editor waiting to see it.

In truth, I was dismayed at the way it grew, untidy as a weed. The first draft rapidly assumed the proportions of 'A Study in Scarlet', which had been rejected as too long by half the publishers in London. (The other half thought it was too short.) I had not forgotten, if Mary had, that it had cost me fifty pounds to publish 'A Study in Scarlet'. Self-publication is no hobby for a married man. I had to do better with 'The Sign of Four'.

The revisions I made to that manuscript! There was a time, I do believe, when it had over twenty chapters. I know it was one of the most disjointed pieces of journalism it has ever been my misfortune to read. There were so many plot lines to juggle, so much tension to capture, so many characters to introduce, manage and dismiss. What drove these people to act the way they did? What motivated them? The story didn't begin to fall into place until I realized that if I telescoped our courtship and let our engagement coincide with the opening of the Agra treasure chest, I would have both the dramatically satisfying ending I needed and the perfect engagement gift for my Mary. Mindful of Holmes's concerns, I remembered to disguise Anthony Smith's name and settled on Inspector Athelney Jones. I foresaw problems in keeping the fictional names clear in my own mind and bought a pocket diary for the purpose.

Through it all, I was seeing Mary, cherishing my writer's dream, and casting about for a medical practice that was within my straitened means, since we were naturally unable to marry until there should be some glimmer of financial security on our horizon. Fortunately, as it turned out, we were not dependent on the sale of my manuscript to make that possible.

It was at about this time that Holmes formed the habit of including me in his cases. [*Note*: Mary must never see this diary.] Those were good days, though not of course as good as the married ones since.

I am beginning to understand why Mary has refused to read this journal. It is a heady experience, writing without fear of contradiction or reproof. If Lestrade were a more lettered man, I would suggest he attempt the exercise himself. Now there's a thought: Inspector Lestrade keeping a diary.

Lestrade is an interesting study. Over the years, Lestrade has been the means of introducing Holmes to any number of practical, intellectually stimulating problems which, while they may not have been financially lucrative as a rule, have been the making of him as a detective. Even the self-taught need others, if only to provide them with the opportunity to perfect their craft. This opportunity Lestrade has repeatedly provided over the years, at a cost to his vanity that, judging by my own experience of Holmes, has not always been outweighed by the gratification of presenting the correct solution—Holmes's solution—to a wider audience than was Holmes's own. It is a pity Holmes is not more grateful for it. At the same time, I may say that Lestrade's concept of what constitutes an adequate investigation does lend a certain amount of credibility to Holmes's oft-repeated assertion that Lestrade would spend his days copying *The Encyclopaedia Britannica* if his superiors at the Yard asked him to do so.

You know what it is, don't you? It is this Jack the Ripper madness and the pure confusion of those who are supposed to be handling it. The full weight of officialdom has been brought to bear upon the matter and officialdom is helpless. Helpless or not, however, it is still not about to put itself in Holmes's hands and only Holmes could expect it to do so. This is not one of Lestrade's little investigations, where Holmes can be smuggled in by a side door. The soiled doves of Spitalfields won't be clubbing together to hire him, the Whitechapel Vigilance Committee is more interested in violence than vigilance (and, in any event, is as disorganized as most amateur efforts), and Scotland Yard has its reputation to protect. Sir Charles Warren is not the man to trifle with tutelage from unofficial sources, were Holmes twice as tractable and only half as abrasive as he is. All the whores in Whitechapel could lie dead at his feet, their entrails affixed to their shoulders like epaulettes, and Sir Charles would still fight for the integrity of the Yard. That is what it is for a man like Sir Charles to be a public servant. He is as undivided in his loyalties as Holmes is in his. They simply have different loyalties.

The letter, when it finally arrived, proved to be from Mr Fitsch rather than Cousin Nat. It was remarkably clear. The *Strand Magazine* is not interested in book-length fiction. This is no reflection on the quality of 'The Sign of Four', which is undeniably high ("one might even say gripping in places"), but a straightforward response to the exigencies of the market. They cater to a population of busy, modern people who require brief interludes of mental stimulation of a fairly intense but not protracted nature. A novel with twelve (12) separate chapters offers their readers eleven (11) separate places to put their magazine down and lose interest in it. *The Strand* prefers short fiction, "adventures," falling somewhere between 6,000 and 9,000 words. If I should care to sign a contract for, say, six (6) adventures deliverable at two-month intervals (six adventures would be the minimum number that they could consider), my contributions would be very welcome.

The standard rate was remarkably appealing. Half for me,

half for Holmes, and Holmes won't have to look for another roommate. I meant it, too.

I believe it was Mary who pointed out that it might be as well to have six adventures in hand before signing a contract committing me to the timely delivery of same.

* * *

"Your diary, John."

I suppose the idea is for me to find myself unexpectedly in possession of a particularly fine spot of prose that I will then feel compelled to share with the immediate world, thus inspiring me to produce yet another "adventure" of Sherlock Holmes. It doesn't work that way. Holmes knows it doesn't work that way. 'The Sign of Four,' 'The Adventure of the Speckled Band,' 'The Five Orange Pips,' 'The Boscombe Valley Mystery,' 'The Adventure of the Noble Bachelor'—I have a drawerful of useless manuscripts at this point. Do I really need to produce any more?

I don't consider myself easily dissuaded by any means, but there comes a point where you have to consider the possibility that the Universe is trying to give you a hint. Maybe the world doesn't need to hear about the adventures of Sherlock Holmes. Did you ever think of that?

Holmes certainly hasn't. He stopped by last night to tell me the story of the *Gloria Scott*. Last week it was the story of the Musgrave ritual. I don't know how to tell him this, but much as Mary and I enjoyed hearing about his third case as a consulting detective and the strange events that persuaded him to invent his unusual profession in the first place, it would be a sheer waste of my time to prepare either of these for publication. A man has to be well-known before his biographer can afford to begin his story with his subject's first faltering steps on the road to glory. Nobody knows who Sherlock Holmes is. Why should they care how he became a consulting detective?

I can't possibly tell the story of Holmes's life in chronological order. What is beginning to worry me is that I may not be able to tell it in any other order, either. It really is extremely peculiar. Mary is committed to my writing (as witness this diary), Mr Fitsch is committed to my writing (as witness his publication offer), even Holmes might be said to be committed to my writing—or why should he have told me the stories of the *Gloria Scott* and the Musgrave ritual? I, on the other hand, have never felt more detached from the process in my life. Too many people are taking too much interest in this. All of the pleasure has gone out of it.

Holmes means well, but if he wanted to encourage me in this work, then he shouldn't have put the kibosh on the four adventures I had completed. There is no doubt in my mind that Holmes's refusal to accept any of the money offered me by the good gentlemen of the *Strand* ("Your friendship is all I require, Watson") would have meant infinitely more to me if he had not simultaneously made it impossible for me to accept that money myself.

Nothing is more discouraging to the would-be writer than a sudden and complete halt to the publication process. I feel all of the satisfaction of a wandering scholar patiently trying out his schoolroom Swahili on his native bearers who only finds out a week into the experiment that they are, each and every one of them, stone deaf. On top of the frustration, I feel foolish. I should have known.

I did know some of it. That is, I knew that 'The Boscombe Valley Mystery' was going to have to wait, first for the autumn Assizes and then for "John Turner's" death. But he was an old man and dying when we knew him, if not from the diabetes that I gave him in my manuscript. It can't be long now. And it's not as though I were planning to come out with this adventure first. No, that honour was to have gone to 'The Adventure of the Speckled Band'.

How *could* Holmes have promised Helen Stoner to keep her story to himself until after her death? She is younger than we are! Or, promising her his silence, how could he have neglected to mention it to me? Suppose I had published the adventure first and shown it to Holmes afterwards? Not that I would have done such a thing. My habit of consulting Holmes over the final version was formed by 'A Study in Scarlet' and I should find it hard to break now—doubly hard since this latest development. But oh, it does hurt to see this one consigned to oblivion. A wicked stepfather, gypsies, poisonous snakes, cheetahs, baboons, mysterious last words, the lovely Helen: it had everything. Everything, that is, except permission to publish.

To think I once thought it was my consummate powers of selection that would make us famous! I spent weeks going over my notes before I made my selection. Now I find that 'The Adventure of the Noble Bachelor' is as unsuitable as all the rest. This one must wait until Lord St Simon has recovered from his humiliation. And how, pray tell, shall I know when that has taken place?

"Tut, Watson, you have only to read the society pages. As soon as St Simon engages himself to marry Another, you may be certain that any objections he may have to the airing of the peculiar circumstances that attended his previous wedding will be overruled by the young lady in question. Whatever other virtues your prose may have (and it paints a very pretty picture of that young man), your report will have the effect of a public proclamation of St Simon's continued bachelorhood. An aristocratic silence on the subject will not serve. They must be grateful to you. Bigamy is an ugly word."

True enough, no doubt, but what guarantee do I have that St Simon will pursue the matter? He has been forty years without a wife and I do not think that his first experience of wedded bliss can be described as at all encouraging. How many husbands lose their wives at their own wedding breakfast, after all? Stronger characters than his have quailed before the possibility of a second disappointment. It is the kind of situation in which the inverse relationship between the magnitude of the embarrassment endured and the probability of its being repeated brings the subject no comfort whatever.

So we are left with only one adventure, the weakest of the lot and a personal failure for Holmes. When I wrote 'The Five Orange Pips', I thought I was providing a little ballast for the series, a touch of reality to offset the staggering success reported in the other adventures. It's not good to give the public the impression that you can solve everything, that no matter what the problem is, you have the cure for what ails them. For one thing, it isn't honest, and for another, it lessens their appreciation when you do succeed. I thought Holmes knew that. Besides, it's not his fault the *Lone Star* went down in the West Indies, cheating the gallows. As long as the villains are dead, what difference does it make how they died? I think he's taking this whole thing too seriously, hedging his permission with one condition after another. Yes, I may publish 'The Five Orange Pips', but not until I have at least four (4) other adventures in print, all showing his cleverness in bringing some villainy home to the villain(s) of the piece. That's a bit thick, isn't it? I felt like I was talking to Cousin Nat, with his first refusal rights and his six adventures at two-month intervals.

I don't know whether Holmes settled on the number five because I had so far completed only four "adventures" including that of the pips (so that I would have to write at least one additional adventure before the issue could so much as arise for discussion) or because my unfortunate title suggested it to him (so that the fifth adventure in the series could be 'The Five Orange Pips'). I only know that the more time I spend combing through my notes, the less sure I am that this is possible to do at all or if it is, that I want to be the one to do it.

I thought I had my six adventures for Cousin Nat, but by the time Holmes got through with the four I had to show him, I was in no mood to interview him about the overlapping footprints for 'The Brook Street Mystery' or the ins and outs of the handwriting analysis for 'The Reigate Puzzle'. He would have liked nothing better, I'm sure, than to reconstruct his thinking for me on these two technical matters, but what would have been the point? Even after I got those stories straight and wrote them up, I would still be three adventures short of what I need in order to take on the *Strand* and two adventures shy of being able to use 'The Five Orange Pips'. There's no other way to think about it. If I write up 'The Brook Street Mystery' and 'The Reigate Puzzle', I will have one less adventure for Cousin Nat than I had *before* I spoke to Holmes and offered him half the money. The more I write, the less it seems I have written. That can't be right.

You know, I'd much rather Holmes had accepted his fair share of the proceeds and shown an intelligent interest in this side of the business, instead of burdening me with gifts I can't accept, like the *Gloria Scott* and the Musgrave ritual. He makes me feel like this is all Watson's Foolishness, this idea I had of preparing his adventures for publication. Why doesn't he just say he'd rather I dropped the whole thing, if that's how he feels about it?

The way I see it, there are the adventures I can't afford to tell, ever, like that business of the Naval Treaty and the Beryl Coronet and the Second Stain: adventures whose telling would threaten the national interest or my hide. I am thinking now particularly of the adventure of Charles Augustus Milverton (a pseudonym, of course), the blackmailer who was murdered before our eyes while we were engaged in burgling his safe. I see no advantage, to me or to Holmes, in bringing that little escapade before the public. That is not the kind of case Holmes needs more of. Then there are the adventures I can't tell for reasons of public taste and morals: the adventure of the Etheric Manipulators and the Jamison case spring to mind. It is no accident that Holmes, hearing from Mary that I was working on "the Cartwright case," suggested that I turn my hand to the Jamison affair. The foiled bank robbery is excellent as far as it goes, certainly I can understand Holmes's preference for this one of all his cases, but how can I possibly accommodate the distraction of poor, soft Rufus Jamison in print? Pornography is no more my style than it is the *Strand*'s. There are the adventures I tried to tell and shouldn't have: 'The Sign of Four,' 'The Adventure of the Speckled Band,' 'The Boscombe Valley Mystery,' 'The Adventure of the Noble Bachelor' and 'The Five Orange Pips.' The adventures that are too complicated to be accommodated in 6,000 words. The adventures that the client would prefer me to keep secret. (I think we can safely include the Jamison case in this group.) And now, the adventures that Holmes would prefer me to keep secret.

Mary was so disappointed. She loved those stories.

"Your diary, John."

And the moral of that is, never impress a woman unless you are prepared to go on impressing her.

Chapter 6

Once again, Lestrade has chosen the better part of valour. I like Lestrade. I really do.

After much searching of his conscience (and his own best interests), Inspector Lestrade has provided Holmes with a fair copy of the two authenticated Ripper letters *in his own best handwriting* and is consequently in deep disgrace.

"You mark my words, Watson: if these foul murders go unpunished, it will be a blot upon the Yard forever. And it will be Lestrade's fault!"

I like Lestrade. Even now, perched on a crag 200 miles away from my Mary, in a miserable situation in which I may say I feel Lestrade has (indirectly, indirectly) some slight responsibility for placing me, I cannot find it in my heart to feel otherwise than warmly toward him. He handles Holmes so badly.

Holmes was in a passion, flinging himself about our sitting room as if he were in Baker Street, where everything breakable has long since been broken, and Mary was in a state, visibly steeling herself every time he passed one of her treasures. As for me, I was more distracted than either of them. I kept picturing the look on Lestrade's face as Holmes deduced from the samples provided that the infamous Ripper was a man of average height, thick-set, with a clubbed thumb, ginger hair, a mild case of amblyopia, and a bad habit of bearing down on his pen until the nib gives way; a man of indifferent education, a probable Inspector at Scotland Yard.

There are times when I think I may have a better memory for the scenes I've missed than for the ones I've witnessed.

A porcelain figurine leapt off the table in Holmes's wake. By some miracle of coordination I should not care to have to repeat, I caught the thing before it hit the carpet: a Meissen shepherdess. Naturally, Holmes was looking elsewhere at the time. He had come to rest in front of the window and was staring out at the fog. I could see his knuckles whiten as he throttled the curtains. It was understandable, I decided. Lestrade would try the patience of a saint.

Holmes was speaking to me. "What do you think of Dartmoor at this time of year?"

"Dartmoor, Holmes?" My mind raced stupidly along the lines provided by that night's *Evening Standard*. Not the escaped convict, surely? I restored the little shepherdess to a more secure place, well behind her more expendable sheep. "You are thinking of taking a holiday?"

He released the curtains. "When have you ever known me to take a holiday?" he snorted.

He was quite right. I had had to drag him to Reigate last year. "I beg your pardon, Holmes. There is a case?" (I was careful not to ask him whether there was a case worth travelling to Dartmoor for. Holmes is not a happy traveller.)

"I hardly know what it is. What would you think, Watson, of a spectral hound that dogs the steps (ha, very good, dogs the steps, Watson!) of a family unto the second, third, fourth generation?"

We were all attention. "A spectral hound, you say, Holmes?"

"By all accounts a fearsome spectacle, responsible for the deaths of one Baskerville after another. There is a family legend, you understand."

It was the only part I did understand. Sherlock Holmes, investigating a spectral hound?

"But Holmes, ..." I began.

Don't discourage him, said the look on my wife's face. They were her mother's curtains, I remembered. I changed course immediately.

"... this is wonderful! There is bound to be an adventure in this one." I let a note of doubt creep into my voice. "You are sure about the family legend?"

"Would I tell you there was a family legend if I were not?

There is a letter extant, early eighteenth century, I was able to date it within the decade,"—is there anything he has not studied?—"one of those morbid 'To be given to my sons on the occasion of my death' exercises that served to enliven the obsequies of that cheerful age. Can you imagine anything more unpleasant, Watson, than a reminder on the occasion of your father's funeral that the sins of that father and his father before him shall be visited upon their sons unto future generations yet unborn? I can't. It's the Garden of Eden all over again. The letter will make a delightful addition to your tale, I have already arranged with Sir Henry for its inclusion. I offer you the traditional warning to the sons of the house, the house itself (a lonely manor within walking distance of Dartmoor Prison)," —you would have thought the Prison was the height of my touristic ambitions—"and a hearty, fresh-faced American heir with one boot. You know how you like Americans, Watson."

"One boot?" I asked. I was reminded of a pair of ears, nestled amid a quantity of salt.

"Two feet, one boot. It is a long story, Watson, and with all due respect to Mrs Watson, these are not the circumstances in which I should wish you to hear it. There is a walking stick, too, which I should be glad to have your opinion of. No, not one of mine, although I would appreciate the return of the one I lent you: I acquired it under rather unusual circumstances. Thank you, Watson—you may keep the neckerchief. It suits you. We breakfast with the last of the Baskervilles at eight tomorrow; the train for Devon departs two hours later. You should plan on a stay of at least two weeks, possibly as many as four. Dear lady," he bowed, "has your husband your permission to join us?"

What could she say? "You make me ridiculous, Mr Holmes, with your remarks. Of course John must go if he wishes to do so."

What could I say? "Eight o'clock, Holmes? At which hotel?"

Holmes was ever a late riser. "If you could be at Baker Street at half-past seven, Watson, that will do nicely. Mrs Hudson will provide the breakfast."

* * *

Because I arrived promptly at seven-thirty, breakfast ("What ho, Mrs Hudson! Mrs Hudson? Ah, Mrs Hudson. Breakfast for four in half an hour, Mrs Hudson") would, I knew, be served promptly at eight. I wish Mary were better acquainted with Holmes and his habits. It could only serve to increase her good opinion of me.

"No need to linger on the landing, Watson. Come in, come in. You're up early. Shaved, too, I see. *And* packed. I shall be ready in a moment. Mind the mat. The left corner is undone, a little trap for the unwary. I must remember to mention it to Mrs Hudson. Remind me, won't you, Watson?"

I wondered how long he had been warning his guests about the mat. Eventually, he would probably solve the problem by tacking a note to his door: "Mind the mat." The same tack would, I knew, serve to secure the mat. The tack hammer was right where I had left it. The tacks were in the Coronation tea cup. The mat was in the hall.

"Watson? Where are you, Watson? He can't have gone far, his luggage is still here. Ah, there you are, Watson. All set? Good. I can't think if you're going to wander off every time I start to talk to you. What are you doing with that tack hammer? We have no time for tack hammers today, Watson," he said severely. He was holding a walking stick. "Go on, take it. I would call your attention to the teethmarks: there and again there. It belongs to Dr Mortimer, purveyor of the Baskerville family legend, executor of the Baskerville family estate, and the closest thing we have to a client at this present. We must see if we cannot bring Sir Henry to a better appreciation of the perils of his situation. It is grave, Watson, very grave, and he is thoughtless, made giddy by the size of his inheritance. Imagine, Watson, a quarter of a million pounds! I must finish dressing before our two young friends arrive."

Ever since he turned thirty-five, Holmes has decided that he is middle-aged. This allows him to adopt an avuncular manner toward any client as little as six months younger than he is (witness "our two young friends") while simultaneously annoying the hell out of me, three years his senior. Mary finds this exquisitely funny, but then she would. Mary's still in her twenties.

Everything about this case has taken me by surprise. Sir Henry, whose sole claim to giddiness as far as I can see consists of his purchase of two plain suits of clothing and one pair of boots to celebrate the occasion (I'd hate to think how Holmes would describe *my* behaviour if I were to come into a quarter of a million pounds), the fact that I am on the case alone, even Dr Mortimer's black spaniel pup, Cerberus. I suppose Dr Mortimer feels that anyone with sufficient education to recognize the dog's name has sufficient education to rise above the allusion, but it would give me a turn to find myself attended by a physician accompanied by a coal-black dog answering to the name of Cerberus, and I do not make the mistake of imagining that I am unique, in this regard or in any other. It was Cerberus ("the other hound from hell," as Holmes so succinctly put it) whose teethmarks were on Dr Mortimer's walking stick.

This demonstration of Holmes's deductive powers will be infinitely more impressive once I make sure it precedes his presentation of the Baskerville family legend. It's a funny thing, but once you introduce the element of a spectral hound into a narrative, the reader will expect that any stray teethmarks of a canine persuasion will be due to that dog and no other. Watson's First Law: Introduce the puppy before you introduce the Hound.

SIR HENRY BASKERVILLE: two feet, one boot, as promised. To be specific, one new brown boot, borrowed and returned, and one old black boot, still missing. Obviously, the thief prefers the colour black.

The real question is why anyone would willingly put himself at risk returning the first boot when he might with perfect safety have pitched it into the Thames instead. If Holmes has any explanation for this peculiar behaviour, he has thus far kept it to himself, inquiring only as to whether in the first case as in the second, it was the *left* boot that was taken. Sir Henry really couldn't say, which all by itself probably accounts for my presence at Baskerville Hall. Holmes can do nothing without data.

My letter to Mary included a full account of the episode of the walking stick and I find that I am in no mood to repeat that conversation here. One post-mortem ought to be enough for anybody. Suffice it to say that as usual, I was wrong and Holmes was right, and here I am in the garden spot of all England (I am speaking facetiously), by myself, virtually without instructions, waiting for a spectral hound to appear.

Holmes passed the muffins, praised the kippers, and gave our two young friends to understand that he could not possibly leave London to its own devices at the present time. Although they remained unspoken, the words "not even for a spectral hound" hovered delicately over the breakfast table. There was no help for it. Holmes had a blackmail case to resolve and the negotiations had reached a critical juncture. Holmes looked knowingly at me. "Watson is the very man. Watson?"

For Holmes, the shortest distance between two points is always a straight line. I was left with my mouth open and my suitcase packed in response to an invitation that Sir Henry had not, in point of fact, issued. I could wish that Holmes would occasionally proceed the way other people do.

To his everlasting credit, with me if no one else, Sir Henry passed this first test of his fitness for his new position in life with flying colours. The invitation was made as warmly as if the idea had been original with him instead of with Holmes.

Sir Henry did not mind saying that it would mean a great deal to him to have me at his side, and so on and so forth. Mary knows what he said—she had that conversation, too, in her letter.

Sir Henry is a true gentleman, who will be a credit to Baskerville Hall and a blessing to the surrounding area, always assuming the Hound doesn't get him first. It will be a pleasure to help him rid himself of his ancestral burden. I only wish I knew what I was supposed to do with myself until Holmes gets here. "Do not let Sir Henry out of your sight!" has a nice ring to it, but it's not very specific.

* * *

This is a gloomy place. I thought at first that the circumstances of our arrival had unduly prejudiced me against the Hall, but I have seen it in daylight now, such daylight as the Devonshire sun is capable of at this time of year, and it is no such thing. This is a gloomy place.

Memorandum. If so be I am ever in a position actually to write 'The Hound of the Baskervilles' (a good title, yes), I must be sure to make it August or September. October is no time to be sitting out on the moor, scribbling in your journal. It's damnably chilly on Dartmoor in October.

About our arrival. There can be few developments more trying to the composure of the uninvited guest than the wholesale resignation of his host's domestic staff. I did not know which way to look. I am here as Holmes's deputy, committed to protecting his interests—his interests and Sir Henry's life. I could not possibly keep Sir Henry in sight at all times from the vantage point of an hotel. I followed Sir Henry into the Hall.

Now I may not have much experience of colonial sons returning to their ancestral demesnes to claim their inheritance, but surely it is just a trifle unusual for the faithful family retainer to serve notice to the long-awaited heir while he is

still on the doorstep, waiting to take possession. There is nothing intrinsically objectionable to Sir Henry, that the mere sight
of him should bring the words tumbling from Barrymore's
lips, heedless of my presence. Sir Henry is as presentable an
heir as the most exacting servant could wish for. A bit more
open in his manner, perhaps, than the good Barrymore is
accustomed to, but Sir Henry has been abroad for some years,
after all. They might have given him a moment to get his bear-
ings. What's the matter with Barrymore, anyway?

"Sir Henry, might I have the favour of a word with you
after dinner?"

That's the way it's done in the novels I've read. The
manservant requests the favour of a private interview with
the new baronet at the new baronet's convenience, and the
new baronet and his friend are shown to their rooms and
given every attention. Fires are burning in the grates, hot
water appears on the instant, and the meals would bring tears
to the eyes of Henry VIII.

The meals at Baskerville Hall would bring tears to the eyes
of Henry VIII, all right, but they wouldn't be tears of joy. This
Mrs Barrymore has no more notion of how to dress a joint
than Holmes does. I wrote Mary a whole long letter last night,
telling her how much I miss her. It wasn't until I read it over
later, about to sign it, that I realized it was really about how
much I miss Cook.

There is something amiss with the Barrymores, I can feel it.

Such is the progress of my investigation, and I can imagine
what Holmes would find to say to me were I to confess as
much to him. "Holmes, there is something amiss with the
Barrymores; she is a terrible cook and he is precipitate in his
actions." No, this particular insight is best kept within the
confines of my diary.

So far, my stay at the Hall has served primarily to reconcile
me to my own infinitely more meagre patrimony. Not twice a
quarter of a million pounds could induce me to bury myself
here and I am not even thinking about the Hound—the

Hound is a separate problem. All I do all day is write. I write to Mary, I write to Holmes, I write in my diary. At least Mary writes back. I haven't heard a word from Holmes since I got here. Sir Henry seems perfectly content for me to spend my time in this way ("I never met a Writer before"), but I cannot say that I am equally contented by it.

Where is Holmes? That is the question. Fortunately, Sir Henry is too polite to ask it of me, but I am under no such constraint myself. Sooner or later, it is bound to occur to a man with a quarter of a million pounds that he can afford to lose one old boot and then where will we be? I have done what I could with the anonymous letter Sir Henry received while he was in London, but there is a deal of difference between a cryptic communication in town and a supernatural communication at home and we have yet to see any least sign of the latter here at the Hall. Where is Holmes? It goes without saying that if Holmes has a blackmail case in town, I am delighted to be in Devon, spectral hound or no spectral hound (it will be a long, long time before I forget the name of Charles Augustus Milverton, I can promise you that), but he should have been able to solve half a dozen blackmail cases by now. He forgets, I know his methods.

I hope Holmes isn't throwing my letters away.

* * *

Mary writes, reminding me that Holmes is depending on me. Am I responding to Sir Henry's impatience or am I simply feeling impatient on my own account? She misses me, too. So far, six patients have opted to hoard their complaints against my return: Mrs Ogden, Mr Dougherty, Mr Peterson, Mrs Carroll's Timothy, old Mrs Randall, and young Mr Jellett. She is sorry about Mr Jellett, she did try to persuade him to see Anstruther but "he knows when he is well-suited." If that isn't a hypochondriac all over! Cook is sorry to hear about "that Mrs Barrymore, spoiling a good roast." Mary doesn't like to promise, but she is of the opinion that Dr Watson can expect a rare dinner to welcome him home when this case is over. She sends her love. (Mary, not Cook.)

I wish this letter had arrived yesterday or, better yet, the day before. I don't know what to do now. Mary is right, of course. The impatience *was* mine. It's a bit grim, having to supply evidence of my friendship for weeks on end while Holmes keeps his own counsel and drops out of sight. I hope Mrs Carroll's Timothy doesn't have anything serious. It would be just like Mrs Carroll to decide that my absence from town was an omen, absolving her from any further efforts on Timothy's behalf. I have abandoned my wife and my practice in order to sit on an egg in Devonshire and, little by little, my fear that it would hatch before Holmes could arrive has given way to the fear that, on the contrary, it isn't going to hatch at all.

The truth is, I am used to a more active life than this and so, I should have thought, was Sir Henry. Something happens: I report it to Holmes, I describe it for Mary, I react to it in my diary. Through it all I remain convinced that Life is not supposed to happen slowly enough for me to be able to take it down in triplicate. Between events—and we are mostly "between events" here at Baskerville Hall—Sir Henry watches me move my pen across the paper. On his infrequent visits, we bring Dr Mortimer up to date. It doesn't take long. The local gentry are staying away in droves, crippling my investigation and playing havoc with Sir Henry's self-confidence, which I am beginning to see has been seriously eroded by Barrrymore's unaccountable behaviour.

I am sorry now that I didn't share my suspicions about the Barrymores with Sir Henry, but it did not occur to me that he would take the coldness of his welcome to the Hall so much to heart. In particular, it did not occur to me that Sir Henry could suppose either his manner or his person so unworthy of the Baskerville family line (a line so depraved, remember, as to make the legend of a spectral hound especially devoted to the destruction of its male descendants seem plausible in this day and age) as to render Barrymore's behaviour upon the doorstep not only excusable, but very nearly justifiable. The Barrymores are not the only servants in the world. I say, let them go—once Holmes arrives and has analyzed the situation, of course. Perhaps I should remind Sir Henry of Holmes's suspicion regarding Barrymore—his suspicion that Barrymore may have been the source of the anonymous letter Sir Henry received in London, warning him away from the moor. Then again, if Holmes has discarded that hypothesis for some reason, he won't thank me for recalling it to his client's mind. Oh, where is Holmes?

Personally, I should have thought Sir Henry could find considerable joy in the prospect of effecting an escape from the listless Mrs Barrymore and her never-ending parade of burnt offerings. I know I do. Sir Henry needs to learn how to look on the bright side. It would not have done for Sir Henry to have begun his tenure at the Hall by turning the Barrymores off, but if they choose to leave, that's another story and small blame to him. If only he didn't take everything so personally!

I'm beginning to see that young Baskerville is actually quite shy under his American bravado. More than once he's told me that he didn't bargain on becoming a recluse when he moved into the Hall. That's the way he talks: "I didn't bargain on this, I didn't bargain on that." One way and another, there is quite a bit about life at the Hall that Sir Henry didn't bargain on. I'm beginning to think that the Hound (if there is a hound) may be the least of it.

Every day, we tramp out on the moor for our exercise and every day, Sir Henry becomes a little bit less American, a little bit more like Heathcliff. He doesn't *walk* across the moor anymore, he *stalks* across the moor. I do my best to keep up, but the terrain is hard on my leg and if I don't stop periodically to rest it, I run the risk of having it give out altogether, which would be ignominious in the extreme. There's no conversation in Sir Henry these days. No pleasantries about the weather, no remarks upon the scenery, no plans for the future. He no longer talks about electrifying the approach to the Hall or looking forward to meeting his new neighbours. He carries his gun everywhere—nearly potted poor Cerberus this afternoon. In mistake for a rabbit, he said. I ask you, does a coal black spaniel look like a rabbit to you?

I didn't know what it was at first, but I do now. And I take full responsibility for it. Because Mary is right, the impatience was mine. The problem is that against all the odds, I have succeeded in communicating it to Sir Henry, who in his natural state, doesn't have an impatient bone in his body.

Sir Henry, always the perfect host, is taking pains to become a more picturesque protagonist for my story.

I suppose that from Sir Henry's point of view, it is a short step from becoming a recluse to becoming a romantic recluse. I have never met—or imagined—a more impressionable young man. I know because I enquired, that Sir Henry was born in Devon and lived here until he was well into his teens. You would think he would have more sense. How can I tell him that Heathcliff is a Yorkshire character, not universally admired?

We have these little discussions, he and I, about the Baskerville family name, the Baskerville family legend, the Baskerville family reputation. When we first came to Baskerville Hall, at a time when it might be supposed that such questions would be uppermost in the new heir's mind, these discussions were spaced with the liveliest exchanges about the prairies of Saskatchewan, the sport to be had there, the unpredictability of the weather, the violence of the gales, the threat of tornadoes. I should like to cross the Atlantic and see Saskatchewan for myself sometime. It sounds a fine life for a young man with no family. Physicians, he tells me, are as scarce as hen's teeth (!) and may be certain of a warm welcome wherever they choose to settle. Mary has no more desire for travel than Holmes does, I'm sorry to say. But I enjoyed hearing about it. All that is at an end. Since arriving at the

Hall, Sir Henry has grown progressively more morose and taciturn. Almost I could believe he had found some evidence of debt or mortgage among the family papers, but he assures me it is no such thing.

"I own it, Dr Watson, free and clear, lock, stock and barrel. I am a wealthy man."

You would have thought he was announcing the death of his dearest friend. Was there someone special he had left behind in Canada, a girl perhaps, that he was missing now? I was as tactful as I knew how to be, and my friendship with Holmes has been a great education in tact.

"No, nothing like that, Dr Watson. There is no one 'special to me,' as you put it, in the whole world." And we were off for another ramble on the solitary moor.

I give up. If there is any more to this than ordinary loneliness and simple nostalgia for the adventure of Canada and his lost youth, I do not know what it is. These two problems, however, are real, and well within the purview of Dr Mortimer. I wonder what his story is? Some domestic tragedy, I fancy. He never speaks about his wife and I know he's married. That's not natural. I begin to wonder about him.

Who told Sir Henry about the Baskerville family legend? Dr Mortimer. Who suspected foul play in the matter of Sir Charles's death last spring? Dr Mortimer. Who observed more about the circumstances of that death than anyone could have, excepting only Sherlock Holmes? Dr Mortimer. What kind of family legend is it that is in the keeping of the executor of the estate, a stranger to Dartmoor and not a family member?

I am surprised Holmes never asked himself these questions. Then again, what would be the doctor's motive? That's easily answered: the boredom of Dartmoor stands surety for any kind of distempered freak. And why, if he is the motivating force behind these unlikely events, has he brought Holmes into it? Wouldn't he be the last person to want Holmes involved? But here we are up against the vagaries of human nature. Maybe he is one of those gamblers who plays less for the stakes in the game than for the pride he takes in beating his opponent. There are people like that, I know. Holmes is like that. I may have created this problem by publishing 'A Study in Scarlet'. Wouldn't that be awful? If that's true, then the Hound won't appear until Holmes does.

One thing at a time. What matters now is not the Hound (if there *is* a hound), but the depression of Sir Henry's natural spirits under the weight of his unnatural isolation. Whether or not Dr Mortimer is the mover and shaker behind the spectral hound, he should be able to do something about the Heathcliff part of the problem. As the local medico, he certainly has the *entrée* into what passes for polite society on Dartmoor and I know he likes Sir Henry, but I don't suppose it will occur to him and I despair of being able to plant the thought between his ears myself. He is too busy examining our skulls, assessing their cranial capacity and estimating the degree of protrusion of our jaws. His hobby: the human skull, theme and variations. "Alas, poor Yorick, I knew him Horatio," and so on and so forth. Not altogether inappropriate for a physician, I admit, but intrinsically no more interesting than any other hobby. He was going on last night about the "vacuous description" of the escaped convict that is being circulated by the authorities, who dared to describe Selden as a red-headed fellow of average height, under-nourished (as well he might be after a year in gaol), with a dark beard. It's not much of a description, I'll give him that, a beard is a very temporary possession and by definition, most men are of average height, but it turns out that it is Selden's red hair that Dr Mortimer finds most offensive.

"Have you ever seen anyone with red hair, Dr Watson? Sir Henry? I'll be bound you haven't. And you never will. Mark my words: if this chap Selden really had red hair, they would have caught him long ago. He's probably quite ordinary-looking, really, with brown hair, a wizened face, low-slung jaw and a hungry look. His skull, now, might prove interesting…"

I've never seen a double chin, either, but I believe I know what one looks like. Oh, I wish I had thought of that last night! It does me no good whatever to think of it now. And what am I going to tell Mary?

* * *

A few more days of Baskerville Hall and my brains will have turned entirely to mush. It's not a *blackmail* case that is keeping Holmes, it is this missing person business of Mary Sutherland. Her "little problem" ("a case of identity," he called it) has turned out to be more complicated than he thought. Well, I'm not surprised. He had mixed feelings about that case from the beginning. I saw the way he refused to set his fee or accept a retainer from the lady. Quite contrary to his usual custom, although Miss Sutherland couldn't be expected to know that. I realize the case had a familiar ring to it (how could it not? it was only six months ago that he was approached by the Noble Bachelor, Lord St Simon; the difference between a bride gone missing immediately after the ceremony and a bridegroom gone missing immediately before it, is hardly overwhelming to the man of science), but the fact that he was successful in solving the one does not mean that he will be successful in solving the other. No two cases of pneumonia take quite the same course and no one knows this better than a doctor. One patient recovers, the next one dies, and the doctor whose patients have the best chance is the doctor who refuses to protect his pride with speculation but resolutely sets his face against death and wills them all to recover. So it is with Holmes. He was as confident of his powers as ever ("If you would care to stop by tomorrow evening, Watson, I believe I will be able to elucidate the matter for you") and yet he would not set his fee. Twenty-four hours later, I am at Baskerville Hall and Holmes is up to his neck in what must have been a fruitless search for the missing man.

On the whole, I am not sorry to be away from London.

Difficult to say what will happen next. On the one hand, it is characteristic of missing person cases that they tend to be solved quickly or not at all. As Holmes explained it to me, "There are always several lines available to the unbiased observer of an investigative disposition. If these have once been tried without positive results, however, further efforts are generally misplaced." A roundabout way of saying that the rare individual who wants to disappear badly enough to sever all known connections and adopt all new habits will probably succeed. Under ordinary circumstances, Holmes would invest two or at most three days in such a search. These, however, are not ordinary circumstances. The timing could not be more unfortunate: the Cathcart case, the Ripper business, and now Miss Sutherland's little problem, with nothing to look forward to but a spectral hound. Holmes has often said that he cannot afford to embark upon a losing streak. He must and he can accept the occasional failure, but two failures in a row he can not and must not accept. He is superstitious, is my friend Holmes.

I hope he will not feel obliged to go to Italy. But no—surely he will not leave the country while Sir Henry is in danger. Miss Sutherland's case is urgent only to Miss Sutherland.

I feel better now. Holmes won't write until he has solved his case of identity and then he probably won't write, either, but will simply take the next train to Devon. He may wire us before he leaves town, but I wouldn't bet on it—he does like to make an entrance. Until then, it is my job to protect Sir Henry. In all fairness, I don't suppose I could have contributed anything to the resolution of Miss Sutherland's "little problem" beyond my sincere good wishes for my friend's success and his client's eventual happiness.

Unlikely in any event that this would have made an adventure for me. Too similar by half to 'The Adventure of the Noble Bachelor', which, as an adventure already available in written form, naturally has pride of place in its author's affections, for all that publication is forbidden me for the present. It was interesting, even so, to observe his two clients' very different reactions to their experience. St Simon, who had had his American (and her antecedents) thoroughly investigated before making her an offer, was nevertheless completely convinced that his bride had disappeared of her own free will, quite possibly with the fixed intention of making a fool of him. Miss Sutherland, who in sharp contrast to Lord St Simon, knew practically nothing about her intended, much less his antecedents, was equally convinced that her fiancé had been spirited away from her against his will and was in grave danger. I wonder why that should be so?

* * *

If Mrs Barrymore's culinary talents are known to the neighbourhood (and I see no reason why they shouldn't be, the Barrymores have been in service at the Hall for time out of mind), that alone may serve to explain our social isolation. There is no reason for Sir Henry to take all of the credit to himself, and so I told him. I am beginning to lose my patience with that young man. God forgive me, but he does not seem to have the temperament for this business. He is as nervy as, as Mrs Barrymore.

We heard the Hound again last night. That is, we heard the call of an animal that Barrymore tells us is believed by the locals to be the Hound of the Baskervilles. Somehow I doubt that Holmes would be as impressed by this intelligence as Sir Henry was. Upon my word, I do not look forward to the prospect of spending Halloween at Baskerville Hall with Sir Henry! Was it only yesterday that I was telling myself that I could put up with my exile if only I knew what was keeping Holmes? I must have been mad. It is impossible to predict how long it will take him to lay the ghost of Miss Sutherland's past. I could be stuck here for months! Patience, Watson, patience.

I keep telling myself there must be some way for me to put

my time here to good use. It is no secret to me that it is the want of any useful occupation that is making the waiting so difficult. I write to Mary, I write in my diary. It is three days now since I have written to Holmes—there has been nothing for me to say. I can't send *Holmes* a description of the moor at sunset or a quick sketch of the furnishings in the dining room. [*Note*: I must remember to inquire into his progress on the Sutherland case when next I write. That will give him something to think about.]

I know what Mary would say if she were here. Sir Henry is happily inured to my writing and too much the gentleman in any case (and in spite of his current Heathcliff routine) to request a recitation of me. I might just as well redd up some old adventure as fadoodle around with this one. I can almost hear her voice.

Mary seems to think—and I am bound to admit, Holmes frequently appears to suffer from the same delusion—that every investigation brought to a successful conclusion is worth the telling, and it is no such thing. Mary would leap at the chance to send me my notes if I asked her to, but I have no desire to raise her hopes by making the request. I know what it must be costing her to write me every day and never once ask me whether I am keeping my journal. Besides, I don't need my notes to remind me of the adventures that I could tell if I would (and if I could see my way past the various plot knots that infest them). The list is nothing if not short. There is the Rufus Jamison case (Holmes's clear favourite) and there is the plight of the lusty King of Bohemia. God knows how he got Holmes's name, but he did.

The only way for me to avoid the King of Bohemia is to appoint myself Holmes's deputy in fact as well as in fiction and do what I can to solve the Baskerville case in his absence. I know what Holmes would think of this, but facts are facts and the one inescapable fact bearing upon the present situation is this: Holmes is not here. If Sir Henry is left to his own devices much longer, he's not going to have any devices. I have never seen such a rapid deterioration in an apparently healthy individual. Never. It must be stopped!

My resolution is made. I will leave no stone unturned in the pursuit of information that may bear upon the death of Sir Charles Baskerville last May and the consequent threat to the health and safety of his nephew and heir, Sir Henry Baskerville; and I will undertake to introduce that same Sir Henry to the charms and distractions of Dartmoor society, if it is the last thing I do.

I will begin my programme by taking my latest letter to Mary (which I will tell Sir Henry is a letter to Holmes) to the Post Office myself immediately after breakfast. It will not occur to Sir Henry in his present state to forego the solitary pleasures of wrestling with the paperwork of his inheritance in order to join me. Anyone I meet will find me gregarious in the extreme—I will assume the personality of my late brother and discover unplumbed wells of fellow-feeling in each chance-met acquaintance. I will issue invitations with a fine disregard for my status as a guest at Baskerville Hall (I can take Holmes as my model for this part) and seize upon any vague hint at reciprocity with all of the eagerness at my command. Why not? I'll never have to see these people again. I suspect that this is one thought I would do well to bear firmly in mind for however long it is that I am to be Holmes's deputy.

I go to bed for the first time since my arrival at the Hall well pleased with my plans for the morrow. Tonight I shall sleep the sleep of the just.

* * *

Ten days of unremitting stress here at Baskerville Hall and night after night, I slept like a top. Now that I have come to a decision as to how to manage the remainder of my stay, I'm broad awake and can't get to sleep at all. Why is irony the very stuff and substance of life? Looking out of my window, I am reminded that when night falls in this part of the country, it takes the whole world with it except for the lights of the prison, twinkling balefully across the moor. The moon is a rumour, hidden in a thicket of clouds. No star shines on my writing. What was Sir Charles doing outside after nightfall on that soft May night, wandering down the gloominess of the Yew Alley to the summer-house, listening to the melancholy sighing of the trees?

Answer: Bachelor that he was, he had an assignation with a lady. I am sure of it.

Watson, you have outdone yourself! In the matter of hypothesis generation, you have no equal. In recognition of the superior quality of your achievement, you may broach the subject of the tears in the night with Sir Henry in the morning. The introduction of the topic of domestic strife will give his thoughts a new direction.

And now, to sleep. I will have less time for writing now than I did formerly. Or so I hope.

Chapter 7

A full day—full of doubt, aggravation and disaster, that is. First, the disaster: Heathcliff has found his Cathy.

It needed only this for the situation to become completely intolerable. Oh, why isn't Holmes here? Practically the only advice he gave me was "Stay with young Baskerville," and how the devil I am to do that when he has found an eligible young lady in the neighbourhood is more than I can say. It is only a matter of time before he moves from giving me a hint to telling me straight out to mind my own business and keep my distance. Sir Henry is not only Holmes's client, he is also my host. Nor is this my only worry. As it happens, I made the acquaintance of the amiable Miss Stapleton several hours before Sir Henry did (blast that solitary walk to the Post Office!) and due to an absurd misunderstanding in which she took me, the stranger on her doorstep, for the new baronet, I know that she was, as they say, "prepared to like him" long before she met him. She was positively clinging to me—clutching my arm, whispering in my ear, rising on tiptoe to remind me how much taller I am than she is. Upon my word, it was prettily done! In a voice that sent a veritable shiver down my spine, she begged me, as the supposed Sir Henry, to leave Dartmoor behind and flee Baskerville Hall for my very life. That makes two people who want Sir Henry to leave his inheritance to the dogs (or should I say the Hound?): Miss Stapleton and Sir Henry's mysterious London correspondent, the one who uses newspaper clippings and a glue pot to compose his anonymous warnings. Since discovering her mistake, Miss Stapleton hasn't said one word to me, preferring to concentrate on the real Sir Henry. I don't want to let my suspicions run away with me, but I do hope that Miss Stapleton hasn't been in the habit of meeting Sir Henry's late, lamented Uncle Charles by the summer-house of an evening.

Sir Henry is well and truly smitten. Beryl Stapleton is "a jewel among women." (Sir Henry is not distinguished by the originality of his expression, save on those not infrequent occasions where he is guilty of an Americanism.) He actually believes that in Miss Stapleton (excuse me, "the sweet, unspoiled Miss Stapleton," I should say), he has found a woman who is able to content herself with the extremely limited diversions available in this locale.

Personally, I don't know what he means by the diversions available in this locale—the view of the prison? All of his interest in the escaped convict has returned. Unless I miss my guess, Sir Henry has visions of liberating Miss Stapleton from the clutches of the evil Selden, bearing her off in triumph to the Hall and marrying her out of hand. Foolishness, all of it. Slippery Jack Selden is probably hundreds of miles away from here by now. It's been twelve days, after all. How could a man survive alone on the barren moor for twelve days?

There is yet another consideration here. It seems to me that a young lady marooned at the edge of the Grimpen Mire by a brother as self-centered as the entomologically inclined Jack Stapleton might well be looking to the Hall for a husband wealthy enough to take her away from the diversions of Dartmoor. After all, if Mrs Barrymore can't stick life at the Hall, what price the beautiful Beryl? It's no use speaking to Sir Henry about this. I know, I've tried. He is still overwhelmed by his good fortune in the matter of his new suits, which arrived at the Hall this morning, just shortly in advance of Miss Stapleton. I don't need Sherlock Holmes to tell me that we won't be seeing Sir Henry's Canadian sunset tweeds any more. Imagine a country where orange tweeds are considered normal male attire. Canada must be a colourful country.

The Stapleton connection is altogether unfortunate and yet it was the sole fruit of my morning's expedition. I met the brother as I left the village grocery cum Post Office, he produced a sister, and every permutation since has been rife with danger.

Mr Stapleton and Dr Watson: he wonders whether my good friend Sherlock Holmes can be far behind. Surely we are looking into the matter of the Baskerville Hound for Sir Henry? It seems that Dr Mortimer shared his copy of A Study in Scarlet with just about everyone in the vicinity of Baskerville Hall previous to Sir Charles's death. So much for arriving in the neighbourhood *incognito*. I can't say I am looking forward to giving Holmes this piece of news.

Miss Stapleton and Dr Watson: she indulges herself in a fit of femininity that would have driven the real Sir Henry right over the edge. Not that his encounter with her brother can have added to his peace of mind. What must the bonehead do but insist on showing Sir Henry ("as a newcomer to our fair neighbourhood and the worthy successor to the estimable Sir Charles") exactly where it was that the infamous Sir Hugo Baskerville, inspiration of the Baskerville family legend, met his death at the jaws of the Hound.

I've left one out. Oh yes, Miss Stapleton and Sir Henry: he falls at her feet. How could I forget that?

Well, so far there hasn't been any less writing to my new approach! My first duty was to prepare my report for Holmes, and that duty, I am sorry to say, is with me yet in spite of two determined efforts to discharge it. I have given Sir Henry notice that I must have a block of time to myself tomorrow for the purpose, and he has kindly promised me the whole of the afternoon. Sir Henry is genuinely impressed by my journalistic duties, than which nothing could be more fortunate—or stand in greater contrast to the attitude of my friend Holmes. Holmes has such rigid ideas of what constitutes a report! Try as I may, I cannot seem to catch the trick of describing (in detail and at length) everything I have observed, while at the same time vigorously suppressing any references to the thoughts, conclusions, plans, and speculations that attended those observations. Holmes does not know what a burden this interdiction of his imposes on me. It feels as unnatural as patting yourself up and down on the head with one hand while rubbing your stomach in a circular motion with the other—a trick my brother could do to perfection, but which utterly defeated me.

There is also the matter of Sir Henry's newfound romantic interest. It may take some time to decide in what words to broach the subject of a possible courtship between Baskerville Hall and Merripit House. Holmes is not inclined to look with favour upon the romantic and I do not want to do or say anything that will cost Sir Henry any least part of Holmes's sympathy or interest. I have to write to Mary, too, who will be most interested in Beryl Stapleton, I know, and the progress of Sir Henry's trammelled courtship. Between them, my two readers (I cannot call Holmes a correspondent) have me covering the ground pretty thoroughly.

There remains the matter of my investigation of the Baskerville family mystery: Sir Charles's death, the spectral hound, etc. There I am on relatively solid ground, if only because no one expects me to solve the puzzle. I must see if I cannot find a way to put Barrymore in my debt. He will know, if anyone does, who it was that Sir Charles was meeting by the summer-house that evening. It will be difficult—Sir Henry did himself no good service when he taxed Barrymore after breakfast this morning for an explanation of the female sobbing that has been disturbing my sleep of nights. What possessed him to do such a thing? It's as plain as a pikestaff that Mrs Barrymore is the weeper. There is no other female here. Along with his other failings, Barrymore must be a domestic brute.

Sir Henry has a kind heart, but I could wish that he were a bit less ingenuous than he is. Then again, I could wish that Sir Henry were less romantically susceptible than he is, too. It will go hard with him, I know, if Miss Stapleton should reject him, or her brother should find some pretext to object to his suit. Sir Henry still hasn't gotten over *Barrymore's* rejection.

I wonder if Miss Stapleton might possibly have been educated abroad? There is something not quite English about her.

Her colouring, too, is darker than is usual. Those flashing eyes, that raven hair—she is much darker than her brother, for example.

More tomorrow, when I may possibly be able to keep my eyes open.

* * *

The odds on my being able to keep my eyes open lengthened last night when I discovered that the elusive Barrymore roams the corridors during the small hours and lingers long-ingly at the embrasure of a certain window, this being the one window of all the windows at the Hall that looks toward the moor. It is suggestive, what? I could not forbear telling Holmes in my letter that Sir Henry and I have concocted a plan to suit the occasion, but in deference to his wishes, I spared him the details. Of course, I must keep the entire inci-dent from Mary, who would certainly worry if she knew we were planning to accost Barrymore when next he walks. There will be no sleep for the weary tonight! I must endeav-our to keep my enthusiasm within bounds—take a lesson from Sir Henry, who spent his afternoon going through mountains of bills and receipts in order to unearth the name of the architect who planned the Hall and every contractor, furnisher, carpenter or plumber that has ever set foot on Baskerville family soil. Sir Henry is going to redecorate the Hall in order to make it a suitable setting for Miss Stapleton, whom he met for the first time yesterday. Take a lesson, Watson. Barrymore's wanderings may have nothing to do with the Hound. He may have some lay of his own. He may be a backstairs Lothario. Remember Mrs Barrymore's tears. Wouldn't it be something if Uncle Charles's fateful trip to the summer-house were in hot pursuit of Barrymore and his sec-ond portion?

Watson, you amaze me. You predicted today's Stapleton debacle to a nicety, without so much as a shred of evidence to show you the way. I'd like to see Holmes do that! There was Miss Stapleton, recoiling in horror from Sir Henry, easily the most eligible bachelor in all of Devonshire, and there was her brother Jack, descending upon that same Sir Henry, furiously demanding that he "Unhand her, unhand her at once, I say!" It makes no sense.

I was not close enough to hear the rest of the conversation, but Sir Henry was and I have it all. I'd like to have seen Holmes handle that situation. A pity I can't write Holmes now, but I can't expect Sir Henry's good nature to be proof against everything. In particular, I can't expect him to sit across from me and calmly watch me report his humiliation to my friend Holmes. No doubt it is trying his temper sufficiently just to see me busy with my journal. I must keep this entry short. Just a few more lines. You see what comes of Holmes's prohibition against sharing my speculations with him—I'll get no credit with Holmes for a prediction recorded only in my journal.

That's it. From now on, Holmes gets letters from me, not "reports." If he doesn't like it, he can damn well come to Devon himself.

I wish he would.

* * *

We have gotten the truth out of Barrymore at last and it sent us out on the darkling moor for a couple of hours of petty convict-baiting. The sky was clear, the rain had stopped, and Miss Stapleton must be protected. That's what we told each other, at any rate. I had my pistol, Sir Henry his hunting-crop (silly weapon, but I wasn't about to take the chance of Sir Henry's potting *me*), and the only difficult moment came at the height of the chase, when Sir Henry decided to ask me what my friend Holmes would say if he could see us now. That froze my blood, all right. I had completely forgotten that we were supposed to be avoiding the moor by night.

Which brings me to our discovery. There were two men out on the moor tonight (besides Sir Henry and myself, I mean) and one of them was not Selden. The stranger's form rose in the west and was outlined against the fitful moon scant seconds after Selden vanished in the opposite direction. Unless the world has gotten a lot smaller since I arrived in Devon, this was a different man. I saw his silhouette distinctly: taller than Stapleton, thinner than Lassiter, with better posture than Dr Mortimer if less presence than the artful Barrymore—it is a rare man who has a better demeanour than a good servant. I was ready to give chase to this second apparition (which I feel in my heart is of London manufacture) when Sir Henry was unmanned by the cry of the Hound—or the boom of the bittern. That's Jack Stapleton's theory about this sound: it's the last of the bitterns (some kind of crane, I think he said), bellowing across the moor in order to attract a mate. I have to admit, it sounded like a hound to me. And, of course, nothing can persuade Sir Henry that it is not The Hound, searching for the last of the Baskervilles. That was the end of our hunting and tracking for this night.

I trust Miss Stapleton will be impressed.

* * *

A dull grey morning, as weary of the world as I am, and I seem to have dozed in spite of myself and the cold ashes in the grate. My letter to Holmes is done and all I want now is breakfast and a couple of hours' sleep in a bed instead of a chair. I don't know how Holmes does it—sitting up with an intellectual problem is infinitely more tiring than sitting up with a sick patient. The last of the bitterns and the last of the Baskervilles: it is all a bit too romantic/nostalgic for the likes of plain Dr Watson. I miss my wife and the last of the bacon. I'm tired of burnt toast and blackened mushrooms.

That glimpse I caught of the stranger on the moor has had me sweating over my notes all over again, trying to decide how many words of my 9,000 word allotment I can afford to spend on the matter of the escaped convict. On the one hand, the convict probably has nothing whatever to do with the central problem of the Hound. On the other, Slippery Jack Selden is undoubtedly real. Small wonder we set off after the poor bastard last night. A man can only take so much sitting around and thinking before it becomes time to do something. What we did was chase Jack Selden up and down the moor for the best part of an hour, until we found ourselves caught between the convict and the stranger, and the Hound (or was it the bittern?) made its spectral presence known. There is something about a disembodied bawling in the near-dark of a deserted place recently determined not to be deserted after all, that is unnerving to the spirits. I feel sure I could capture that sensation with my pen.

I can tell you one thing: Mr Lassiter of Franklin Hall is going to be a problem. Dr Mortimer will be easy enough, the Stapletons will be manageable within limits (I shall, for example, have to exercise discretion in the matter of the description of my passionate introduction to Miss Stapleton, that goes without saying), and Sir Henry will be all that is agreeable, I'm sure. Mr Lassiter, however, is going to be a problem. Unless—no, I can't think it likely that he will oblige me by proving to be the villain of the piece. He is too portly, for one thing, and too well-established in years for another. Crime is a young man's game. I can't see Mr Lassiter scrabbling over the tors, baying like a hound in the moonlight. Then, too, Mr Lassiter is litigious to a fault.

If Mr Lassiter had a grievance against Sir Henry or an interest in the Hall, he would be bringing suit for a certainty. Every man of violence has his weapon; the poisoner does not think to reach for the axe. If Mr Lassiter were the culprit, he would be setting the law on Sir Henry, not a spectral hound.

Ordinarily, I'd say this was a problem with a simple solution: leave Lassiter out of it. With any luck at all, he'll be a minor character, no great loss to the plot, dead wood eminently suitable for pruning. If anything is clear about this case at all, it is that I am going to have to leave something out if I am to be left with a 9,000 word adventure. Lassiter is so litigious, however, that he is capable of anything. In particular, it seems to me that he is capable of bringing suit against me for leaving him out of the piece. You should have heard him on the subject of property rights!

Mr Lassiter is going to be a problem.

* * *

Progress at last: Barrymore has taken umbrage over our persecution(!) of poor Selden and I have turned the situation to our advantage, I think. It is best that I not say how, I am afraid that it is not quite legal. (Am I committing a felony? I must ask Holmes.) Barrymore then returned the favour with a piece of news that confirms my original hypothesis—Sir Charles did indeed have an appointment with a lady that evening, a lady with the initials "L.L." *Not* Miss Stapleton, I conclude. That's a load off my mind. Best of all, Sir Henry has sent me off to my room to compose my report for Holmes. A lucky chance, since it means I have leisure for a little nap. My report is done, it won't take but a minute to add the news of Sir Charles's erstwhile lady friend. I knew Mr Lassiter was going to be a problem. Five will get you ten she's a relative, a cherished daughter for preference. He's been a widower for some years, so it can't be his wife. That's something, at all events. At least we won't be dealing with a case of adultery again.

For what it's worth, I don't believe Barrymore's tale of the burnt letter for a moment, his wife cleaning out the grate after Sir Charles's death, finding the charred remains with only the

"L.L." signature still legible, in (of course) a lady's hand—it smacks of Wilkie Collins—but I expect the information itself is accurate enough. Why should Barrymore lie to me? No reason at all, particularly now. It's just our careful Barrymore, salving his conscience by giving me the lady's initials instead of her name. He didn't betray the lady. Oh no, of course not.

I must ask Dr Mortimer whether Mr Lassiter has a daughter. It is going to be a beautiful day after I get some sleep.

* * *

I can tell you exactly what he said. He came in out of the cold and wet, whipped off his coat and hat, and asked me a question. "Would you say I was irascible?" he asked. And I answered him. "Why, no, not to your face," I said. The cleverness of my response woke me up directly. Now I'll never know what Holmes would have answered me. I tell myself it's just as well. Judging from Holmes's behaviour when I am awake, he would not have been at a loss for words for long.

In one of those eerie coincidences that so often superintends the proximity of the waking and the sleeping worlds, I have learned that while I was evading Holmes in my dreams, Sir Henry was evading me in reality. Leaving me (as he supposed) engaged in composing my report for Holmes (but actually composing myself for sleep), Sir Henry slipped away to Merripit House for a clandestine visit with Miss Stapleton. It's wonderful what love can do. Last night, Sir Henry was shaking in his shoes at the sound of the Hound. This morning, he is haring off across the moor, by himself, without a second thought. I don't know which Sir Henry I like better: the one who is not ashamed to be afraid or the one who is not ashamed to be in love. That young man is a bundle of feelings and no mistake. It makes quite a change from dealing with Holmes.

I have been as stern with Sir Henry as I knew how to be but even so, I am afraid to leave him until I am assured that he is properly penitent. I am in no mood to lose Holmes's client for him now that I am beginning to believe that there may be a case in all of this. Better I should wait for Holmes to investigate the mysterious "L.L." than that I should permit Sir Henry to jeopardize his safety again.

So here we sit, on either side of the fire, Sir Henry occupied with the everlasting paperwork of the estate, I with my diary, each of us wishing only to be shut of the other so that we might pursue our several goals. I wonder if I might be able to interest Sir Henry in a friendly little game of écarté?

* * *

A letter from Holmes! No date, no salutation, no signature, and practically no message. My word, but Miss Sutherland must be keeping him busy! It's a good job I know his fist when I see it. Listen to this: "The Hound is real. Sir Henry is in mortal danger. Avoid the moor by night at all costs."

Even when he doesn't send a telegram, he does. What does he mean, the Hound is real? The peasants here speak of a supernatural force dedicated to the destruction of the Baskerville family line, a force that takes the shape of a gigantic hound whose slavering dewlaps and maddened eyes drip hellfire. I will not believe this apparition is real. Besides, if the Hound is real, what will it avail us to avoid the moor? I may not know much about the supernatural, but surely it is not so easily thwarted as that.

I know Holmes does nothing without a good reason, but it would certainly be easier on his friends if he could, upon occasion, bring himself to tell us what those reasons are.

"The Hound is real. Sir Henry is in mortal danger. Avoid the moor by night at all costs."

* * *

Well, it took the better part of the day, but I think he's got it now. For the longest time, Sir Henry couldn't seem to understand the object of the game, that he was supposed to try to win. Finally I told him that he should simply *pretend* that he wanted to win. For the sake of his opponent, I told him. Because unless I believe that he wants to win, I can get no pleasure from beating him. This explanation, which begs the question in at least two places that I can think of, seemed to satisfy him. It certainly improved his play.

I don't know why I didn't think of this before. A couple of hands of écarté with Sir Henry, and Dr Mortimer will be unmasked for the villain he probably is. It's a plot worthy of Holmes himself. Dr Mortimer doesn't stand a chance against him. Over cards, young Baskerville's overdeveloped graciousness is not far short of an incitement to riot, as I saw myself this afternoon.

"Your Queen, man! Play your Queen. I'm out of clubs, as you'd know if you'd kept count as you should. Play your Queen!" I was actually shouting at him.

"Which Queen should I play?" he asked. As if I could know he had more than one Queen!

I have only to wait until a suitable lull in Dr Mortimer's skull lecture, interject a comment to the effect that Sir Henry has been learning to play écarté, and await results. Sir Henry's overdeveloped notions of courtesy will not let him deny the charge in front of me, his teacher; Dr Mortimer will be obliged to oblige; and I will be free to watch the proceedings from a safe distance. Twenty feet or so ought to be close enough.

It may be weak of me, but I find that I would rather take my conversational chances with Barrymore than try for still another convivial evening in the company of my host and Dr Mortimer.

* * *

Cerberus is missing. Now do I write that to Holmes, as a piece of potentially valuable data, or do I keep it to myself, knowing how he feels about lost lap-dogs? I have no other news for him. Barrymore wasn't exactly a fountain of information tonight and Dr Mortimer stands revealed as the harmless eccentric he appeared to be, innocent of any machinations against Sir Henry.

I must have something to tell Holmes, and that as soon as may be.

Chapter 8

It was in order that I might have something to tell Holmes that I proposed the following plan to Sir Henry: if he would remain within the confines of the Hall during my absence, the whole of my absence, I would undertake to interview Lassiter's daughter Loretta (initials "L.L.") of Miss Lassiter's Typewriting in Coombe Tracey. Whatever deficiencies of judgement or intelligence Holmes may see fit to charge me with in regard to my handling of this case, I hope I may hold myself excused from any imputation of disloyalty or deficiency of purpose. And so I told him.

It was not an easy interview. In fact, it was awkward beyond belief, trying to introduce the topic of Sir Charles Baskerville and the summer-house into the conversation. Miss Lassiter kept smiling and thinking that I was in need of her typewriting services; I would show her my manuscript if only she could be reassuring enough.

"You are a Writer?" she prodded.

Has everyone on Dartmoor heard of 'A Study in Scarlet'? Dr Mortimer has much to answer for, I thought, all unconscious that a corner of my journal was protruding from my pocket.

Holmes may be right about this. It is possible that I would find a life of deception difficult to sustain.

I was making my way back to the Hall, ignoring the muck (we've had our share of rain) and going over my words, trying to put a more flattering construction on my interview with Miss Lassiter, when I was accosted by her father, fairly bursting to tell someone of his find upon the moor. After conning the barren wastes for weeks with his telescope, he has discovered that a gentleman has set up housekeeping in one of the neolithic huts. No, not a warder, the warders gave up the search for Selden almost a week ago. (The more fools they,

I thought.) A gentleman it was, a gentleman who keeps a boy running errands for him to Coombe Tracey.

"See for yourself, Dr Watson."

To my eyes, the boy looked to be about twelve.

I abandoned my previous occupation with alacrity. This would be something I might be proud to share with Holmes. Half a moment, though. Why tell Holmes the beginning of the story when with a little exertion I might have it all? I had many questions about this gentleman. Who was he? What was his purpose on the moor? I would go out to the gentleman's hut and ask him. I had been successful with Miss Lassiter, after all. I didn't know whether or not to believe her, but I did have her version of last May's events: a late-night appointment made but not kept, Sir Charles waiting vainly at the appointed place, the appointment kept by Death in the form of a gigantic Hound. It was for Holmes to decide how much truth there was in it.

I approached warily, the more warily because I could not be certain, now that I was here, which of the several huts in the vicinity was the hut I had seen through Mr Lassiter's telescope. I burst into three of them before I found the right one. By then I had modified my original strategy, calmed my nerves with tobacco, and was making my entrance with a "Hello? Anyone at home?" on my lips.

As soon as I saw how the place was furnished, I had the answer to all my questions: Holmes. I would have known that orderly disorder anywhere. No doubt Holmes would be able to tell from a cursory examination of the interior when the occupant was due back, but I confess it was beyond my powers. I settled myself to wait for his return.

I have said that I had the answers to all my questions, but in point of fact, I found that I had a whole new set of questions. What had I ever done to him that he should serve me such a trick? I took inventory of his meagre belongings. So, he had been here some days, a week at least. Why would he hide here, so dark and damp as it was? I lit his dark lantern. Does he want to give himself rheumatism? One thing and one thing only I regretted: that I had insufficient light to turn to my diary. It would have helped me give shape to my feelings.

Time passed. I thought of my reports, making their way to an empty apartment in Baker Street. I thought of Mary's reproaches at my impatience. I thought of Mrs Ogden's Timothy; sick with what?, I wondered. Well, I was right about one thing: Holmes wasn't in London working on a blackmail case. I wondered what had been the outcome of the Sutherland debacle. I felt like a fool, twitting him about it. All my sympathy had been wasted. When I write Mary about this, I decided, I will stress the humour in the situation: Lassiter watching Holmes watching Watson watching Sir Henry. So this is what a bachelor has to do for entertainment. Who was watching Lassiter?, I wondered. Dr Mortimer, probably. If I do it right, Mary will laugh.

My face grew warm as I recalled chasing Selden across the moor. It grew warmer when I remembered the stranger's outline, Holmes's outline, against the moon and recalled his near-telegraphic communication to me the next day. He must have sent that note off to Baker Street by first light, in order for it to have come back to us so quickly. The afternoon was wearing away. It grew chill. My recognition that this was his lair would mean very little to Holmes, I knew, without some detailed bit of evidence that I could point to—a laundry mark in a shirt, a distinctive bit of cigar ash, a footprint. The more I tried to pin down the reasons for my certainty, the less certain I became. Certainly, there was nothing distinctive in these possessions. What if it were not Holmes? What if this were Selden's hiding place after all? Slippery Jack Selden, the Notting Hill murderer, and me armed with my journal! Wouldn't it be better to wait at some distance from the entrance so as to confirm my hypothesis in safety? The thought was father to the deed. I shut the lantern.

"Well done, Watson! But what have you been doing in there these two hours past? I was beginning to think that I should have to come in and get you after all." He had my discarded cigarillo in hand to justify his hypothesis.

Well done, Holmes. I did not even try to tell him that I had recognized his home away from home. He would not have believed me.

Holmes's reasons for my deception could not be admitted without argument. Oh, there was the usual blather about the need to keep his presence secret so as to lull the villain(s) into a false sense of security. My lack of guile, his reputation, and so on and so forth. Where does he get this stuff? His fame is hardly greater than mine in this part of the country. Anyone who's heard of Sherlock Holmes in this neck of the woods has heard of him by way of 'A Study in Scarlet', written by one John H. Watson. Stapleton made the connection immediately, as did Miss Lassiter, with very little help from me.

"You can't be serious," I said. "How can anything lull a spectral hound into a false sense of security?" I had him there. He changed the subject immediately. It seems that Holmes is worried about his biographer. Of all the infuriating nonsense!

"You have been working in the wrong length, Watson. Your forté is the long story. What we have here," and he fanned his letters at me, "is the makings of a serial, Watson. Think of it!"

My forté may be anything you like, but what they will buy is *adventures*, short stories of at most 9,000 words. I have Mr Fitsch's word on it. Holmes doesn't know what he is talking about. 'A Study in Scarlet' isn't "a long story," it's a short novel.

A serial must be carefully planned. The plot must lend itself to segmentation. There must be a train of narrative segments, each segment approximately the same length, each segment ending on a note of suspense, that suspense resolved in the next instalment and a second, related conflict introduced and carefully heightened in its turn, until the final chapter comprehensively restores the moral fabric, social order, and family peace that were so wantonly disrupted by the narrative play. It is not easy to write a serial.

Even if I could write a serial, I am not persuaded it would

be the most advantageous means of introducing Holmes to the general public. Imagine the burden of information the first instalment would have to bear! Imagine the number of introductions that would have to be made: myself, Holmes, Sir Henry, Dr Mortimer (I *must* have Dr Mortimer), the Barrymores, Selden, the Hound. Imagine the amount of plot that would have to be accommodated, the degree of interest that would have to be aroused to carry the reader from one issue of the magazine to the next. No, this time Holmes has gone too far. I enjoyed the role of biographer when there was some reason why the story should be told, some doubt that I could tell it, and some recognition that when it was told, I had done something. Now that it turns out that serials can be created willy-nilly out of correspondence (at which point no doubt they go out and create their own market, too), I have lost my taste for the part. And so I told him. God knows how our discussion might have ended had the Hound not chosen this particular night to make his appearance.

"Ah, the boom of the bittern," I observed.

"The boom of the bittern? Watson, it is the Hound!"

All our differences were forgotten in the chase. Well, almost all. I confess I had a rather powerful emotional reaction to the question, "How came you to leave Sir Henry alone and unprotected? When did you leave the Hall?"

Rather than say, "This morning," I concentrated on keeping my footing.

I had every reason to suppose Sir Henry firmly fixed at the Hall, I told myself. Didn't I have his word? By following my advice, hadn't he beaten Dr Mortimer at cards last night? Didn't I have his word? You may say that I had had his word before without observing its having any material effect on his behaviour, but that would be to deliberately miss the point. Sir Henry is not an habitual liar. On the previous occasion, the provocation had been strong. A marriageable female as attractive as Miss Beryl Stapleton in an area as devoid of attractions as Dartmoor is, must be allowed to be strong provocation. Since Jack Stapleton's three-month embargo on Sir Henry's attempts to attach her affections, however, Merripit House could not be allowed as a temptation. Where else could he go? Sir Henry must be found safe at the Hall, I told myself, clutching my side.

"You are out of condition," was Holmes's next observation.

I flatly refused to leave Selden's body at the foot of the tor, to be savaged by the Hound. Every feeling revolted against it. We made shift to carry him to one of the neolithic huts, at a little distance from Holmes's. He was pitifully light.

Sir Henry had spent the day indoors, at the Hall, and was discovered playing cribbage with Dr Mortimer. Cerberus is still missing. I have deferred further conversation with Holmes until the morning.

* * *

If he says, "Elementary, my dear Watson," one more time, I shall not be responsible for my actions.

Nothing is as I had imagined it to be. Miss Stapleton is actually Mrs Vandesomething and married to the man who has been passing her off as his sister these two years past. What she must have suffered, being forced to hope month after month that she had not conceived, and she his lawfully wedded wife. How she must hate him! Holmes has not told Sir Henry. No doubt he has his reasons. Miss Lassiter meanwhile has reportedly had hopes of attaching Mr Stapleton, alias Mr Vandesomething, and is in Holmes's opinion, lucky to be alive. So much for romance on Dartmoor.

"Watson, do you tell me that you have passed that portrait morning and evening for two weeks and never once noticed the resemblance?"

Dr Mortimer did not notice the resemblance, either, I am happy to say, in spite of his hobby and his greater familiarity both with the portrait in question and with Mr Stapleton, a Baskerville born on the wrong side of the blanket, as the saying goes. It's like something out of *King Lear*, with Mrs Barrymore cast as Cordelia. Holmes has promised that I may be present at the *dénouement* of the Sutherland case, scheduled for twenty-four hours after our return to Baker Street.

"You know that I never willingly interrupt the unravelling of one case to tackle another. In accepting Dr Mortimer's kind invitation, I determined to put the Sutherland case altogether aside until the Hound might be laid to rest. I have my hypothesis for that case. It remains only to confirm it."

Other men may speak of hypothesis testing. Holmes speaks only of hypothesis confirming. In his words: "I do not expect to be disappointed."

The Hound is real. Sir Henry is, was, has been in mortal danger. On Holmes's advice, Sir Henry is to dare the moor tonight, alone, at all costs. Holmes thinks I don't know what this means, but I do. A child could tell you what that means. I have written to Mary, advising her to expect me the day after tomorrow.

It has been an adventure.

Chapter 9

Are all wives given to these sudden flashes of insight, do you suppose?

Mary and I talked for hours last night, catching each other up on our separate doings. I was telling her about Mr Lassiter and his telescope, my discovery of Holmes's lair in the neolithic hut and the way Holmes caught me out, when she broke in on my story (very unusual for Mary), saying in a wondering voice, "You must want to write these adventures of yours very badly, John." I began to apologize for my selfishness, but again she cut me off.

"No, John, I don't blame you! To want to be heard is very natural and the silence surrounding Mr Holmes begs to be broken. He feels it himself. And his own fumbling attempts at that side of the business have flown very wide of the mark. Articles on the taxonomic classification of the human ear do not begin to do justice to his deductive powers. You said so yourself. But I think it would be good for you to realize that your heroic perseverance in this matter is a measure of your own desire for publication. Not mine, not Mr Holmes's, but yours, John."

I wonder that I did not realize this myself. The admission comes hard, though, for all that Mary says ambition is a fine thing in a husband. I had not thought of myself as an ambitious man.

Holmes, now, Holmes is ambitious. For myself, I know that my next adventure will come more easily if I can bring myself to believe that telling that particular story will serve a more general purpose than my own aggrandizement.

* * *

My desk is prohibitively tidy this morning. In this corner, my letters to Mary, secured with a business-like India rubber band. A number lightly pencilled below our address tells me (I suppose) the order of their arrival in Paddington. She should see the greasy bundle of correspondence Holmes surrendered to me as we came down on the train yesterday.

It seems that Mary, like the rest of us, had high hopes for 'The Hound of the Baskervilles'.

* * *

One of the things it is going to be difficult to adjust to now that I am back in London is the sudden reduction in the amount of time I have for keeping my diary. Every time I bid a patient goodbye, I expect to be granted the indulgence of a short paragraph in my journal. This is a hard thing to lose.

* * *

Finally, Mrs Ogden's Timothy, with nothing worse than a sprained ankle, thank goodness. That's a relief. I believe I have been holding my breath, figuratively speaking, about that boy ever since Mary wrote me about him.

* * *

I am glad I thought to bring Mary those flowers last night. Lovely dinner—roast beef, Yorkshire pudding, green beans and baked onions, I wonder if there is any left?—and Holmes did not stay very late, after all. Something about a letter he had to send with regard to the Sutherland case. I have been invited to present myself in Baker Street at a quarter to six this afternoon if I would like to see how it comes out. I expect I'll go.

* * *

Bills, bills and more bills! Where is the money to come from? If it is to come from my practice, then I must refrain from investing my time in spectral hounds on Dartmoor. If it is to come from my writing, then I must not grudge the time I spend in pursuit of a story, but must work to develop the ability to turn a greater proportion of my material into adventures I can publish. Meanwhile, neither solution is advanced by the amount of time I spend with my diary. This truly is time spent to no financial purpose.

* * *

Found my notes on the Sutherland case, which tell me nothing I did not already know. I wonder why Holmes calls it a case of identity?

* * *

A quarter to six. No time to walk to Baker Street, plus I shall be late no matter how quickly I manage to get there. Holmes will have to understand, my time is not my own. Passed all day from pillar to post (Mrs Ogden as the pillar, Mr Jellett as the post), I am forced to admit that I have very little to show for all the claims on my medical attention since I returned from Baskerville Hall. What would I not give to have been spared this last half-hour with that hardy perennial, Mr Ambrose Jellett?

Holmes will never understand if a late arrival on my part spoils what would have been one of his dramatic moments. I suppose I must hope that Miss Sutherland's stepfather will be equally delayed. There, I've found my notes at last. Five to six—I must fly!

Chapter 10

Not a word to Mary! My best strategy must be to wait and see what Mr Fitsch has to say to my submission. He may have forgotten all about his very obliging offer. It has been several months, after all. Time enough to tell Mary about my triumph when Fitsch has accepted 'A Case of Identity'.

Up all night writing, then round to Baker Street at first light to hear the verdict. Breakfast under the sustaining influence of Mrs Hudson, a brief but mutually satisfying arrangement with Peterson the commissionaire, and the deed was done. I was back in my surgery by ten o'clock in the morning and if all the world is different-seeming, well so it is. Different, I mean. It must be nearly an hour now since Peterson delivered 'A Case of Identity' to Mr Fitsch, Editor, at the offices of the *Strand Magazine*.

Holmes can adjust to a new situation faster than anyone else I know. "Have you given any thought to your next adventure, Watson?"

"Holmes, please," I sputtered, "that is months away."

"Yes, I know, two months away, to be exact. But what is two months, Watson? Winter will take the city in its jaws, November will give way to December, and December will slip away, taking the old year with it. Then January will be upon us and your new adventure will be due at the *Strand*."

Holmes made a steeple with his fingers. "'The Sign of Four' is too long. You agree with me, Watson?"

Actually, I don't, but I know Fitsch does and as I recall, the sentiment was original with him, not Holmes. Holmes was almost as pleased as I was by 'The Sign of Four' when it was new. Holmes took my fidget for assent and began to tick the remaining candidates off on his fingers.

"'The Sign of Four' is too long, 'The Speckled Band' is out of the question while Helen Stoner is alive, 'The Boscombe

Valley Mystery' must wait for the demise of John Turner—you are reading the obituary column daily, I hope, Watson?—and it is not yet time for 'The Five Orange Pips.'

"You may not realize it, Watson, but 'A Case of Identity' puts paid to two adventures which were otherwise eminently suitable: 'The Hound of the Baskervilles' and 'The Noble Bachelor.' In the case of Lord St Simon, your noble bachelor, it is the nature of the problem which is too strongly reminiscent: social embarrassment and personal disappointment at the nuptial event, occasioned by the disappearance of the client's newly wedded spouse. For Mary Sutherland, it is true, the disappearance was in advance of the wedding, she lost a spouse-to-be, St Simon an apparent spouse, but this distinction, important though it may be to the client facing the necessity of instituting formal annulment proceedings, cannot be of comparable significance to the casual reader. In the case of Sir Henry Baskerville, it is the pattern of the solution which provides the damning echo. One case of identity is very like another, I'm sorry to say."

I reminded myself that 'The Hound of the Baskervilles' would be as long or longer than 'The Sign of Four'. "Lord St Simon?" I asked weakly.

"Engaged to Another," he confirmed. "As I predicted. Another American, I believe. Wait, I have it here—yes, an American, from Philadelphia this time, the only daughter of a purveyor of tea and comestibles. How the mighty have fallen, eh, Watson? One can but hope that she will be equal to the challenge. Unlikely that St Simon's recent experience of American womanhood will have gone very far toward sweetening his disposition. Haven't you been reading the Society pages?"

"I thought it would take at least a twelvemonth before he was ready to test the waters again," I said.

"So it would had his affections been engaged the first time, Watson. No, I fancy he returned to the field in very short order. Well, he must have done if he managed to bear off a second prize so nearly on the heels of the first. It is a pity you didn't wait."

I don't think so. Had I known about St Simon's engagement, I hope I should have done the same thing. It was important that 'A Case of Identity' be told. Besides, it is a better story than 'The Noble Bachelor'.

* * *

Not a word to Mary, indeed! Five minutes after she's popped her head into my surgery to wish me "Good morning" and make sure I've had my breakfast, I've told her everything. She thinks it's wonderful. Imagine, A Case of Identity, what a wonderful title! When can she read it? I felt a momentary pang, telling her that I'd already sent it to Mr Fitsch, but she made nothing of it. "That's as it should be, John. This way I'll get the full effect, seeing it for the first time in print." Of course Cousin Nat will like it! What could I be thinking? No cousin of hers could possibly be so lacking in discrimination as to reject one of my adventures. "Now, John, I know what you're thinking and I don't want to hear a word about 'The Sign of Four.' You know Cousin Nat explained why that was not suitable. It was a technical problem, a problem of length pure and simple. It's a poor world where the painter must cut his canvas to fit the size of the frame, but if that's the world we live in, there's no sense in repining. 'The Sign of Four' is a beautiful story. Now how shall we celebrate your first sale? And shall we invite Mr Holmes to join us?"

I told Mary I'd have to think about it but the truth is, I don't have to think about it at all. I know exactly what I want to do: I want to take Mary to see Annie Oakley in the American border drama, "Deadwood Dick, or The Sunbeam of the Sierras." We saw the Peerless Lady Wing-Shot last year in Buffalo Bill's Wild West (With Fifty Hostile Indians) at the American Exhibition, and I still remember her famous mirror shot—and the Attack on the Deadwood Coach! I wonder if they'll do something similar here? I don't see how they could, really. This is a dramatic presentation on a stage in a theatre, not an exhibition in an outdoor arena. I wonder what her voice sounds like? We can do without Holmes on this occasion, I think—a man who had no interest in seeing a demonstration of Miss Oakley's marksmanship will have no interest in seeing a demonstration of her thespian abilities.

Afterwards, we'll eat oysters and drink champagne and talk about the play. Mary will toast my first sale and I will toast her blue eyes. Maybe she will be able to help me plan my next few adventures. She's already solved the St Simon problem for me.

"Is that all, John? There's nothing else? Without telling me all of the details of the Sutherland case (I do so want to read it in the *Strand*!), is that the only point of similarity between that case and Lord St Simon's? Because if so, I don't see why we shouldn't leave it to Cousin Nat's judgement. You've already written 'The Noble Bachelor,' haven't you? So what will it cost you to submit it to Cousin Nat, say a year from now? He'll know better than any of us whether the coincidence is apt to strain the credulity of his readers. But you know, John, I doubt that this will prove to be the insuperable obstacle Mr Holmes imagines it to be. Hardly anyone is as disturbed by repetition as Mr Holmes. And the *Strand* is a monthly magazine, after all. Who is to say how many of those who read the December issue this year will still be reading the magazine next year or the year after that? As I understand it, Mr Holmes has been known to complain himself about the sameness of the problems presented to him by his clients. I may not be as logical as Mr Holmes, but I fail to see how he can expect you, who are only his biographer after all, to select from a pool of similar problems, problems that are all different from each other. It seems impossible to me.

"You know, John, one might even argue that a certain similarity in the opening paragraphs of your adventures was motivated by an admirable attempt at verisimilitude on your part."

Trust Mary to see it from my point of view. We'll go Sunday afternoon. Holmes almost never drops in on us of a Sunday and when he does, it is always in the evening. With any luck at all, he'll never know we've gone and we won't have to hear his scathing comments about the decline of the theatre, or his opinion of Buffalo Bill's Wild West, which he's never seen. Holmes has no taste for popular entertainment. He's told me so many times. I see no reason to issue an invitation I know will be refused.

Besides, Holmes is no doubt under the impression that he and I have already accorded the possible publication of 'A Case of Identity' all of the celebration it deserves. That's Holmes's idea of a party, anyway: poached eggs and porridge *à la* Mrs Hudson. His spare and meagre habit (all the more spare and meagre since I removed to Paddington, I might add) have led him to equate any early morning meal more substantial than a cup of coffee with riotous living and ruinous self-indulgence. By his rarefied standards, I was gay to dissipation this morning, downing two kippers and a piece of dry toast. Personally, I like breakfast.

I can't wait to see how 'A Case of Identity' looks in next month's *Strand*.

Chapter 11

"Are you happy, John?"

"Not as happy as I am going to be," I replied gamely, tossing my newspaper to one side. I am a man who believes in seizing his opportunities. It was good to be home again.

"Not now, John! Please be serious," she laughed. "It's broad daylight."

The thought crossed my mind that I had rarely been more serious, but I held my peace and hid my disappointment. The ladies have their own way of looking at things, bless them. Her blushes told their own story. I can be patient.

She regarded me thoughtfully and I felt the first faint pangs of uneasiness. Mary was uncommonly pensive today.

"Are you happy with me, John? Do I make you happy?"

"Mary—Darling," the correction was immediate, "Darling, of course you do. How can you ask me that?" (I give you my word I did not know what she was leading up to.)

"Do you think Mr Holmes is happy?"

I stopped short. This must be what they mean by feminine intuition. The thought of feminine intuition applied to Holmes appalled me. Even had I known what to say, I am not sure my voice would have obeyed me. I could feel the hairs on my arms prickling to attention. Just a moment ago, things had been going so well. Now, without any warning, the conversational ground had been cut away at my feet, by my wife. There yawned before me a pit of immense dimensions and I stood stupefied on the brink of destruction. I had lodged with a man who could read my thoughts long enough to know that I did not look for the same accomplishment in my wife. How had she tumbled to my friend's secret? How? That was the question that gnawed at me, to the perfect exclusion of more practical considerations.

I know Holmes for the most private of men. Whatever

progress he has managed to make in his lonely battle with cocaine will be lost forever if he once realizes that he has an audience, and a female one at that. Mary's manner must not develop even a hint of sympathetic understanding. I know Holmes. Which does not explain Mary's sudden insight. All these months we have been pretending, he and I, that it is for the sake of our great friendship that he haunts my home. It is a polite fiction, nothing more, and its major prop (I confess it freely) is Mary's unquestioning acceptance of our supposed friendship. She can have no way of knowing that I have seen more of Holmes in the six months since our marriage than in all my years in Baker Street, that he almost never shared his cases with me then.

To be sure, part of it is the excuse afforded by Mr Fitsch of the *Strand Magazine*, whose princely advance, split fifty-fifty with Holmes, held out the promise that he might be able to retain his rooms without having to subject himself to the vagaries of another and possibly less congenial fellow lodger. He is not easy to live with, is my friend Holmes. As for me, I was husband enough to welcome his intrusion into our family circle. It has been a long time since I last lived among the ladies and these after-dinner reversions to our cheerless days in Baker Street have lent a certain piquancy to the married state that I have been grateful for on more than one occasion. If I was husband enough to welcome him, I was also doctor enough to know why this man with no great talent for company should suddenly crave the distraction of strange surroundings and familiar faces on an almost nightly basis. I rejoiced to see it, buried the joy out of sight so as not to provoke him—I had learned my lesson over 'The Sign of Four'—and...

Of course, 'The Sign of Four'! Absurdly simple, once you see the intuitive chain in its entirety. I cursed myself yet again for having ended that tale by disclosing the syringe in his hand. Of all of the adventures that have emerged from my pen, that is the one Mary knows best, as that is the one that brought us together. She cannot have forgotten how he turns to the drug when I announce our engagement to marry on the last page.

She was waiting for my answer.

Do I think Holmes is happy? Well, do I?

I cast about frantically for something neutral to say about Holmes and the pursuit of happiness, but all my thoughts led directly to cocaine. Holmes would like, I know, to believe himself above such mundane considerations as mere earthly happiness, an artist content to live for his art, but in that case I think he should be above such mundane considerations as mere earthly *unhappiness*, and that I know he is not. He can tolerate anything but boredom, or so he says. Boredom, the common lot of mankind, and rather more common for Sherlock Holmes than for the rest of us.

The entire topic of Holmes and happiness is fraught with apparent contradictions. Once possessed of a worthy problem (perhaps I should say, once possessed *by* a worthy problem), he seems happy enough, I suppose. Assuming that one can be quite tense with happiness. And that this happy nervous tension is sufficient recompense for the overwhelming weariness of the rest of it.

What I remember best from our years together are the frequent, lengthy bouts of determined inanition that he would enliven with a little morphine or a little cocaine, just often enough to keep the medical man in me, not to mention the potential friend, perpetually on edge. It was calculated to a hair's-breadth and I can only hope that my marriage and consequent removal from Baker Street came early enough for him to be able to give it up now that I am no longer on hand to shock and impress. I have lately felt justified in that hope by the amount of time he manages to spend with us. I see no sign of the indulgence in his eyes and of course I know better than to think he would abuse Mrs Watson's hospitality so.

I must not discuss this with Mary.

I imagined myself telling her that happiness is too static an expression to sit comfortably on his face, which specializes in the more mercurial emotions of impatience, excitement, frustration and irritation, but I gave it up. She has sat across from him often enough these past few months to know how whey-faced he is. If only she could see how flattering it is that Holmes should seek us out like this! It is a great compliment to her, and to the marriage that we have made between us, that he can take his ease here. The pure clarity of vision forced on him by his analytical gifts unfits him, practically speaking, for the emotional rigours of normal social interaction. It must be as difficult for Holmes to close his eyes to the sordid undercurrents of ordinary family life as it is for those of us gifted with normal hearing to ignore a factory whistle. For years it was his habit to protect himself from the strain of inconsequential conversation by repairing to our rooms for literally weeks on end…

I must not discuss his morphinism with Mary.

I could feel myself beginning to panic. The need to protect my friend warred with my inability to dissemble before my wife. I could find nothing whatever that it was safe for me to say, no red herring to offer in propitiation of her curiosity.

"I agree with you," Mary said softly.

I waited for more, reflecting that it is difficult to argue with a woman who agrees with you.

"You are so thoughtful of Mr Holmes."

It is even more difficult to argue with a woman who admires you. I began to relax. She stroked my moustache. Arguing was now out of the question.

"That is why I have invited Miss Hughes to tea tomorrow."

I struggled briefly. There was a *non sequitur* here somewhere, if only I could find it.

"You remember Miss Hughes, John. Celia Hughes, my particular friend from school?"

I had never met Miss-Hughes-my-particular-friend-from-school, but I had heard of her. How I had heard of her! She was beautiful, was Miss Hughes. And clever, far more clever than my Mary. Miss Hughes had the most splendid ideas, none of which I understood very well. They were pranks well enough, but the point of the pranks always seemed to elude me. Mary would abandon her story in mid-stream, saying vaguely that it was a very good joke on the geography mistress, who *would* talk of America in the most condescending way.

"I shall look forward to meeting her," I said carefully. My relief at having been delivered from the conversational shoals of Holmes's cocaine crisis lent my voice a passable imitation of sincerity for which I was momentarily grateful. Momentarily, I say, because Mary's next words, said in all innocence, shattered my peace completely.

"Mr Holmes and Celia may deal very well together."

"Holmes? *Sherlock* Holmes?" My voice cracked as the full enormity of the situation burst upon my brain.

"Yes, dear, of course." She looked at me in wonder. "Mr Holmes and Celia. What have we been talking of all afternoon?"

What, indeed. Clearly, the question was rhetorical. I debated answering it anyway.

"John, are you sickening with something? You have been very quiet this past hour and you hardly touched your mutton. Here, let me feel your brow. I can postpone the tea party..."

Choosing the moment, as always, with a fine disregard for my own best interests, I stood firmly upon my dignity, reminded her that I am after all a doctor ("I will let you know when I am 'sickening with something,' Mary") and stalked off to my study, where I have beguiled these two hours past scribbling this journal entry and achieving an amused resignation to tomorrow's social event, which promises to be something quite out of the common way.

I wonder how Holmes will take it.

Chapter 12

Holmes is not taking it well, and I begin to wonder why I ever thought he would. Of course, in my own defense I may say that I never thought it would go so far. One little tea party, I thought, and Mary will see her mistake. Holmes is a bachelor more by definition and design than by circumstance or inclination, anyone can see that.

Except, apparently, my wife.

Mary has approached the problem of Holmes's domestic happiness with a single-minded obliquity of purpose that would bring a Caesar to his knees. This is not going to be easy. I emerged from my study that first evening all prepared to forgive her, only to find that she was the one whose feelings had been hurt.

"I don't understand you, John." Stitch, stitch, stitch.

"I should have thought you would be pleased by my concern."

"All I want is your happiness."

"If you feel that you can not abide the thought of a visit from my friend Celia in your home, then there is no more to be said." Stitch, stitch, stitch, snip.

I prefer not to recall my side of this particular argument. It was hopeless from the beginning. I strove to take the philosophic view. I reminded myself that I had preserved my silence regarding my friend's battle with his unhealthy habit, at considerable personal cost: Mary's feelings were definitely hurt. One little tea party, I told myself. Surely it was not too much to ask that Holmes give up an hour of his time in the interest of preserving what was after all no secret of mine. Perhaps it is Destiny, I told myself. Holmes and Miss Hughes were destined to meet; they were made for each other; Holmes is grown weary of his solitary life.

I did not believe it for a moment. On a sudden I found

myself wondering how Mary would contrive his invitation. We did not normally see Holmes until the shank of the evening, and then only when the fit for company was upon him; he came when it pleased him to come, knowing he was welcome. What pretext would she offer my friend the consulting detective? With that thought, my capitulation was assured. I would not have missed this for the world. Never let the sun set on a quarrel, I told myself solemnly. We made it up.

"So you will see to it that Mr Holmes arrives promptly tomorrow?"

And quarrelled again.

And made it up. We compromised: neither of us would take any steps to secure Holmes's presence at this event, prompt or otherwise. She was my own Mary again.

By morning she had it all worked out. Celia would come to tea tomorrow, as planned, and would with my permission (a nice touch, that) be invited to pass the following week with us, during which time Holmes would be bound to put in an appearance. By only inviting one of the two parties to be introduced, we would ensure an easy, informal atmosphere for their introduction.

I suppose she had to tell her friend Celia something.

By the end of breakfast, it was positively providential that circumstances had fallen out in just this way. Poor Celia was come to the end of her engagement as governess to Master Edward Sternbridge and was in consequence a bit mopish. She had no reason to be as cast down as she was, she said so herself in her letter. Certainly it was good news that her charge was fit enough to return to school, it had been understood from the beginning that this was a temporary measure, the Sternbridges were ever so grateful for her help, but there it was: she was mopish. The prospect of a week with us, in the soot and fog of a London tight in the grip of the worst winter since 1866, with the tempting prospect of Sherlock Holmes, bachelor, on the horizon, would set her up finely.

"It will be something for her to look forward to, John."

Quite so. I was in no hurry for the ordeal, myself.

* * *

Miss Hughes proved to be a taking little thing, with masses of soft, silky hair foaming above her heart-shaped face. How do they make their hair *do* that? Mary has never been able to explain it to me properly. I know I gave her a very thorough grounding in the mechanics of the flying buttress that time she asked me whether that cathedral was quite safe. I hardly think "Hairpins" is sufficient to return the favour. Mary's elbow was in my ribs. I made haste to pass the plate of cakes, inadvertently tipping several of them into our guest's lap. I suspect that this trifling accident lay behind Mary's remark later that evening to the effect that if Holmes were only half as impressed with Miss Hughes as I was, next week should go off very well. Sometimes there is no pleasing Mary.

I had been agreeably surprised to find no sign of Miss Hughes's self-confessed mopishness in either her manners or her conversation, which were uniformly as pleasing as her very pleasing person. Since I was still of the opinion that the historic meeting of Holmes and Hughes would offer significantly more in the way of consolation to the spirits in the offing than at the dock, I was naturally pleased to make the acquaintance of a Miss Hughes who was prepared to be cheerful going into the experiment. She was pretty, she was sweet-tempered (she forgave me for the cakes immediately), she was well-informed for a woman, and she was interested in anything and everything. I felt that Mary had done very well by my friend in that first essay, little though I expected to come of it. She was altogether charming.

I think Mary should have felt complimented by my reaction.

I promised myself that I would do what I could to make the anticipatory portion of the coming week a success. With any luck at all, Holmes would not put in an appearance until Tuesday or Wednesday.

In fact, it was Thursday before our uninvited but hardly unexpected guest happened upon the party in his honour. If my calculations are correct, that means that we had then passed three very comfortable evenings together discussing matters of general interest (the state of modern medicine, the politics of the Indian situation, and various sporting events). We were in a fair way to bringing a fourth such evening to a contented close when there came a decisive knock at the door. I reached for my medical bag, hoping for the best—a difficult confinement or a simple household accident, perhaps. But it was Holmes, smelling of nicotine and creosote, as usual. At least, the nicotine was as usual. The second component of the aroma was as likely to be formaldehyde or sulphuric acid as creosote. His collar was awry, his suit looked as if he'd slept in it (at a guess, because he had), and his waistcoat had two buttons missing. Fortunately, he is not a heavy-bearded man. I could feel Mary's palms itching to set him to rights.

Within moments of his arrival, all of the awkwardness inherent in the situation had boiled over. I was immediately aware that far from providing us with an easy, informal atmosphere, Mary's stratagem had given me, at any rate, a pale and panicky sensation I can only describe as stage-fright. I felt over-rehearsed and under-prepared all at the same time and as Mary stumbled over the necessary introductions, I knew I was not alone in my predicament. Holmes looked at us narrowly—a most unpleasant sensation—before favouring Miss Hughes with a nod. As I may possibly have mentioned in passing, Holmes is not a convivial man. It was with a very real sense of relief that I watched her engage him in conversation.

"Mrs Watson tells me you have an interest in the unusual, Mr Holmes."

Did he say, "And the beautiful, Miss Hughes"? No, he did not. He helped himself liberally to my whisky, ignoring the gasogene. That night he took his whisky straight. "So do many men, Miss Hughes."

Celia glanced at Mary. And persevered. "But a professional interest, Mr Holmes?"

"*Touché*, Miss Hughes."

She looked puzzled, as well she might. Charmingly puzzled, I thought. Holmes sighed softly and resigned himself to the pleasures of a little instruction.

"'*Touché*,' Miss Hughes, is a fencing term which signifies that your practice partner has brought his foil, the button which protects the point, into sufficient proximity to some vital organ, the heart for example, to have won the match."

"Not your heart, I think, Mr Holmes," she said sweetly.

After that, conversation was a trifle strained. Holmes left even before he decently could, while Miss Hughes showed a marked propensity to linger over her sherry, which mystified me until Mary caught my eye.

It seemed my presence was no longer required.

Chapter 13

Eight days. I have eight days to deliver a story, "an adventure of not less than 6,000 or more than 9,000 words" to the editor of the *Strand Magazine*, or stand in violation of my contract. Eight days and not an idea in my head apart from this business of Holmes's mysterious partiality for the single state, which partiality seems less mysterious to me all the time. You would think there was a scandal in Bohemianism, to hear Mary tell it. I can remember when all she wanted was to see me happy. Now all she wants is to see Holmes happy, that is to say, "to see Mr Holmes settled." It is not the same thing. Holmes is easily the most settled man of my acquaintance. Why can't she see how unsettling all of this is?

I have to keep reminding myself that it is for his sake that I am watching Mary plan her plans and plot her plots. I have an obligation to preserve his secret and no way to do that save by accepting Mary's construction of the situation. Meanwhile, the campaign to relieve Holmes of the burden of his bachelorhood divides its attentions and multiplies its effects, evolving at such a breakneck pace that I cannot think how to combat it.

"Do you think Mr Holmes is happy?" is as unanswerable today, shining grimly in her eyes, as it was when she first raised it above a month ago. The mortifying fact that however unhappy he was then he is far less happy now, fairly trembles in the air between us. It cannot remain unspoken forever.

"Mary... Dearest." My arms are about her waist and I am nuzzling her cheek. "Can't you be satisfied with making one man perfectly happy? Now, for instance?"

She melts against me (Mary never says very much in my fantasies) and I know that Holmes is safe and all is well between the Watsons again. It is the perfect line and I am justly proud of it, but the casting is all wrong. What if she should laugh? Mary has had some very strange reactions lately.

At least with Holmes I know where I am. His reactions are logical: he hasn't dropped in on us of an evening since his impromptu sparring match with Miss Hughes ended in a technical knockout in the opening round. After last night, I know better than to expect that he will suddenly reinstate the habit or, for that matter, willingly accept a concert ticket from me for years. Miss Blish took care of that. As for my dropping in on him, it is impossible. Mary is my responsibility; I can't go there empty-handed; I need a plan. For all I know to the contrary, Holmes may be constrained by the same consideration. This is not going to be easy.

In a matter of a few short weeks, we have gone from private embarrassment at home to public embarrassment at the theatre. I do not call it progress, but then I do not pretend to have my wife's intuition for these things. Her view of the matter has been different from mine from the beginning.

"I hope you are not feeling badly about this evening, John? I promise you, I thought it went very well for a first attempt and so does Celia. It is not as though Mr Holmes had been *expecting* to meet a Miss Hughes here this evening…"

I was too quick for her that time. Snatching up the button-hook, I began furiously on my boots and did not look up until the danger had been averted. I have grown very fond of that buttonhook lately.

"Frankly, I am disappointed in Celia. They might have had quite a pleasant conversation had she resisted the impulse to take him up in that very unbecoming way. In a man whose intentions are so uniformly of the best, I had hoped she might make some small allowance for an awkwardness that is never coarse or vulgar. Well, no matter. Clumsiness is not inexcusable, but it was perhaps a little optimistic of me to expect it to appeal to Celia, of all women. I shall do better next time. The important thing is, Mr Holmes spoke to her, for several minutes in fact. That must be accounted a gain. It is more, certainly, than I hoped for when I first broached the subject with Celia…"

I can only say that it did not seem like much of a gain to me, considering the nature of their conversation. Besides, I knew Holmes well enough to be reasonably certain that he would not speak to her again.

There have been times when my (mis)understanding of a situation has been sufficient to justify even Holmes's opinion of my deductive abilities. This was one of those times. I had put my trust in Watson's Law of Emotional Inertia: bodies at rest tend to stay at rest, I comforted myself. I forgot that the law of inertia has a second part: bodies in motion tend to stay in motion. And I haven't had a restful moment since.

I seriously underestimated my Mary and I am not too proud to admit it here, in my private narrative journal. The activities of the past few weeks have taught me more about women than the entire previous thirty-eight years of my existence. Of course, I have also met more women in the past few weeks than I have during the entire previous thirty-eight years of my existence. Governesses, in particular, come and go here with a rapidity that is astonishing, considering that we have no children. Not that Mary is unreasonably prejudiced in favour of her former profession. Far from it. So far this week, I have made the acquaintance of three governesses, one typewriter, a hearty equestrienne newly arrived from India, a gifted poetess, and one elegant widow with two young daughters and a small independence, suitably invested. Mary tells me she knew nothing about the children and I believe her. It takes more imagination than I hope either one of us possesses to envision Holmes in such a setting. That still leaves us with three governesses, one typewriter, the equestrienne and the poetess for this week, however, not to mention whoever will be sharing our tea this afternoon. Are *none* of Mary's friends married?

I wish Mary could simply have accepted the fact that her friends are always welcome in our home, if only so as to forestall her from putting it to the test on a daily basis like this. It is not a principle which lends itself to an inductive demonstration, being true solely by virtue of the generosity of the husband, which generosity is, like all generosity, diminished rather than enhanced by the demands placed upon it. Most wives know this instinctively.

In the interest of domestic harmony, I was pleased to approve of the overall suitability of the various candidates for Holmes's nonexistent affections. I was sympathetic. I was optimistic. I never once noticed the sudden and possibly pointed plunge in my friend's fortunes, the incontrovertible fact that none of the young ladies I have met in recent weeks can hold a two-inch candle to Celia Hughes.

As equestrienne follows poetess follows governess follows typewriter follows governess follows governess, I find that each addition to our social circle signals some minor but unpleasant expansion of my role in this chapter of errors. Every breakfast is devoted to planning ways and means of arranging the necessary introductions to Holmes and as often as I have resolved to hold myself excused from this exercise in futility and attend to my newspaper, just so often have I fallen into the trap of providing an intelligent answer to some seemingly innocent question which then embroils me in a full-scale discussion of the matter. It was a positive pleasure for me to be called away from the table this morning to lance a carbun‧ cle for one of Dr Anstruther's patients.

Believing as I do that none of the young ladies stands the least chance of engaging Holmes's romantic interest, I suppose I must accept the proposition that Miss Blish was as good a choice as any for Mary's second attempt. The admission comes hard, though, and not merely in the light of further events. Flora Blish is a little, wispy, fluffy woman, with a perfectly ordinary face, a sweet if slightly startled expression, and all the nervous energy and intellectual powers of a day-old chick. She clings. She darts away. She requires reassurance.

I don't mean to suggest that she is unattractive, I am sure she is very well in her way, but it is not Holmes's way and it puzzles me mightily that Mary should ever have thought it was. Perhaps she thought that Flora's mildly worried look, all shy and retiring, hesitant and unsure, would evoke the chivalry in Holmes. If so, she was sadly mistaken. Poor Flora! Holmes *has* no chivalry. Then again, Mary may have thought that Flora, as the antithesis of Celia Hughes, would be the perfect counterweight for that experience, I don't know. I'll never know now.

Neither will I ever know what possessed Holmes to greet Miss Blish with a string of personal deductions on our way to our seats at the theatre. Why couldn't he deduce that she was high-strung, given to outbreaks of hysteria, liable to let forth a piercing shriek, clutch vaguely at his sleeve, and pitch forward into the aisle in a dead faint? I promise you, this was a good deal more obvious than that her beloved brother, initials WHB, William Henry for preference, had been lost at sea, leaving his orphaned sister to make her way in the world by her needle, an exercise for which she had little love and less ability, possibly in the capacity of a milliner? She is, in fact, a milliner's apprentice.

As Holmes and I wrestled her unconscious form out of the public gaze and into the comparatively empty lobby of the Alhambra Theatre, I resolved to make the purchase of smelling salts a condition of any further romantic introductions to my friend the detective. The difficulties attached to maneuvering a lady in a dead faint through a crowd of people all moving in the opposite direction, half of them persuaded that she must be the worse for drink ("Disgusting, Frederick, that's what I call it"), and the other half idly wondering what our connection might be to her and thinking the worst, can hardly be over-emphasized. As usual, Mary was wonderful, fanning Flora's face, referring to her in strategically pitched tones as her little sister, and scolding us roundly for bungling the operation ("Mind her foot, John, she may be insensible now but she will need it later"). Nothing convinces a crowd of the propriety of a compromising situation so quickly as the combination of a hectoring wife and a hen-pecked husband. I must remember to ask Holmes whether the combination is as rare among the criminal classes as it is popularly supposed to be.

Under Mary's command, we won the lobby and laid our burden down in an overstuffed chair surmounted by enough potted plants to disguise her condition. A small plaque identified the chair as the gift of someone with more money than good taste. I don't know who provided the aspidistras. Holmes surveyed the situation as from a great height.

"She is remarkably pale, Watson," he said in a judicious tone.

I did not deem the moment right for a lecture on the dynamics of fainting, the inevitable pallor of the victim until the free flow of blood to the brain should be restored. Mary chafed Flora's icy hands.

"If I can be of any further assistance,…" he said, letting his voice trail off.

"No, Mr Holmes, I think you have done enough for Flora," Mary admitted with a rueful smile only I could see. "John and I will see her home. Perhaps it would be as well if you were gone when she recovers. She will not like to be reminded of her foolishness, I know. You are not offended, I hope?"

Is it any wonder that I love her? Holmes made good his escape, Flora slowly surfaced from oblivion, and Mary spoiled what could have been a perfect moment by whispering in my ear, "Did you notice, John? Mr Holmes has replaced the buttons on his waistcoat!"

I am beginning to think Mary could have found a silver lining to the clouds that hovered over Noah's ark.

Flora sat bolt upright. "Where is he?"

"You are in the lobby of the Alhambra," Mary said soothingly, answering the question Flora should have asked. "You fainted. From the heat," she added firmly. "You will feel better directly."

Flora should have been putting herself to rights, struggling

120

to sit up, pronouncing herself very well able to return to the theatre, apologizing profusely for something over which medical science knows she had no control. Her hair was still up and relatively tidy, her dress neat. Thanks to that attention-getting shriek of hers, I knew she had crumpled cleanly onto the carpet, without striking her head on anything along the way. Still, she persisted.

"Where is he, Mary?"

"He is gone home, Flora. Surely you would not wish to prolong the evening?"

"Certainly not," she agreed in a doubtful voice, "but I must hear more about dear William from Mr Holmes."

Nothing we could say to her on the subject of Holmes's penetrating observations could persuade her that she had already heard the whole, that Holmes was no spirit rapper gathering his information from The Great Beyond but a man of logic and science, that it was her costume, the mud on her boots, the set of her shawl that had told him all. She was politely unconvinced.

I suppose we made a muddle of it. I know it did not help matters when Mary insisted that I tell Miss Blish how Holmes had deduced all that, I am familiar with his methods, I am a man of science, I would explain it to her: go ahead, John. She folded her hands expectantly in her lap.

Is anything more completely inconvenient than the mis-placed confidence of a woman, and that woman your wife? I could see the cause well enough, what with Flora lying in state on the sofa in our drawing room sipping sherry, and I had heard the effect, Holmes's swift dissection of Flora en route to our seats at the theatre, but I could no more divine the connection that linked this cause to that effect based on my past observations of Holmes the consulting detective than I could have picked up his Stradivarius and executed a flaw-less rendition of Bach's "Partita" based on my past observa-tions of Holmes the violinist. I am not Holmes. I could not bring myself to point to her badly darned gloves and deduce her inadequacies as a seamstress, I am sorry. All I could do was repeat my conviction that there was a perfectly logical explanation for my friend's performance, that it was an analytical skill developed over a period of years which was to the best of my knowledge his alone, and that it was indeed the details of her attire which had told him her story. Flora listened patiently to everything we had to say and, sipping her restorative, quietly played her trump card.

"Tell me then, Dr Watson. How could he know that William Henry is dead from my mode of dress when I did not know his fate myself until Mr Holmes told me? I wear this commemorative riband to remind myself that he may be dead, but Mr Holmes knew right away that he *was* dead. How do you explain that?"

Her voice was heavy with irony, the voice of a person unskilled in debate but secure in her position. Her little speech revealed such a profound lack of perspective on this evening's events that I knew myself defeated. I heard myself giving her Holmes's address ("221B Baker Street, from about 11 a.m."), hoping there might be some actual mystery attached to brother William's departure so as to enable Holmes to assist her in a practical way. I heard Mary remind Flora that she should wire for an appointment and wear the same costume so that Mr Holmes would be able to explain his behaviour; her outfit was evidence, Flora, evidence that Mr Holmes needed in order to pursue his inquiries. It was a fortunate phrase, I could see. Mary pressed home her advantage and by the time Flora was deposited with due care on her doorstep, she was as rational as someone of her limited intellectual attainments could be after ten minutes' exposure to Sherlock Holmes. Poor Flora.

Poor Holmes.

Upon my word, I did not anticipate spending the first Christmas Eve of my married life feeling sorry for Holmes and deceiving my wife! Every time Mary passes the study door and smiles encouragingly at me, the tide of guilt moves that much closer to the high water mark. I know what she thinks. She thinks I am hard at work fashioning a suitable adventure against my deadline. She has never really understood that I must have a story to tell before I can tell the story. With the best will in the world, I can't describe an adventure I've never had. I am not that kind of writer. I need grist for my mill and where this grist is to come from now that Mary is so briskly attending to the matter of Holmes's domestic happiness, is anybody's guess.

* * *

"Mr Holmes is here, John, and look what he's brought us."

Personally, I think it is as well for Holmes that he should have no marital ambitions, given his limited understanding of the fair sex.

"A goose," she added unnecessarily. I could see it was a goose.

Holmes must have made his presentation in the hall, for Mary's arms were full of goose. She was trying not to cradle it like a baby, I could tell. One hand was tightened gingerly over the thoracic region, the other hugged it below the belt; the head drooped fetchingly over the crook of her elbow. I was irresistibly reminded of Flora and our adventure at the Alhambra. I must warn Holmes.

"Isn't it a fine one?" asked Mary in the prodding voice reserved by Eve to recall her husband to his social duties. ("Say 'Thank you,' Adam.") She joggled the goose for emphasis, setting off a soft flurry of feathers, not to mention a strong smell of goose.

The goose was not of the freshest and my primary duty was to my friend Holmes. How to make clear that Flora's latest start should not be laid at the Watsons' door? It was a delicate matter. I had no time for geese.

"Miss Blish…" I began carefully.

"Ah yes, Miss Blish!" He saluted a distant memory. Holmes

has never had any compunction about interrupting me. He turned to Mary. "I must apologize for our little contretemps at the theatre last night. I did not realize that she would be so affected by my obervations. I had supposed her recovered from the tragedy or I never should have venture to remark upon it. She is no longer in mourning, it must have happened some time ago. She is extremely emotional, isn't she?"

Naturally, he disapproved.

I rescued my wife. Her eyes were wide with discovery and the goose was obviously heavy. "May I?"

I made quite a ceremony of it, hefting the animal as if to gauge its weight, pinching the down at the breastbone the way I had seen my grandmother do when I was a boy, trying not to pull a face at how sodden it was. It must be snowing again, I told myself charitably.

"John has been writing all afternoon," Mary said into the silence.

She was not herself. Holmes tried to look interested, but it was beyond him. I concluded my examination and made the only comment possible under the circumstances.

"It is a fine goose, Holmes."

Even now, sitting calmly at my desk assessing the damage, I find it difficult to blame myself or to formulate a more cogent compliment for a dead bird. It was a fine goose. I second his motion, support his selection, confirm his choice, endorse his candidate, approve his judgement, applaud his taste and accept said goose *in toto*: beak and feet, liver and lights. It was a fine goose. The inadequacy of the remark revived Mary's social instincts beyond all reason.

"It is a fine, fat, *family-sized* goose, Mr Holmes. Much too much for John and me to eat by ourselves. You will join us for supper? I'm so pleased. There is someone I should like you to meet. No, no details now! Let's just say that I am sure you will like her. We shall discuss this excellent goose of yours together, shall we? Will eight o'clock be convenient? At eight o'clock then." And she ushered him out.

As I waited for her to come and collect tonight's *entrée* from me for plucking, I wondered blankly who would be free to make a fourth at supper on Christmas Eve, with only a few hours' notice. Any number of them, I was forced to admit. No doubt we would be expected to sing carols after supper. Mary looked ready for anything. Good God, not charades! Roast goose is so indigestible, perhaps I should try to talk to her about this evening's entertainment. As a physician if not as a husband. For the first time, I wondered whether "Least said, soonest mended" is as infallible a guide to a happy marriage as it has been to my friendship with Holmes. She was back.

"I hope you are fond of goose, John," she said, her lips twitching. "We'll have this one for supper tonight with Mr Holmes, it won't keep longer, and the little one ourselves tomorrow. Sage dressing tonight, oyster stuffing tomorrow, we'll manage. Don't look so stricken, John! A man who chooses to apologize to a married couple by presenting them with a Christmas goose at four o'clock in the afternoon of Christmas Eve, a family-sized goose with enough meat on it to feed half a dozen healthy people, has to expect to be invited to supper. You'll see, it will be fine. It is indeed a fine goose," she teased, "and I will vouch for its being at least twice as fine in its cooked state. I can manage, John. Truly. Why don't you go back to your writing?"

There is nothing like an unexpected dose of the truth to undercut your position in an argument. Who but Holmes could have failed to see the danger in such a gesture at such a time? That he failed to see it is no doubt also the truth, but not one that I can very conveniently point out to Mary. We already had one goose in readiness for the occasion and now we have two, his goose looking somewhat the worse for wear, I must say. If I did not know better, I would think he had obtained the bird in a pot-house brawl, it looks so bedraggled. The likeliest explanation, of course, is that some client has paid him in trade as it were (it can't always be diamond rings and gold snuffboxes, after all), and that he has taken the opportunity to pass his windfall on to us, in the true spirit of the holiday.

"What will discharge one obligation will discharge another."

I can almost hear him say it, his brow furrowed, his fists jammed into the pockets of his dressing gown, rocking back on his heels in front of the fire as his own wit strikes him with the force of a blow. The goose looked as if it had heard it several times already, under duress. Unfortunately, when the gentle courtesy of a woman like my Mary is involved, what will discharge one obligation will nearly always simultaneously incur another. I hope it will not be the equestrienne. I still haven't decided what, if anything, to do about Miss Blish.

* * *

"John! John! Oh, John, you're here." She fell upon me in as near to panic as I had ever seen her. I held her at arm's length while I scanned her for signs of injury, her screams still echoing in my head.

I had made it from the study to the kitchen in a little under six seconds. My heart was pounding and the blood was drumming in my ears. You would not think six seconds would be sufficient for a person to have formulated any very clear hypothesis as to the nature of the problem, but I found that I was checking them off one by one: the kitchen was not on fire; she had not been scalded; the knife had not slipped; Cook was standing at the foot of the table; they were alone; no one had been hurt. I was needed as a husband, not a doctor. I folded her in my arms, rolled my eyes to heaven, and promised myself I would wait it out. Least said, soonest mended. I nodded my dismissal to Cook. Let her eavesdrop from the pantry, if she is so inclined. She wasn't needed in the kitchen.

"Jules, John. Jules. In the goose."

She had never called me "Jules" before, but then she had

never been hysterical before, either. I raised her chin off my waistcoat.

"Who is Jules, Mary?" She made a visible effort at composure.

"John, there are *jewels* in the goose. Jewels! I don't want any more jewels. Pearls in the post, diamonds in the goose, I won't have any more, do you hear me? I won't, I tell you!"

I suppose, from her point of view, it was rather trying to be persecuted in this fashion. First the yearly pearl from her father culminating in the deadly 'The Sign of Four' and now this.

"Some women would be glad to find diamonds in their Christmas goose, Mary," I said, trying for a lighter touch. She caught me eyeing the modest diamond chip in her wedding band and kissed me, saying, "This is the only jewel I ever wanted, John. Don't you know that?"

I think we both needed the reminder.

"You don't believe me," she accused. "There, in the crop. I was cleaning it to make the gravy. A diamond, John, as big as, as big as my thumbnail. A blue diamond." She was at the crossroads now. The relief of laughter or the relief of tears, it depended on what came next.

She pointed at the denuded goose and I sidled up to the animal with the caution she seemed to think it deserved. I half-expected (I can confess it now) that it was all a trick of the light, a rough lump of quartz that had caught the light for a moment as she worked it out of the crop. If I have learned one thing from my years with Holmes, however, it is that prediction is a dangerous game, waiting on future events a safer. Sweeping the liver and heart slowly aside, I saw a gemstone whose worth it is beyond my ability to estimate. I have never seen such beauty. Very nearly the size of a pen nib, it was cut with literally dozens of facets and flickered in the gaslight like blue flame. I cannot be sure it is a diamond, but no cutter ever achieved an effect like that with quartz. I said the first thing that came into my head.

"I will never complain about your giblet gravy again."

"I thought you liked my giblet gravy!"

We laughed until she cried and no doubt it did us both good. She wiped her eyes on her apron.

"You will have to take it to Mr Holmes," she said unsteadily.

"How many people," I mused, "finding a jewel like this in their goose, would have someone to turn to in their social circle?"

"Oh don't, please, John. I can't laugh any more. I can't. I'm sorry I frightened you by screaming like that. But please, if you love me, don't make me laugh any more."

I promised readily enough. When she sits on my knee like that, I will promise her anything and this was a small thing.

"It is odd, though, that Holmes should be the one to have given us this particular goose, don't you think? Some woman who was feeding the geese must have lost this from a brooch or ring. It fell into the feed; birds are attracted to shiny things; this one gobbled it up. The poor woman must be half mad with anxiety. What a calamity, right before Christmas, too."

"John, you must go right away. That poor woman!"

"If anyone can trace this, it will be Holmes. You realize we will probably be unable to attend your supper party?" I was very proud of that "probably."

"Yes, John, yes. Only hurry. I will make your excuses to Miss Tate"—imagine, it was the equestrienne, after all—"she will understand perfectly how it was. Your diary, John!"

Which is how I came to be seated in Holmes's consulting chambers by myself, in front of a roaring fire, alternately contemplating a jewel which may be a diamond or a pale sapphire or a blue topaz for all I know about gems, and a battered billycock. I had no idea Holmes had taken to wearing a bowler. Perhaps it is for one of his disguises. If he doesn't arrive soon, I shall have to consider the wisdom of returning in time for the unveiling of the goose that laid the sky-blue egg. It would be a pity, particularly now that I have bespoken supper for two from Mrs Hudson, but it would not do for me to linger here while Holmes goes directly from wherever he is to his rendezvous with destiny and Miss Tate. One half-hour more.

Chapter 14

Damn Holmes. And his women! [*Note*: Mary must never see this diary.] Whatever peace of mind his peculiar brand of misogyny may have brought me during my years in Baker Street—and I admit it was considerable—I have paid for since, you may be certain of that.

Holmes has unwelcome news for a female client? Let Watson tell her. He even quoted Hafiz at me. And I walked right into it. I was so incensed that I had the remedy in my hand the very next morning, as I recall, and knocked him up a good two hours before his usual time. It will do him good, I thought, to see the sun rise.

Oh, I was quite short with him, I'm afraid, full of the virtue that only a sleepless night spent in the performance of some noble duty can confer. I thrust the manuscript at him, refused a cup of Mrs Hudson's excellent coffee, and stood at the window in apparently rapt contemplation of the sylvan charms of Baker Street, which consist of one stunted ash that is a disgrace to its species and a half-grown evergreen that was provided by the Teutonic tobacconist across the way in a fit of unaccustomed generosity shortly after we established ourselves here.

I was impatient, Holmes was thoughtful, and we spoke in unison.

"Are you sure you want to do this?" he wanted to know, while I asked, "Have you any objection to make?"

We answered each other in unison as well. "Quite sure," I asserted. And "No, not in the least," he said.

Then, glaring at each other, we agreed: "That's settled, then."

He might have told me what would happen, but that's Holmes all over. As long as the inevitable consequences pose no threat to his own convenience, he is satisfied. *Caveat author*, or whatever the Latin word is. He takes an Olympian view of history, does Holmes.

"Have a kipper, Watson?"

Writing is hungry work. I ate the kipper.

The exercise of recollection, like the keeping of a diary, is apt to be its own reward. As the diary grows with the keeping, so the range and power of the eidetic memory grow with the prompting. One memory begets another and facility follows upon fatigue until I find that I can wander at will, reconstructing entire conversations, complete with gestures, tones of voice, and all the rest. If, as Holmes has so often remarked, I see but do not observe, then I may justly say in my own defense that I remember as few others do. How many "observers" would be able to remember a conversation as apparently trivial as this at two months' distance, and remember it well enough to be able to analyze the conversational cross-currents?

Holmes wanted me to write that adventure, that "case of identity," as he called it. I can see that now. I can see that now that I have been accosted in my own surgery by this selfsame client. Damn Holmes! He pursues his profession in accordance with his eccentric whims and I interrupt mine to cope with the consequences. He safeguards his privacy in conformity with his reclusive tastes and I take my tea in an atmosphere redolent of the schoolroom. Governesses to the right of me, governesses to the left of me, and every last one of them expecting me to be able to produce the eligible bachelor at a moment's notice, like a rabbit out of a hat.

I recognized her, of course: Mary Sutherland, from 'A Case of Identity', whose stepfather had taken such cruel advantage of her myopia. There I was, struggling with the opening paragraphs of what I plan to call 'The Adventure of the Blue Carbuncle', due I might add in two days' time, and there she was, brandishing the December issue of the *Strand Magazine*. No visiting card, no introduction, no curtsey, no apology for disturbing me at my work: it was our parlourmaid's finest hour. The chit is impossible, I don't care if she is Cook's second cousin once removed.

Mary Sutherland, Mary Sutherland, I thought frantically. What was Mary Sutherland's *name*? I could not imagine. I could not remember. I rose to my feet.

"Is this true?" she asked.

"Please," I said, indicating the chair to my right. "Annie, will you see that we are not disturbed?"

Mary Sutherland, Mary Sutherland. Asking me if it were true that the man who had left her at the altar was her own stepfather. Asking me if it were true that the man she had hired to trace her lost lover had discovered this fact and chosen not to tell her. Asking me if it were true that I had chosen to tell the world her story in this month's *Strand*. Damn you, Holmes.

"Yes, it is true. I am so sorry. Please sit down, Miss…"

"Morrison," she said absently, "Sarah Morrison. I suppose you think of me as Mary Sutherland. Of course you do. We are all disguised, are we not, Doctor? I become Mary Sutherland, Angelo becomes Hosmer Angel, his Italian accent becomes the after effect of a childhood attack of the quinsy, the typesetters' ball becomes the gasfitters' ball. You made a mistake, though, when you made me a typewriter. I am far too shortsighted for that. It is not enough to memorize the keyboard, you see. One must be able to read the hand-written copy with both hands placed securely on the machine. No, I do not think I can become a typewriter."

If Miss Morrison's case held no great mystery for my friend Holmes, who maintained from the first that it was the merest commonplace, it has held nothing but mystery for me, his biographer. The greatest mystery of all was the attitude Holmes chose to take toward his client. From the beginning, he counseled her in the strongest possible terms to forget her lost love, make a new life for herself, concentrate on the future, leave the past behind. Sound, practical advice, certainly, but advice the jilted bride must have received free of charge from the vicar on the church steps, assuming the man had even a modicum of sense. She had expected more from Holmes, and she still expected it when she had quitted his office: he would do his best for her but he was very much afraid that she had seen the last of Mr Hosmer Angel. So she had, of course, but to my mind that did not excuse Holmes from his obligation to his client.

It was a mystery to me how he could justify solving the case simply in order to satisfy his own idle curiosity, Hafiz or no Hafiz. If it had been a more interesting problem, I suppose he might have felt some slight responsibility toward the woman who had been the means of bringing it to his attention. Once events had confirmed his preliminary hypothesis, however, he lost all interest in it and in Miss Morrison, whose situation was of course in no way improved by his enlightenment so long as he chose to keep it to himself. By his rarefied standards, the case was thereby proven to be the twice-told tale he had stigmatized it from the first, he was vindicated, and good old Watson was a godsend. He was more than happy to surrender the obligation to me and very clever about arranging for me to wrest it from him, too. It was entirely my own idea to pick up the cheque. Will I never learn?

I should have done better to wrestle with the Jamison case, after all.

It is a great pity that there is no way for me to warn the public of the danger involved in bringing Holmes what he will consider a pedestrian problem. Not that the average person confronted by a peculiar combination of circumstances of a disturbing or even downright threatening nature would have any way of knowing whether it will strike Sherlock Holmes as pedestrian. Miss Morrison certainly found it extraordinary to be suddenly minus one fiancé from his hansom cab *en route* to their wedding, particularly in view of said fiancé's having earlier taken the trouble of extracting her solemn promise to keep faith with him no matter what untoward event might transpire to wrench them apart. I do not suppose she found it

133

any less extraordinary once she was informed by the *Strand* that the man was her own stepfather, either. The professional always sees these things differently from the client.

I have known doctors like this in my time. Give them a rare tropical disease and they will work night and day to arrest its progress. Break your leg on their front steps and you can lie there until it is your turn in the queue. "Where is the challenge in modern medicine?" they cry, stepping over your body. But I digress. I was talking about Holmes.

Holmes might have told Miss Morrison (with perfect truth) that Hosmer Angel had cruelly deceived her—that he is legally (and to all outward appearances, happily) married under a different name which it is to be hoped is his own; that his household includes one very healthy wife, as well as her daughter from a previous marriage; that he had balked at the crime of bigamy, for which cause she should give thanks to heaven; but that having once laid eyes on her at the gasfitters'/typesetters' ball, he had not been able to rest at the thought that she would ever give herself to another.

I wish I had thought of this at the time. It is romantic, it is technically true if happily misleading, and it would have made an admirable preamble to that little speech of his about the wisdom of putting the past behind her, which might have been repeated *in toto* and to some positive effect at that juncture. It certainly fell on deaf ears the first time.

This carefully constructed version of the truth has the further merit of answering all of the questions Miss Morrison asked Holmes in the first place: "Where is Hosmer Angel? What has happened to him? Is he all right? Is he coming back to me?"

She never asked Holmes, "*Who* is Hosmer Angel?" That question Holmes asked himself. A lesser detective would not have asked the question at all, but a better man might have shared the answer with his client instead of with me.

I did not have the luxury of choosing my audience. Nothing less than the whole sordid truth could serve my turn as a writer. Once I was involved, it was in very truth 'A Case of Identity' and all hope lost.

"I do not think I can become a typewriter," she said.

I do not think she can become a governess, shop assistant, clerk or nanny, either, and I shudder to think of the dangers her short sight would expose her to in a textile mill or manu-factory, but I felt obliged to ask the question even so.

"Why should you wish to become a typewriter?"

"I must do something, Dr Watson. I cannot return to live quietly under the same roof as my mother and stepfather now that I know the truth. Surely you can see that?"

I could, of course. I am only sorry that I did not see it two months ago, when I wrote that wretched story. We had come to a lull in the conversation just when we could least afford a lull. In another moment, she would be thanking me for my time, gathering up her possessions, and going out into a world I had inadvertently stripped of all its promise. The fact that the promise was false suddenly meant less than nothing. Where would she go? What would she do?

What would Holmes do in my place?

At last, a question I could answer: Holmes would never permit himself to be in my place—or what's a Watson for?

She was collecting herself. Tucking her magazine under her arm, searching for her gloves. Found them. Tugging on first one, then the other. Her hands were slightly puffy, I noticed. I longed to tell her to eat less salt. She rose to her feet. She was about to speak. I was on my feet myself when I heard a familiar rap on the study door and saluted my salvation.

"Mary, I am so pleased to see you. I did not expect you back for hours, else I should have asked our guest to wait. May I present Miss Sarah Morrison? Miss Morrison, my wife, who may be able to be of some material assistance to you. Have I your permission to tell her your story?"

Mary's entrance had been precipitate—prompted, no doubt, by what must have been a wonderfully lurid account of the lady's arrival by our Annie. Mary was all over wet, the wool steaming gently in the overheated room (I do like it warm for writing), the lone feather on her second-best hat dripping nicely down her astrakhan collar, and she was white to the lips. I was pleased to think that these details would not be apparent to the myopic Miss Morrison, who was acknowledging the unwanted introduction with a meaningless smile and a perfectly numb and incurious, "How do you do, Mrs Watson?" She gestured helplessly, as much with her copy of the *Strand* as at it, which I did not scruple to interpret as consent.

"Mary, I have introduced you to Miss Morrison as if she were a stranger, but what if I were to tell you that Miss Morrison is none other than Mary Sutherland?"

"Mary Sutherland? Whose stepfather… Oh, John!" Her eyes flew to the *Strand* in sudden recognition. She fairly tore the dripping hat from her head and I watched the colour wash across her face as though released by a spring concealed in the constricting ribbons. I steadied her for a moment. "Miss Sutherland, Miss Morrison, you have had a great shock, you must let us offer you some tea. Please, I insist—if for no other reason than to get Annie away from the keyhole while we consider what is best to be done. John, you were absolutely right about that girl, I came home to find her polishing the doorknob with her ear, she will have to go at quarter-day. Excuse me, Miss Morrison, I realize that the inadequacies of our maidservant is not a topic of general interest but if you will let me take your things and—thank you, John, I will add mine to the pile. Do you have them? There. Annie, you will please hang these up and tell Cook that we require tea for three, immediately. Yes, in the study. And we should like some of those scones Dr Watson is so fond of. That will be all, Annie."

Annie bobbed a very inadequate curtsey and dropped a glove and then a hat, but she got the door closed eventually and I blessed Mary for her seemingly inconsequential chatter. Miss Morrison looked far less stricken than she had a few short moments ago. She actually laughed when Mary announced that she hoped neither of us was particularly fond of scones because she happened to know there wasn't a currant in the house and Cook being the perfectionist she was, Annie was probably halfway across town now, searching for them. When Miss Morrison said, "Mrs Watson, I don't care if I never eat another scone," it had all the force of a religious conversion. Holmes has a lot to answer for, I thought.

"Good. Now tell me everything, from the time you first read my husband's account in the *Strand*. How long had it been since you last saw the man you thought of as your fiancé?"

"Our wedding was to have been June 30th, that is six months ago now."

"Good, good."

"Good?" I could not imagine what was good about it.

Mary smiled pityingly "The first six months of *any* marriage are the hardest, John."

I could not argue with it, we have been married for seven months ourselves, but I felt obscurely insulted and resolved to watch the remainder of the proceedings from a safe distance—and I do not regret it. The onlooker sees most of the game and the man who doesn't know that is not a writer. Besides, the game of women's conversation has definite points of interest. When a pair of swifts sets out to build a nest in a new location, they do it as if no swift had ever built a nest before. One of them starts the job in a mood of almost comic desperation, using twigs, gobbets of mud, sodden pasteboard, bits of moss, dead leaves, whatever likely materials are at hand, while the other one twitters encouragement and scrutinizes the result, removing what does not seem to belong and adding other promising bits and pieces, which the first one twitters over, scrutinizes, embraces or repudiates, and augments in her turn. To the impartial observer, the guiding principle seems to be one of unflagging, ruthless, inspired despair. "I'll know it when I see it," they seem to assure each other and oddly enough, they do. Quite suddenly, they will both stop to survey their composition, let whatever they have in their beaks fall unregarded, and move in without exchanging a glance. Now that's a nest. The same principle appears to guide the progress of women's conversation.

"You don't look like Mary Sutherland," was my wife's next contribution.

"I don't?" she asked.

"No, not at all. I am not denying that you *are* Mary Sutherland, you understand. I am merely observing that you do not resemble her." Mary approached Miss Morrison and made a careful study of her subject's physiognomy: left profile, full face and right profile, and repeated her declaration. "No, not at all. I had the impression from reading the case—forgive me, John—of a much larger and altogether more forbidding young lady. A creature with three chins and two timepieces, upholstered in horsehair and trimmed with merino. I beg your pardon! I don't know why I am asking John's forgiveness when the description is so much less flattering to yourself. All I meant to say was that no one reading John's story would be reminded of you. Did he do any better with your fiancé? Excuse me, your stepfather?"

"It is difficult for me to say. Perhaps if I were to tell you about Angelo…"

"Ah, he was Italian, then?" asked Mary helpfully.

"Yes, no, he certainly seemed to be but of course he wasn't. He was just Mama's husband, pretending to be Italian and romantic and operatic."

"Operatic? With a voice damaged by the quinsy? Oh, I see, the quinsy was John's idea. How very clever," she said flatly. "And your stepfather, does he resemble the Mr Windibank John described—slight and pale and rather rabbity, as I recall?"

I perked up at this. I remembered Mr Strong perfectly. A windy little banker, I thought him, with an incongruous family name. Would Miss Morrison see the justice in my description?

"No, not at all. He is considerably above middle height and barrel-chested with it, so that I cannot think why I did not recognize him in the event, although—"

"Just so, no one would anticipate such a cruel masquerade. It could have happened to anyone," Mary assured her.

"Hardly *anyone*, Mrs Watson," she said sadly.

"No, for hardly anyone is so unfortunate in her relations, Miss Morrison. More tea? Now, we must be practical. And we will be. You came here straightaway?"

"I went first to Baker Street, but Mr Holmes was out and the hour of his return not fixed. I could not bear to wait and so conceived the notion of applying to Dr Watson directly."

"You did not confront your mother or your stepfather?" asked Mary.

"I never thought of it."

"Well done, Miss Morrison! Oh, you shall have your revenge, never fear. Another piece of bread and butter, John?"

Sometimes, Mary makes me quite nervous. It took twenty minutes of cross-questioning on the subject of who in Miss Morrison's immediate circle customarily reads the *Strand* and might be depended upon to make the connection before it was borne in upon me that Mary was endeavouring to persuade Miss Morrison that she could safely return to the family nest for the nonce, as long as she did so before her absence was remarked upon and an explanation sought. Mary seemed to think Miss Morrison could obtain considerable amusement from the exercise of watching her mother and stepfather's continuing performance in support of a charade that no longer claimed her as its victim. There was a unanimity of feeling that the longer this continued and the more doubt that could be cast in retrospect over the moment of her awakening, the more complete her triumph would be. It was a subtle point, one I never would have thought to make. Nor would Holmes. I could imagine the sort of interrogation (one could not call it a conversation) Holmes would have conducted in Mary's place.

"What sort of employment have you had before? I see. And your education—you speak French and German, perhaps, know the rudiments of Greek and Latin? (Not a governess, I think Watson!) You cannot type, of course: quite impossible with your poor sight. [He would not miss that.] A *dame de compagnie*, Watson! The very thing. How many elderly people have you nursed through a lingering illness, Miss Morrison? Not even your late father? Well, well, lack of experience need not be a positive barrier, eh, Watson? Everyone must start somewhere. As a physician, Watson, you will be in the best position to help Miss Morrison to her goal. Really, you could not do better. I rely on Watson absolutely."

Certainly, Holmes. Whatever you say, Holmes. Any number of people are looking for a paid companion in Paddington! The people of Paddington nurse their own. Well he knows that the only possibility I could have encountered in my professional capacity was met in his company, in Kensington, as the senior member of an investigative team of etheric manipulators!

I am rambling. This conversation never happened; Holmes was out when Miss Morrison called; he did not send her to my door; she came of her own accord. No one has said anything about her becoming a *dame de compagnie*, least of all Holmes, who may not even know the phrase. Anyone reading this would think me addicted to Mrs Radcliffe's novels.

Lately, all roads traversed in my capacity as Holmes's friend or even his Boswell (detestable phrase) seem to lead to a young lady with marriage on her mind. Today's acquisition is Miss Morrison, who needs to be persuaded out of her independent notions. I look to Mary for that. They have been closeted together in the parlour on the subject of ways and means of employment for upwards of two hours and I do not doubt that reason will prevail. A woman who cannot be depended upon to recognize her own stepfather without the help of a consulting detective, a woman who routinely leaves the house in mismatched boots (she did it again today, I noticed), is a woman who requires more than the usual degree of male protection. It should not be impossible for Mary to convince her that all men are not like Hosmer Angel.

The path of the biographer is fraught with peril, and insanity may not be the least of its dangers. I no longer think, if I ever did, that it is merely a matter of recording the truth as it happened. Recording the truth is a risky business at best, to be justified only by the most extreme circumstances, as in 'A Case of Identity', and even there I should have done better to have exercised some restraint. Fortunately, the issue of too much truth is unlikely to arise relative to 'The Adventure of the Blue Carbuncle'. I seem to be making this one up out of whole cloth as I go on. First Mary doesn't want to be mentioned, then Holmes wants me to disguise the size of the stone, the site of the goose farm, the source of the billycock, the name of the thief, and the thief's disposition.

"There is no point in drawing the attention of the authorities to the passenger lists, Watson."

What it comes down to is that I am free to use the deductive chain in its entirety—I merely have to make up the people, the crime, and the conversation. I begin to think it is only fair that he has refused his share of the remuneration for this activity.

I wonder if Peterson would enjoy a morsel of fame? He's always been good to us. The important thing for me to remember is that for everyone I meet who would resent playing a part in one of my adventures, I must know dozens who would relish the office, dine out on the story, and be forever grateful to me. I have it in my hands to become a very popular fellow and it behooves me to remember it.

I have almost decided to let Holmes suffer from an excess of Christmas spirit in this one, freeing the repentant thief in order to mark the holiday. Lestrade will know it for a fiction at once but I can cope with that objection. It is an advantage, is it not, to give Lestrade the impression that I deal in fiction? So that's settled.

May it bring a little holiday cheer to the hearts of those who need it.

1889

Chapter 15

'The Adventure of the Blue Carbuncle' is done and if I may be
excused for saying so here in my private narrative journal, it is
exceedingly well done, too. The plot advances at a sprightly
pace, the characters are interesting without being obtrusive,
and the point of view is steady as she goes. Not only do I
manage to be on the scene to witness first-hand everything I
need to be able to tell the interested reader (Mary is right, it
does help to imagine that the reader is interested), but for once
all of my characters resist the temptation to seize the floor and
entertain my audience without me. Holmes himself speaks
briefly and to the point, instead of in those brutal periods he
favoured in 'A Study in Scarlet' and 'The Sign of Four'. I ask
questions, he answers them, and the illusion of conversation
is maintained. I must remember this technique: the result is
masterly.

The pacing is good, too. For the space of 5,000 words, the
deductions of my friend Holmes open new fields of inquiry
and then, just as the anxiety of Mr Fitsch the word-counter
may be supposed to reach fever pitch, the long arm of coincidence intervenes to save us a tedious journey and the mystery
unravels in a 2,000 word coda that precisely complements the
statement of the puzzle. Facts, 5, Logic and Coincidence, 2: a
very palatable mixture.

I only hope Holmes will like it half as much as I do. Watch
him ask me why I keep interrupting him in this adventure!

* * *

Well, I'm not sure what I have accomplished here beyond the
destruction of my casebook, but my intentions were good. It
came to me in the middle of the night, driving me out of a
sound sleep and my warm bed: why are my notes about

Holmes in chronological order? It doesn't matter to me when his cases happened. What matters to me is how experienced a writer I have to be in order to turn a particular case into an adventure suitable for publication in the *Strand*.

I put on my dressing gown and crept down to my surgery. I didn't need a fire. I lit the lamp, took out the casebook I began in Baker Street, and ripped it apart at the spine. I would need four piles, I decided: Tell Now, Tell Later, External Events, and Maybe Never. Fortunately, I had always begun a new case on a right-hand page and was not quite halfway through the book—there were no leaves with multiple cases on them.

'The Adventure of the Speckled Band,' written but not publishable until Helen Stoner's death: External Events. 'The Brook Street Mystery': Tell Later. (I don't know why, but I have totally lost interest in this case.) 'The Adventure of the Second Stain': Maybe Never. 'The Naval Treaty': Maybe Never. 'The Reigate Squires': Tell Later.

'Retreat to the Island of Uffa': Tell Later. 'The Five Orange Pips', written but not publishable until four adventures have preceded it: External Events. 'The Boscombe Valley Mystery', written but not publishable etc.: External Events. 'The Noble Bachelor', written but not etc.: External Events. 'The Plight of the King of Bohemia': Tell Later. 'The Rufus Jamison Case': Tell Later. 'The Adventure of the Etheric Manipulators': Maybe Never.

A pattern was definitely beginning to emerge, I thought, as I considered my four categories and contemplated my three piles of paper. Where were the cases I could Tell Now? The remaining cases added materially to the existing piles without making a start on the missing stack. I still had nothing to Tell Now.

The urge to shuffle all the papers together and try again was very nearly overwhelming. At length, I decided that it would be better to take the time to describe the outcome of my experiment than to confound the data by running the experiment again. External Events and Maybe Never I have bundled together and put away; in six months' time or thereabouts, I shall look at them again. Tell Later, which was much the smallest of my three piles, I have placed squarely on my desk, to the left of my journal, for easy access at odd moments during the day. It is just barely possible that with the right twist or turn, one of these might be converted into a Tell Now. Change a name, adjust a character, move someone from the beginning to the end of the story, orchestrate a shift of sympathies. It needn't be a big thing, I tell myself—if I keep looking for the key, I'm bound to find it.

Knowing Holmes, I would of course prefer to be on the last page of my next adventure before subjecting myself to the ordeal of hearing his opinion of this one, as good as it is, but even if that is not possible (and I don't see how it could be, writing takes time), I still have two days to make a start on it. Two days to secure Holmes's grudging approval, to make any minor nominative adjustments that may be necessary, and to convey the final, authoritative version of 'The Adventure of the Blue Carbuncle' to the estimable Nathaniel Fitsch, who will be delighted and say so with the promised princely advance against my four remaining adventures.

This is an odd arrangement, which I shall have to look into when it becomes time for me to renew my contract. Had I failed to produce my second adventure as agreed, I should not have been paid for my first. No doubt that is how Mr Fitsch manages to make ends meet at the magazine, but I fail to see why his financial difficulties should be mine.

* * *

Talk about a busy day—I saw the Ogden child twice today. Once for a mysterious rash on his stomach (not so mysterious—impetigo) and once for a bloody nose that wouldn't stop bleeding because every time his mother turned her back, he had to show his little brother (the one who threw the block at him) how it hadn't stopped bleeding yet. It made perfect sense to me, but then I had a brother myself once.

Another day, another governess. Today's candidate was a Miss Pamela Lampley, a lovely girl with a bone china complexion and delicately arched brows, whose penchant for scholarly quotations would have whipped Holmes into a frenzy inside of an hour. "Wasn't it Alexander Pope who said…?" Usually, I was pretty sure it wasn't.

Ordinarily, I'd probably be feeling irritable after an encounter like this, but Mary has made me one of her father's famous hot toddies (to celebrate the New Year) and I can see why they're famous. This thing must be three parts rum to one part cider, warmed over a candle so as not to take the edge off.

What can Mary possibly be thinking of? I know Holmes is an unusual man, but that does not mean that he is looking for an unusual woman. That, my dear Mary, is a fallacy—a false inference. I don't know why we must suppose that he is looking for a woman at all, but granting this very remarkable premise—that Sherlock Holmes is in need of a wife—we are yet some considerable distance from understanding precisely (or even generally) what kind of a wife he could possibly be looking for.

I don't understand Mary. She wasn't discouraged by Celia Hughes, she wasn't discouraged by Jo Tate, she wasn't discouraged by Flora Blish. She wasn't even discouraged by Mrs Weekes of the two daughters and a small independence, suitably invested. To my mind, she should have been discouraged by Mrs Weekes. If you cannot imagine a man the proud Papa of a brace of daughters, then you have no business looking out for a wife for him.

Perhaps Mary thinks it would be different if they were his daughters but what I say is, where is the evidence for that belief? Where is the evidence?

Stimulated by my introduction to Miss Lampley (not to mention the hot toddy), I asked Mary to look at the evidence with me, but I might as well have spent my time whistling the wedding march for all the good it did me. You would have thought I was speaking in tongues. She never sticks to the subject—it's like trying to wrestle with an eel. She agrees with me every step of the way, except of course for the conclusion. There I was, resolved from the very bottom of my heart that we should not have the well-read Miss Lampley to deal with, and there was Mary, agreeing with me. "I saw the look on your face, John," she teased. "You have a very mobile countenance."

Do you suppose they learn this technique from their mothers? I'll go bail she never learned this one from her father! Mary will be guided by me in every particular, but as for the scheme itself, all she can say is: "Did you want marriage before you met me, John?"

Of course not, but we were talking about *Holmes*.

Chapter 16

Today I invented Irene Adler. With a little coaching, Holmes may perhaps be persuaded to remember that to him, she will always be *the* woman. I hope so. The strain of watching Mary comb her acquaintance for *the* woman is beginning to tell on me.

I can't believe how simple it is. I was beginning to think that nothing could discourage Mary when she unwittingly made me a present of the one infallible means at my disposal. She was stitching at the time—something white, I think. I was reading an article about the manifold uses of iodine during the American Civil War. Apparently, no soldier was allowed to die (except in prison, where conditions were appalling) without being subjected to a course of iodine treatment, generally at near-toxic dosage levels. War is a terrible thing.

"John?" she asked. "John, how long did you live with Mr Holmes?"

I looked up. "Six years, dear. Why do you ask?"

"As long as that? I did find myself a crusty old bachelor, didn't I?" (Mary *will* have her little joke.) "Well, John, can you not think back over your time in Baker Street and give me some indication of the type of female beauty Mr Holmes is most sensitive to? He must have admired some young lady over the course of six years."

Her question fell on me like the proverbial thunderbolt. I closed my medical journal. "Will you excuse me, Mary? I am in the middle of a very tangled adventure and it is calling me. I will be in my study."

The problem with the King of Bohemia's scandalous predicament has always been that it is not romantic. If that seems like a silly thing to say about a discarded mistress blackmailing her former protector, all I can say is that blackmail is not a romantic subject. Sordid, yes—romantic, no. Thanks to Holmes, there's plenty of action in the case, with plumber's smoke rockets, riots in the street, secret compartments, cries of "Fire!," loyal maids, and impenetrable disguises, but the fact remains that all the plot in the world can't compensate the reader for an unattractive case of characters. It is absolutely essential that the lady in the case engage the reader's sympathy, however thoroughly that sympathy may war with our better judgement. We must want the lady to win, and not merely because we so dislike the gentleman. It would help immeasurably if someone in the story, someone actually on the scene as it were, evinced a strong admiration for the lady, so that we might follow that character's lead with our own admiration, our own loyalty. But who? I can't do it, I'm a married man. That has been the sticking point for this adventure for months. In all that time, I never once thought of Holmes. That just shows you, doesn't it?

Let us review the situation. The discarded mistress is in a difficult position—and we must be made to feel the difficulty of it. She is without hope of any mitigation of her circumstances—and this must be seen to be a consideration. (Yes, I can do that.) She is young and beautiful, and she has the deductive powers of Sherlock Holmes ranged against her. She is helpless before him—or is she? Oh, I will have my readers sitting on the edge of their seats for Irene Adler!

Speaking of which, "Irene Adler" was certainly an inspired choice. It is a beautiful name, a beautifully believable name. Little did I know how important this name would be when I referred to her ladyship in the introductory section of 'A Case of Identity'. I shudder to think how easily I might have kept the original or fixed on something even less suitable: "Trina Fiedler," for example. It would be impossible to believe that a Trina Fiedler or an Eileen Sadler could be an opera singer from the backwoods of New Jersey, with a voice to make the heavens weep and a face and figure to rival—well, let us just say, a face and figure to rival her rivals'. Talk about killing two birds with one stone! By the time I've finished with Irene Adler, Holmes won't recognize the old harridan.

There is an element of poetic justice in all of this that appeals very strongly to me. After all, I know Holmes very much better than Mary does. In fact, Mary hardly knows him at all. Of the two of us, it makes sense that I should be the one to present him with his heart's desire. We shall want none of her Nora Nelligans or Pamela Lampleys after this! If my friend Holmes has a taste for fallen women, the cast-off consorts of foreign kings, that is a taste that Mary cannot very well attempt to supply. She must retire from the field. But stay a moment—what am I to make of Miss Adler's final capitulation? So farcical of her to leave the wrong photograph behind, in order that the King might have something to remember her by, when (as she well knew) all he wanted to do was to forget her.

The ending needs work, I can see that. The title, on the other hand, is perfect. Not even Holmes can fault 'A Scandal in Bohemia'. It's so clearly a reference to the Bohemian stratum of society. Who would dare to imagine that this really happened to the King of Bohemia, of all places? And yet it did.

Before I forget: Holmes vetted 'The Adventure of the Blue Carbuncle' for accuracy yesterday and it passed with flying colours. That is to say, it was not too accurate. I packed it off to Mr Fitsch on the instant. Theoretically, that means that I have two months to polish 'A Scandal in Bohemia' to its final form. Personally, I'll be surprised if I last a week without showing it to him.

* * *

Snatching twenty minutes and a couple of sandwiches before I begin my rounds of those too ill to attend me in my surgery: six households tonight, perhaps twice as many by the end of the week. Last month, no one had the influenza. Last week saw a few isolated cases. This week, it seems that half of

152

London is laid by the heels. There was a damfool editorial in the *Times* today, too, discussing the outbreak in terms of Darwin's evolutionary principle of survival of the fittest. Darwin was writing about the origin of species, not the death of some poor Granny in Paddington! If I had the time, I'd stop that foolishness with a few well-chosen words of my own. Too tired to do that now. Up half the night working on 'A Scandal in Bohemia'. Strike while the iron is hot, they say. Besides, if this epidemic blooms the way they say it will, I'm not going to have a moment to myself. So far, Anstruther's practice seems to be harder hit than mine. I see him starting his day earlier and ending it later than I have had to do.

Odd how often it's the young who die of it. They nurse an elderly parent through the crisis, perhaps a child or two, and just when everybody seems to be on the mend, they take it themselves and rapidly go from bad to worse. It's as if they had used up whatever reserves of strength they had before taking the illness.

Not that I look for anything like that this evening. It's early days yet, none of my families is too badly hit. Mostly I see people pulling together in time of trouble, relatives lending a hand, neighbours helping neighbours. That won't last, of course, it never does, but it warms the heart whenever and wherever I meet with it. More tomorrow.

* * *

I have finished it: 'A Scandal in Bohemia', and I am better pleased with it than I can say. Unless I am very much mistaken, it is superior in style and execution even to 'The Adventure of the Blue Carbuncle', and that is saying something. I will fight for this one. Let Holmes try to tell me that the title could be improved or the casting adjusted. (I take my plots from life, he cannot touch me there.) Sometime during the dark reaches of the night, I was visited by one last inspiration—in response to which, I have dated the incident back two years and placed myself under a pledge of secrecy only recently raised. Let Mary chew on that thought for awhile.

The case is about as airtight as one poor writer could make it. I have taken care not only to marry the lady off, thus putting her forever out of his reach (I am taking no chances that Mary will attempt to locate the lovely Miss Adler for my friend Holmes), but also to place him at the wedding itself as an impromptu witness. There is no getting around that. Impossible to believe that Sherlock Holmes could be taken in by a mummery; the lady must be well and truly married. I then sent the happy couple out of the country for an extended honeymoon on the Continent. Who knows where they are today? I don't. Mary will be so understanding, so solicitous of his broken heart, so touched that he could ask the King for her photograph. It is the most romantic thing I've ever heard. There won't be a dry eye in the house. Holmes must enjoy the humour of it.

You know, it is no mean feat to have invented a plausible past for my friend Holmes, a romantic past that I may reasonably hope will serve him in lieu of the domesticated future Mary otherwise has in store for him.

In a way, it is a great pity no one but Holmes will ever know what I've done for him.

Chapter 17

He doesn't like her.

It was positively the last thing I had ever thought to hear. What's not to like? "What possible objection can you have to her?" I asked him. "She's a fictional character! She sings, she dances, she had the King of Bohemia at her feet. All of the men in the neighbourhood go in awe of her. She is an opera singer, retired from the stage, slender enough for breeches parts. An American, with Continental polish—I made sure you would like that. You can give her any face you want, Holmes. What possible objection can you have to her?" I had Godfrey Norton, bachelor, throw up a promising career as a barrister with chambers in the Inner Temple in order to marry Miss Adler, knowing her history. What more does he want?

Don't tell me he's upset because she overlooks him as a possibility! He can't be as unreasonable as all that, can he? Surely not even Holmes can be as unreasonable as all that.

Irene Adler is the picture of refined gentility. Holmes appears before her in the guise of an out-of-work groom, pickled in stout and tobacco, probably tubercular, and almost certainly a slave to demon drink. Meanwhile, there is a successful lawyer already on the scene, with a full moustache under his perfect aquiline nose (Holmes's nose is not at all distinguished) and a special license in his pocket, ready to whisk her away from all of this unpleasantness as his lawfully wedded wife.

Why should Irene Adler, the daintiest trick in shoe leather for miles around, take His Horseyness into account? She'd be bound to see him, if she saw him at all, as a potential housebreaker rather than as a potential suitor. Didn't he spend his day examining her ground-floor window locks? Didn't he way, "Thank you, mum," when she tipped him a penny for handing her out of her carriage?

What does he expect me to do? I put in the fire trick right enough, he can have no objection to that, he saw himself it doesn't work in real life. People don't rush about, calmly securing their valuables in times of crisis. They grab whatever's handy and rush out into the street with it. I saw it myself, with him: one clock, a vase of flowers, and a tureen of soup. Now that we know it doesn't work, surely I am free to use it in my adventure—I'm not giving away any valuable secrets with this one. What does he want from me?

"Did you see the obituary column in today's *Times*, Watson? John Turner is dead."

And what if he is? I can't release 'The Boscombe Valley Mystery' for his family to read on the way home from his funeral. A decent interval has to elapse. Say, six months.

"This arrived this afternoon," he told me. I looked sharply at him, but as usual with Holmes, to no purpose. His face keeps its secrets.

It was a letter, from Alice Turner—one I thought at first she must have written before her father's body was fairly cold. I was wrong. She had written it while he still lay dying.

The old reprobate! It was a plea for information and it was addressed to Holmes.

4 January, 1889

Dear Mr Holmes,

It is now seven months since you were kind enough to come to Boscombe Valley to assist Inspector Lestrade in his investigation into the mysterious death of our neighbour, Mr McCarthy, with an eye to the eventual release of his son, James, from all suspicion in that regard. Perhaps Mr Lestrade did not make that part clear to you—I realize, of course, that he never fully believed in James's innocence. But you, Mr Holmes! You offered us hope from the beginning. Why, it was exculpatory evidence of your production that led to James's release at the autumn Assizes.

My father tells me I do not understand business—that you,

Mr Holmes, are a private enquiry agent, with no more serious loyalty than to the man or men who have hired you. Is that true? Oh, Mr Holmes, do you know of any reason why I should not pledge myself to marry James? My father has this afternoon in the extremity of his suffering (which it is terrible to see), wrung from me a promise to the effect that I will not engage myself to marry the man who killed Charles McCarthy.

He has dinned it into my head that your departure from the scene was in consequence of your discovery that James was in very fact the murderer—that, under the circumstances, you could do no more toward exonerating him of his crime than to point to whatever bits and pieces of material evidence at the scene of Mr McCarthy's sad demise might be twisted and turned to divert suspicion in sympathy to your client's cause. Is that what happened, Mr Holmes? My father says it stands to reason. Else why should you have concealed your own suspicions of the murderer? You have named no other man, offered no other explanation, spun no alternative theory of the crime. You appeared among us for the space of several days, dispensed reassurances with a prodigal hand, and retired to the metropolis once more, where you have preserved your silence and your opinion from any stain of popular judgement.

I do not well know what I am saying, Mr Holmes. But I beg of you—if you have any least encouragement to offer my hopes of happiness, I should be forever in your debt.

Distractedly,
MISS ALICE TURNER
Boscombe Valley Hall

Never have I been able to read a document through to its conclusion in Holmes's presence.

"You will notice that I stand accused of two mutually exclusive offenses," he said. "Perhaps I didn't understand what it was I was hired to do: Lestrade did not explain things properly. Alternatively, perhaps I understood precisely what it was I was hired to do and did it. I am not certain which of these two prospects pleases the young lady less. Would you care to venture an opinion?"

I ran my eyes over the remainder of the letter, wondering wherein lay the mystery. The young lady, Miss Turner (why can he never remember their names?), was beside herself over the realization that unless and until some other party was accused of the slaying of Charles McCarthy, suspicion would continue to hover over young James. James was with his father shortly before the fatal attack; they were quarreling; he was discovered cradling the dying man in his arms, muttering broken words of comfort; when questioned by the authorities, he had nothing to say for himself beyond a ritual protest of his innocence. Half the amount of circumstantial evidence would excite public opinion against him.

By now, Miss Turner knew just how much the dismissal of the charges at the Assizes had done to quell the local reaction—not much, I'll be bound. The extensive investigative efforts of Sherlock Holmes and company, imported at considerable expense from the metropolis for this grim occasion, had failed to produce the name of a second suspect and the deathbed promise exacted by her father had confirmed the intolerable nature of her situation. No doubt young James is finally behaving as a suitor, too—a development which would have been gratifying in the extreme in any circumstances less trying than these.

If I were to venture an opinion, it would be that what rankled most was her father's claim that she did not understand business. Miss Turner must be delivered from the sensation of being enmeshed in secret social conventions. I know what that is like. The occasions that can recall my Army days to my mind are indeed striking in their diversity.

"Will you let me handle this?" I asked, returning the letter. (Foolish question!)

"Willingly," said Holmes, handing it back to me.

All in all, it was a typical visit to my old rooms in Baker

Street. I arrived at eight o'clock believing I was an adventure to the good with Irene Adler and 'A Scandal in Bohemia', and I made my exit thirty minutes later knowing it was no such thing, burdened with an unrelated writing assignment: 'The Boscombe Valley Mystery'. Again. I expect I shall have a fair amount of rewriting to do to fit the narrative to this special case.

It goes without saying that I was unable to think of a way to suggest to Holmes that in the light of this further service of mine, he might without undue generosity, reconsider his position on the matter of Irene Adler and 'A Scandal in Bohemia'. Given how he feels about it, I can't even show it to Mary.

Chapter 18

I shouldn't have inflicted another adventure on him so soon after 'The Adventure of the Blue Carbuncle'. That's what Mary tells me. At another time, in another place, knowing that another deadline was upon me, he might have been more understanding. More tolerant. Sometimes Mary positively astounds me with her wisdom—what she would call her "motherwit." How can she possibly see all this and still believe Holmes to be in need of a wife? To say I do not understand it is to understate the case by a wide margin, believe me. Ever since 'A Scandal in Bohemia' was ruled out of court, I have felt like a fly trapped in a web of misunderstanding, a web from which no effort of mine can possibly extricate me.

"Never mind," said Mary. "You have two months to persuade Mr Holmes to your point of view and I have two friends I wish you to meet. They are coming to tea this afternoon: Jane Purchase and Elizabeth Tarrant. Seed cake today, John. Mind you're on time."

"Yes, dear."

I wonder whether Mary could possibly be right about this—about 'A Scandal in Bohemia', I mean. The question is, can I hope to raise this adventure for reconsideration at a later date or have I with my poor sense of timing, managed only to put it beyond the pale? Certainly, my timing was poor. In my eagerness to get an adventure ahead of myself (and the ubiquitous Mr Fitsch), I completely lost sight of the fact that for Holmes, the press of external circumstance is practically essential for acquiescence. How could I have been so foolish? Holmes won't even get dressed in the morning without a good reason!

Holmes prides himself on rising to the dramatic occasion and does everything in his power to heighten the sense of alarm permeating his cases. He thrives on excitement, looks for it, relishes it, and actually seeks to manufacture it when he can get it in no other way. He uses it to stimulate his deductive powers. My mutely enquiring face acts as a goad. How could someone with that emotional constitution possibly understand the medical temperament? They are diametrically opposed. Unlike Holmes, I look always for the space in the clearing where I can go to hear myself think. By temper, training and experience, I value the ability to take emergencies in my stride, with a becoming lack of fanfare. The entire medical profession rests on the efficacy of a lengthy preparation for a barrage of crises whose general dimensions can be gauged and analyzed in advance. I want method, I want peace, I want formulae—a prearranged response to an anticipated demand. Of course Holmes reacted badly. How could he help it? He probably thinks that if he waits until my deadline is upon me, I will pull another and to him, possibly more congenial adventure out of my files. He seems to have my files confused with a bottomless pit. I suppose it is inconceivable to him that I might do my best work while my deadline is yet some weeks away. After all, it is not as though he'd found my last effort entirely to his taste.

"But, Watson, why a blue carbuncle? The carbuncle is a species of ruby, ranging in colour from deep orange to blood red. There *are* no blue carbuncles."

There is no Duchess of Morcar, either. Really, sometimes Holmes tries my patience. Does he think this is easy? I should like to see him try his hand at this some time.

I have written to Miss Turner, offering her our condolences on her sad loss, urging her to do nothing in haste, reminding her that I was with Holmes when he answered Lestrade's appeal for help, promising her a full account of the circumstances of Charles McCarthy's death within the week. It will take me that long, I judge, to discover how to work in the story of James McCarthy's entanglement with that barmaid. I will leave it to her judgement, I told her, whether the facts uncovered by the unremitting efforts of Sherlock Holmes preclude a marriage with young McCarthy. That gives him about a week to make his confession to her. In all conscience, I can do no more for the lad. My first duty must be to the lady, who also happens to be our client—or, rather, Lestrade's client. It is a material consideration, as Mr Turner's reflections on the nature of business remind me.

Miss Turner seems to be a sensible girl, one who may (I hope) be tactfully encouraged to accept the happiness that Life offers her. As Holmes's reluctant intermediary, I emphatically reserve the right to so encourage her. It would be too cruel if with one blow, I were to shatter both her memory of her father and her hopes for the future. John Turner was a long time dying and it is a great pity he chose to use that time to try to spread the enmity of his generation like a blight onto the happiness of the next. He shall not succeed if it lies within my power to prevent it.

I suppose it is too much to hope that Alice Turner suspects the truth. Imagine promising the old reprobate that you would not marry "the killer of Charles McCarthy"! Logically, John Turner would have to be content with that wording of the promise. Cold comfort for the dying man, seeing that he was himself the killer. Interesting that he should have remained convinced to the end that the son of a blackmailer was no fit husband for the daughter of a murderer.

I must do what I can to bring the truth home to her in a gentle way. I must put a good face on it. Perhaps I can put the text of Charles McCarthy's providential 'Memoirs of Ballarat' into John Turner's mouth—have Turner confess his guilt freely and openly to Holmes as if to ease his conscience, sue for mercy on the grounds of failing health, vow that he always intended to come forward in the event that young James was forced to stand his trial. Recent events may make that last part a bit difficult for Miss Turner to credit, but it's worth a try.

This is 'The Boscombe Valley Mystery', not *Romeo and Juliet*. John Turner is dead. May God have mercy on his soul.

And now we have a communication from Mr Fitsch:

The *Strand* is unable to accept 'The Adventure of the Blue
Carbuncle' for publication at this time and begs that you will
supply the deficiency with another of your excellent adventures of Sherlock Holmes (not less than six nor more than nine
thousand words) by the 12th inst. at the latest. We are presently
working on the February issue of the Magazine—'The Blue
Carbuncle' is a Christmas story and no light editing of mine
will serve to make it anything else. Exchange the snow for a
spring shower, the goose for a ham, and you have the makings
of an Easter story in deplorable taste. Your protagonist may
pardon the good thief in a Christmas story, but hardly in an
Easter fable, don't you agree? A little reflection will, I am sure,
convince you of the truth of what I am saying. We will be most
pleased to accept 'The Adventure of the Blue Carbuncle' for
our December issue, should you care to resubmit it to us at that
time. I return the manuscript to you forthwith. I trust that you
and your wife are keeping well and managing to avoid the
influenza.

Remember, I need the new adventure by the 12th—if it's a
bit over 9,000 words, I won't say no, but spare me that "Sign"
thing. I noticed you referred to it again here. Are you trying to
create a demand for book-length fiction within the pages of my
magazine?

Yours etc.,
NATHANIEL FITSCH

I didn't think it was so obvious. Well, what is obvious to Mr
Fitsch may not be so obvious to Mr Fitsch's readers. If I intend
to create a demand for the long story that is languishing in my
files, I shall have to look sharp and slip in my references
where Mr Fitsch's infamous light editing can not easily take
them out. Were I more like Holmes, no doubt this would add

to the excitement of the task confronting me at this time but as my readers are bound to discover, I am not like Holmes, and it is not excitement that I am feeling. How does Fitsch imagine that a doctor is avoiding the influenza? So far I have avoided *taking* the influenza, it is true, but I can hardly avoid seeing it, hearing about it, talking about it, thinking about it.

Curious how much busier Anstruther is over this epidemic than I am. He goes about half-shaved, with dark circles under his eyes, and I know it's not for effect. For some reason, his practice has been much more affected by the influenza than mine has. My six cases have grown to twenty or so, but from the look of him, he's wrestling with fifty cases, half of them at the crisis. I offered to do his evening rounds for him so he could get some sleep, he can't go on this way, but he tells me he's very well, hard work never killed anybody. A lot of nonsense! Hard work among the infected has killed more than one physician who neglected his own health. He'll be lucky to escape the influenza himself, at the rate he's going. Then I'll have him to care for as well as his patients.

Today is the 10th, my new deadline is the 12th, the influenza is everywhere. Realistically, I cannot expect to write a new 6,000 word adventure in two days, in between influenza cases. And why on earth should I have to? Setting aside the 44,000 words of 'The Sign of Four', I now have six adventures of the requisite length complete and to hand, not one of them simultaneously acceptable to Holmes, Fitsch, and myself. I shall have to throw myself on Holmes's mercy—'A Scandal in Bohemia' or 'The Five Orange Pips', one or the other, it is up to him. I cannot sanction publication of 'The Boscombe Valley Mystery' until June at the earliest, and then only with Alice Turner's permission.

Mary is right. I will stop by Baker Street this evening.

* * *

"Dr Watson, as I live and breathe. The very man we were

wishing for. Dr Mortimer, Sir Henry, you remember Dr Watson."

Holmes, affable? Something was wrong. I turned from Holmes to his guests, searching for the explanation. "You are not well, Sir Henry?" (My question was just pardonable, I judged, coming from a medical man.)

"Nothing that an ocean voyage won't cure," Dr Mortimer said heartily. "Salt air, the sea breeze, new faces, a complete change of scene, and a gradual transition to an active life. It was Dr Bruder's recommendation."

It was not for me to question the eminent Dr Bruder's recommendation, I reflected. "You are going to Canada?" I asked.

"To Canada? Why should we go to Canada? There are no interesting skulls in Canada, Doctor. We sail for Africa! In easy stages, I assure you: London to Liverpool, Liverpool to Tenerife—on a passenger liner, not a merchant ship. We must consider Sir Henry's comfort. We will recruit our strength in the Canaries. Hiking, canoeing, exploring, sleeping rough, with regular excursions to the mainland. When Sir Henry is feeling more the thing, we will embark for the West Coast, wending our way south. We do not have our hearts set absolutely on reaching the Cape, do we, Sir Henry? But the mouth of the Congo, the coastal site of Stanley and Livingstone, that we must venture or call our trip a failure."

Holmes said, "Dr Mortimer and Sir Henry were kind enough to stop by on this, their last evening in London, for a pipe and a chat. Doctor?" I accepted a fill of tobacco from him.

"She deceived me, Doctor," said Sir Henry.

"Not as badly as Irene Adler deceived me," said Holmes proudly. I listened, stupefied, to the recitation that followed. "Watson is calling it 'A Scandal in Bohemia,'" he concluded. "Isn't that right, Watson?"

I had just enough presence of mind to add, "You will find it in next month's *Strand*."

Dr Mortimer was smiling. Holmes must genuinely like Sir

Henry, I realized. I had not suspected it of him—he always holds himself so aloof from his clients. Dr Mortimer pointed out the moral of the story for us: "You see, Sir Henry, however much these things may hurt at the time, they do pass. It is two years now and here we have Holmes, as heart-whole as ever."

Neither of them knows anything about it. My thoughts flew to Mary. "I am sorry you will not be spending more time in London, Sir Henry. I should have liked you to meet my wife. You, too, Dr Mortimer." Moved by some impulse I don't understand even yet, I picked over my words, rejecting my half-formed references to Mrs Stapleton and the terrible position she had been in, finally insisting, "You must promise to give me the pleasure when you return to London, Sir Henry. Mary would never forgive me if I let you put up in an hotel on that occasion."

I owe Mary a bachelor in any case, I thought wildly. By any reasonable standard, Sir Henry Baskerville, romantic baronet and West African explorer, late of Baskerville Hall, would make an admirable substitute for Sherlock Holmes, misogynist and intermittently employed detective.

I was grasping at straws and I knew it. Now that it had come to the point of publication, I found I was not altogether happy about 'A Scandal in Bohemia' as a solution to my domestic problems. It made a marvelous adventure, though— the best of all the ones I'd written. Holmes was so human in it.

We smoked in silence for a little. Sir Henry stared into the fire. His thoughts were easy to guess. Dr Mortimer might not be such a poor choice of attendant, I thought hopefully. He will be cheerfully oblivious to his companion's pain and that, together with the distractions of the Canary Islands and West Africa (money helps, there's no doubt about it), should take Sir Henry over the worst of it. Mary, I knew, could be trusted to do the rest. Weren't we planning to introduce Mary Sutherland to young Stamford next week? Dr Mortimer and my friend Holmes appeared to be looking for a way to introduce the subject of the Hound. Holmes was the first to find the key.

"What did you think of Selden, Dr Mortimer? Camped on the moor in full view of Lassiter's telescope for over two weeks, dodging the warders and harrying his reluctant relatives for supplies—he certainly didn't lack courage. An uncommonly resourceful villain was Jack Selden, don't you agree? You saw the body, Mortimer. What did his skull tell you?"

This unleashed a flood of reminiscences on the part of Dr Mortimer, culminating once again in a discussion of the pure impossibility of red hair.

"You're a scientific man, Holmes." (Holmes raised an eyebrow in token of the compliment.) "You must have noticed that it is a mere figure of speech. Red hair! You might as well describe someone as having a double chin or a turned-up nose. Of course we all do it, but to the scientific mind,…"

If Dr Mortimer has his way, I shall have to resign myself to descriptions of our subjects' skulls. Red hair, double chins, and a turned-up nose are only the beginning. What about grey eyes? Flashing teeth? Bushy eyebrows? A piercing gaze? Don't tell me there's no such thing as a piercing gaze. I have been impaled on the one Sherlock Holmes carries around with him often enough to know better.

I could have listened to Dr Mortimer for hours. I could see Holmes was impressed. He was bored, certainly (Holmes is always bored in company), but he was also impressed—impressed and entertained. It was a new thought and if there's one thing Holmes likes more than another, it is a new thought. Once or twice I fanned the flames with a carefully modulated objection, raising Holmes's other eyebrow, so to speak (I wonder whether Dr Mortimer permits eyebrow raising?), but I would not have challenged him seriously for the world. Not then. Not there. I would choose my ground. A practical demonstration was in order, I thought, and I wanted a bigger audience for it than the scientific Holmes and the abstracted Sir Henry. I'll take Mr Fitsch for my arbiter, I thought: Mr Fitsch and *vox populi*. I had no doubt that they would be on my side. Wasn't "red hair" an expression of the people? The salient points, to my mind, were these: (1) Selden had had red hair; and (2) I had had an idea for an adventure.

Holmes shall have his Jamison case. That was a kindly gesture on his part, toward me and Sir Henry both—it should not go unrewarded. And I know the Jamison case would be Holmes's first choice. I shall call it 'The Adventure of the Red-headed League' and send a copy to Dr Mortimer—no, better yet, to "Sir Henry Baskerville, Poste Restante, The Canary Islands." I will have to change Rufus Jamison's name (what do you think of Jabez Wilson?) and restore to him the hair of his youth, hennaed out of all recognition, but I believe the device will answer. The problem with that case was always how to account for Rufus Jamison's absences from his shop, as regular as clockwork, in a family magazine. It was obvious from the start, even to Holmes, that the truth would not do. The question is, will he be amenable to a fiction of such major proportions? An epic fiction, greater even than the one I created for 'A Scandal in Bohemia'? I think so. It is a hard call, but my best guess is that Dr Mortimer and his scientific mind have antagonized Holmes enough for anything. I have wagered substantial sums on riskier propositions than this in my day! Nothing ventured, nothing gained. And Holmes is an irascible fellow.

For once I need not worry about his client's reactions to my literary plans. Mr Jamison must approve his disguise. What man has ever objected to acquiring a full head of hair? It would be like objecting to a sudden surge of virility. Rufus Jamison is not the type to object to that. He will probably dine out on the story for months—in bachelor circles, of course. It is irresistible.

The fact of the matter is that Dr Mortimer, like my friend Holmes, has very little respect for the power of the written word. I'll show them. By the time I've done with my description, no one will question the flame red hair of our Mr Wilson. Jabez Wilson will not only have red hair, he'll have the reddest hair in all England. No, don't exaggerate, Watson—the reddest hair in all London. Exaggeration would be fatal to my story. Wait until they see the line of red-headed men I intend to assemble in, I think, Pope's Court, to compete for a place in my League. The position will be a sinecure, yes, moderately well-paid. I've got it! I'll have him copy *The Encyclopaedia Britannica* for me, in honour of Inspector Lestrade of the ginger hair. (I want to secure Holmes's approval, don't I? An inside joke at Lestrade's expense will be the quickest way to do that.)

It's perfect. It even has the flavour of a schoolboy punishment about it. I particularly like the idea of sending Rufus Jamison to Pope's Court for his sins. I hope it does the old boy good.

Chapter 19

"Mary, I'm sorry, but I tried to tell you it wouldn't answer." Oh, why didn't she let me show her 'A Scandal in Bohemia' before sending it off to Mr Fitsch? Of course she felt betrayed.

"How did you try to tell me? When did you try to tell me? I had no idea, John. None. You were most approving of Celia Hughes. You never missed an opportunity to take tea with her, talk to her, admire her. Are you telling me that this was on your own behalf?

"And Flora Blish. I know you did not precisely admire Flora, but we were not trying to suit you, John. Presumably, you had already been suited. We were trying to suit Mr Holmes, and that is a very different kettle of fish. I could not know that Celia, as forward as she was, had yet been too modest in her behaviour to attach him! Without a hint from you, I must have moved in the wrong direction. That hint never came. At least I did not fix on a shy, retiring type, all blushes and coltish capers. You may not appreciate poor Flora, John, but she has seen her share of trouble and she has met it with the resources at her command. If those resources, intellectual and emotional, seem as insignificant to you as they did to Mr Holmes, you might at least have the decency to admit that that is not her fault.

"Jo Tate! I suppose you will not tell me that you made yourself clear over Miss Tate? You avoided Miss Tate, it's true but that is hardly the same thing." She appeared to have done for the moment.

"Mary, please. You are upset. It is very natural. For several weeks—very well, for several months, many weeks—you have been trying to accomplish something you can see now had much better have been left unattempted. But Mary, no great harm was done. Holmes does not lack understanding.

170

He knows that I was under a pledge of secrecy, that I could not speak to you."

"Holmes does not lack understanding!" she repeated. "Mr Holmes may not lack understanding, John, but *you* don't understand anything. Oh, go to your surgery! We will talk further of this tonight, after supper."

Is that any way for a loving wife to speak to her husband? And another thing: do you suppose all wives make appointments to do battle with their husbands? And what about their husbands? Do you suppose their husbands meekly present themselves at the time appointed? I give you my word, I have half a mind to drop in on Holmes this evening.

There's the bell: my first patient. I have certainly timed this to a nicety. More later.

* * *

It was while I was listening for the fourth time to Mr Jellett's moving description (no pun intended) of the mysterious pain in his vitals that is sometimes on the left and sometimes on the right but never in the middle, that I gradually came to realize that whether or not all husbands present themselves at the time appointed, one who loves his wife might well choose to be obliging in such a sensitive matter. Surely it is in our best interests as a couple to put this behind us as soon as may be? I could wish it were behind us already but there, that is always the wish of the party in the wrong. I can sympathize with Mary's resentment in this case, indeed I can. I can see her point.

It is one of my many failings that, finding myself in a quarrel, I can nearly always see my opponent's point, often to the extent, over a couple of hours, of losing sight of my own. I could never have been a lawyer. Holmes would have made an excellent lawyer—never does he lose sight of a single advantage attached to his position and he hates to lose an argument—but that is neither here nor there. I owe Mary an apology. I had felt constrained to place the demands of friendship temporarily above the demands of marital openness and that is bound to be a source of hurt and confusion to a wife. I wouldn't want it any other way.

* * *

All is forgiven.

A few tears fell, I told her my idea for 'The Red-headed League' ("Oh, John! Do you think you should?"—very gratifying), and we have made a solemn pact: henceforth, Mary will read each of my adventures as they come from my pen, in advance of my friend Holmes. I am not sure why that should have made everything right between us— it is only what I have been asking for since I began this diary with my account of the adventure of the etheric manipulators, after all—but so it proved. I gave her the revised version of 'The Boscombe Valley Mystery' on the spot.

"After all," she said, "I may be able to suggest ways in which to make the written adventures more palatable to Mr Holmes." Isn't that sweet? I am glad I told her how reluctant Holmes was to see the Irene Adler story in print.

"But John, he is so human in that one!"

My sentiments exactly, but then we all know that Holmes's humanity is not his most prized possession. I even told Mary about Mr Jellett's latest complaint and do you know, she was able to make a very worthwhile suggestion.

"John, why do you not refer Mr Jellett to a specialist? You can do nothing for him, he takes up valuable time that might be better spent in any number of ways" (at which point she gave a delicious little wriggle), "and it is an awesome responsibility to have to tell yourself over and over again that he is not really ill. After all, Mr Jellett is going to die sometime, like the rest of us. At some point, certainly, he will be ill. Why not now?"

Why not, indeed. Mary may not be reliable on the subject of Mr Holmes, but she is lucidity itself on the subject of Mr Jellett.

I'll do it.

Chapter 20

I need a new chapter for this one.

This afternoon, I sustained a visit from two young readers of the *Strand Magazine* who were inspired by the exploits of their hero, Sherlock Holmes, to the utterly unexpected extent of consulting their uncle's *Medical Directory* to search out the bona fides and current address of Dr John H. Watson. They actually called on me. I can't believe it. At their age, I should not have dared! Of course, at their age, I couldn't have done it—my favourite author was long since dead. In answer to my question, they told me proudly that they did not want to disturb Holmes at his work in Baker Street. I congratulated them on their thoughtfulness and was rewarded with two of the brightest smiles I've seen in ages.

They were very polite, it's true, but they stared a great deal and wanted to know how they might obtain a copy of 'A Study in Scarlet' and 'The Sign of Four'. I distributed autographed copies of my first novel and suggested that they apply directly to Mr Nathaniel Fitsch of the *Strand Magazine* for information regarding my second. They seemed disappointed that the autograph was mine and not Holmes's.

Mary says that it is a great compliment to "the persuasive power of my writing," and I suppose that in this, she is saying no more than the truth (it has not escaped my notice that the adventure which brought them to my door was the Irene Adler story, 'A Scandal in Bohemia'), but I am moving my practice in consequence. Readers of 'The Red-headed League' will find me hard at work in Kensington and conclude that their directory is out of date. This technique will not discourage a Mary Sutherland or a Jabez Wilson (not that I look for a visitation from Mr Wilson alias Rufus Jamison), but I expect it will answer for at least some of the

William Smiths and Mary Browns who might otherwise track me to my surgery.

I have always wanted a practice in Kensington.

Chapter 21

"Kensington, John? We are moving to Kensington?" asked Mary.

"Only to avoid my public," I explained. Perhaps I should have asked her first? I have only been married a short while, but I know that Mary expects to be consulted about many more things that my mother ever did. "I should have asked you first, I know, but it was very late and besides, I thought you'd like Kensington."

"I'm sure I should, John. You have often spoken of it." My ear detected a note of doubt. Oh well, I could afford to be generous.

"Come, Mary, where would you like to live? All of London waits at your feet. It's not often that a man can say to his wife, 'Your wish is my command,' and mean it from his heart." I teased. "Now where shall it be?"

"Kensington is fine, John, truly. I know you have always wanted a practice in Kensington. I was simply a little startled to hear you have one, that's all. I must adjust my ideas a little in the wake of this very remarkable adventure. I hope you found us a nice big house," she teased. "I expect Mr Holmes will have to adjust his ideas a little as well. I suppose you must show it to him before you publish it?"

"I don't know about 'must,' Mary, but certainly I had thought to do so. You don't think he'll like it?" It always hurts me when Mary speaks slightingly of my work and I had taken more trouble over 'The Red-headed League' than any of my other adventures.

"I'm sure I think he *should* like it! It's a wonderful story, John. My heart was in my mouth when he tapped that sidewalk. Then, later, in the bank—you have a great gift for description, John. I mean it. By acknowledging the preposterousness of your Red-headed League, you made it impossible for me to doubt it for an instant. I don't know how you did it, but you made me see your Mr Jabez Wilson's red hair stand out like a flame against a long line of drab pretenders to the distinction. It was as if he were Royalty and they, commoners. I had no problem with it at all, even knowing the spuriousness of it. I can see Mr Wilson's red hair yet. Later, I could feel the tension mount as you waited for John Clay in the dampness of that bank vault. Did Mr Holmes really bring a deck of cards with him that evening?"

By now, Mary should know both her husband and his friend well enough to understand that I am never driven to exert my powers of invention on his behalf. My friend Holmes is unique. I could not begin to imagine how to embellish his behaviour for my readers. He is the one fixed star in a sea of invention.

Mary was right about one thing, though: I shall have to choose the time and place for sharing my adventure of 'The Red-headed League' with Holmes very carefully. I am glad I have 'The Boscombe Valley Mystery' to fall back on in case of need. Reader, she married him. That's right, Alice Turner is now Mrs James McCarthy. Mary was so proud of me.

Mrs McCarthy wrote to me from Scotland, where she and her husband have fled to avoid the tongues of the Boscombe Valley gossip brigade, stimulated to new heights of activity by her "precipitous" marriage. (She has only known James all of her short life. I wonder what they would have made of my marriage to Mary? Not much, I'll be bound.) And while she has asked me to convey her "sincere appreciation" to Mr Sherlock Holmes, Mrs McCarthy's letter made no secret of the fact that she reserved the greater part of her gratitude for the author of 'The Boscombe Valley Mystery', an adventure that she for her part would be only too glad to see in print. "For however unpleasant it may be to see our fathers' crimes uncloaked in the public press, I can only rejoice to see my husband vindicated before our family, friends, and acquaintances." She went on to say that she must think of the future. Their children, if any, should live in a world where the truth was honoured and made known. So I am one adventure to the good, anyway. Holmes won't quibble with me over this one, I'm sure. He will be as glad to see the end of it as I am.

It's a pity I can't count on his feeling the same level of detachment regarding the Jabez Wilson case but there, a man's acknowledged victories always loom larger in his memory than his secret successes. I reveal that, far from being one of Holmes's rare failures, the Boscombe Valley Mystery was no mystery to him at all, and I am a hero. I describe the ins and outs of the detective process that led Holmes from Jabez Wilson's unsavoury leisure-time activities to John Clay's criminal ones, unmasked before a grateful Bank Manager and an Inspector at Scotland Yard, and I will almost certainly be told that I have failed miserably at conveying the magnitude of his achievement. Practically speaking, it is inevitable. Besides, it would be just like Holmes to decide that my Red-headed League was distracting the reader from the inherently much more interesting matter of an overly dedicated shop assistant with grubby knees to his trousers, working for half wages at a shop whose pavement sounded different from that of the surrounding shops. Those were the points of interest that recommended themselves to my friend Holmes, as I recall.

And Mary suspects me of embroidering Holmes's idiosyncrasies! She must be mad.

* * *

"Miss Morrison, may I present Dr Stamford? Dr Stamford, Miss Morrison." I marvelled at the ease of Mary's manner as she made the necessary introductions. "Tea, John?" She seemed to have no sense of the falseness of the occasion. I wondered that she could keep her countenance in the face of the astonishing transformation that had befallen Mary Sutherland. *Miss Morrison, Miss Morrison, Miss Morrison:* the correction thrummed in my ears. Mary would not thank me if I were to call our guest by the name I had given her in my adventure.

I accepted a cup of tea and during the interval of passing the cups, examined our guest. Discreetly, I assure you. And I promise you, this was not the Miss Morrison I knew. Or rather (I must correct myself again), the Miss Morrison I thought I knew. That Miss Morrison, better known as Mary Sutherland, had fallen prey to the unscrupulous designs of her stepfather, who had masqueraded as one Hosmer Angel (to give him the name I gave him in my adventure) in order to attach her affections to his absent person and secure her little income to his household on a permanent basis. It was a vile, contemptible trick and she had been its victim. She even looked like a victim. Defeated in her lovelorn ambition to become a typewriter by her short sight, she had no particular style or grace, regularly wore mismatched boots, and beat the air with a breathless, untidy staccato that spoke equally of entrapment and escape. That Miss Morrison had been all abroad in her behaviour, all distress and distraction, at once bereft of her hopes for the future and the security of her past. There was every indication that her mother had joined with her stepfather in her deception.

This Miss Morrison, by contrast, had apparently never known an unquiet moment. She took no cream, no sugar, but stirred her tea as though to keep us company. Her new—and very modish—costume was a welcome breath of spring on this raw day. I specifically checked her boots: new and very daring, being made to match not only each other but also her bottle-green hat with the butter-coloured feathers that crowned the whole. I knew that the vagueness of her gaze was attributable to the ravages of myopia, but I doubt that explanation occurred to young Stamford. She kept her gaze softly focussed on what little she was able to see of the room, while he fell all over himself trying to attract her attention. Stamford always was a specialist at heart—the respiratory system was and is his special area of concern. She was undeniably alluring. She spoke when spoken to and seemed as grateful for the attention as for the tea, but initiated no conversation and was well content with silence. Her unaccountable ease of manner would have melted stronger hearts than young Stamford's.

Perhaps nothing will come of it. Mary says that it would be most unusual if her very first introduction were to bear marital fruit and I can see the logic in that, but I can also see the light in Mary's eyes and that light tells a different story. We are promised to escort Miss Morrison to the surgeons' ball next month, as Stamford's guests, so that he might pursue the connection. I don't know why we need all of these contrivances! When I was ready to marry, I met my Mary and we managed to reach an understanding in spite of the very considerable handicap of Holmes's constant detecting presence. Of course, it's not everyone who could have brought that off as well as I did. And Mary Sutherland does have some claim on my good nature. Oh, bother the woman! I hope she does manage to attach young Stamford. It will be easier to remember to address her as "Mrs Stamford" than as "Miss Morrison."

Finally moderately well pleased with the adventure of 'The Red-headed League'. All told, it has taken almost twice as long as I had anticipated, but in this case I think the extra labour was justified. I want the reader to understand that Jabez Wilson's hair was of such a consummate redness that the most casual observer (that is to say, Dr Watson) would be immediately struck by it. I had to work the description in early, direct the reader's attention to it smoothly, and let the significance of my description build to a crescendo against a fast-moving adventure in which every loose end fits, and the conjuring trick fades into the background.

The worst part of the creative writing business is that when you finally manage to do it and do it well, no one has any idea that you've done anything at all. In this regard as in so many others, it is the exact opposite of the deductive process.

Chapter 22

Bumped into Holmes in, of all places, an opium den—and what would I not have given to have had my manuscript of 'The Red-headed League' with me! He *was* fuzzy-minded. Kept telling me he had a new adventure "for my ears only" and then forgetting what it was. Something about a beggar, a good woman, and a missing husband, but where the opium den comes into it I don't know. I hasten to add that I, too, was there in my professional capacity or rather, what is beginning to feel like my professional capacity, as Mary's husband. It was this way.

It seems that Mary does have *one* friend who is married, and this friend's husband is an opium eater. Abel Hucknell had been gone since Friday and by Sunday, Mrs Hucknell was frantic. Frantic on Sunday, she thought of Mary on Monday: wasn't Mary's husband supposed to be a doctor? Mrs Hucknell brought their wedding photograph with her, for purposes of identification. "Brown hair and blue eyes," she said tenderly, conferring it on me like a gift. She knew exactly where her husband was: Upper Thames Street, the Silver Bowl; Madame Chang would know. Naturally, I left at once. Hucknell, Hucknell—wasn't there a couple by that name at our wedding? I wasn't sure.

Not the best part of town, Upper Thames Street. Idleness is the universal affliction of the poor and evidence of that affliction was everywhere. Saucy city pieces darted out of doorways to accost lonely gentlemen in hansom cabs and passed rude remarks when I ignored them. Young toughs melted in and out of back alleys. The gin shops did a brisk business. We travelled the length of the street twice before I spotted it: on the corner, below a cooper's shop that had seen better days, the Silver Bowl. It seemed fitting that the entrance should be below the level of the street. With more foresight than I am usually given credit for (and, to be honest, more foresight than I am usually prepared to exhibit), I instructed the cabman to wait.

"Don't be more foolish than you can help," I said shortly. "If I'm not out of there in five minutes, ten at the outside," Holmes says it is as well to be precise, "you may go to the police with my blessing."

As Holmes says, the secret is in the timing. Be brief, be prosperous, and be sure you reach your exit before your last syllable reaches his ear. Above all, resist the impulse to tip your unwilling assistant as a token of your good faith. He may pocket the tip in lieu of his fare and write off the difference to pride and independence. Holmes says pride and independence should cost a man everything.

"Madame Chang?" I inquired and realized my mistake at once. Two men loomed out of the shadows behind her—this was no place for polite introductions. "My name is Dr Watson. I am looking for—this man."

"You are his friend?" she asked, making no move to take the photograph. Her words came slowly. "I think you will not have to come for that one more than a few times. I think he sees his death in the smoke." That was Madame Chang's opinion and who can doubt she knows whereof she speaks?

Loyalty to Abel Hucknell kept my face impassive as I digested this information. The old woman sighed. "The fifth bench on the left," she said, indicating the curtained entrance to the next room.

Ordinarily, a new scene resolves itself for me very easily into foreground and background. My impression of the Silver Bowl, however, was that it was all background. The floorboards, badly warped, were bare and dirty. No pictures relieved the monotony of the walls, which were of an indeterminate colour tending toward brown and running with river damp. The lighting was uniformly dim and the atmosphere, naturally, was poisonous. I kept my breathing soft and shallow as I picked my way to the fifth bench. "Abel?" I whispered.

Abel Hucknell had been a tall, strapping man. No more. With brown hair and blue eyes, according to his wife. Bleary eyes and matted hair would have been more to the point, I thought as I helped (or rather, hauled) him to his feet. I wondered briefly whether he had had anything to eat since Friday. There was a small bowl of congealed rice next to his pipe: untouched.

"Abel, it's Dr Watson. Can you stand? Abel? Abel, can you stand? Good. No, don't sit down, Abel, we're leaving. No, don't sit down. Abel? Stand up, Abel! That's it. Claire is waiting for us, Abel. We must go to her." I looked around. We did not seem to be disturbing the rest of the clientele: a verminous lot, I thought. "Abel? Can you hear me, Abel?"

"Claire?" His eyes slid off my face. "Where's the photograph?" he asked.

"The photograph?"

"Claire. If you're from Claire, you must have the photograph. Where is it?"

Light dawned. The wedding photograph was not given me in order that I might identify Abel, but so that Abel might identify me.

"Take me to Claire." he said. And slid from the bench to the floor.

"It might be easier to sling him over your shoulder, insensible as he is, and rely on the fresh air to revive him." The whispered words were so exactly what I was thinking myself that it was a shock to realize that they were not mine. Yes, it was Holmes. "He owes the management two bob for the last pipe," he added helpfully.

I don't know whether 'The Man with the Twisted Lip' will prove at all suitable for my pen but if so, I certainly have an attention-getting opening for it.

* * *

No word from Holmes, which may mean that he has already

solved his case, or it may mean that he is on the verge of abandoning it for lack of evidence. But if his case is solved, why hasn't he appeared to tell me of his cleverness? And if his case is at a standstill, why hasn't he arranged to use me as a sounding board in order to clarify his thinking? Last night's activities didn't clarify anything.

In disguise, his life probably not worth a brass farthing should he be recognized, the disreputable sailor who was Holmes made ready to quit the Silver Bowl as soon as I arrived to provide an alternate means of passing the evening. It's not my fault that Abel Hucknell's condition made that impossible. It may have felt like the hand of fate to Holmes, meeting Watson in an opium den, but I knew it was the hand of Mrs Hucknell that was responsible. "Not now, Watson. Outside. Do you have a cab?" Yes, I had a cab. I needed it for Abel Hucknell.

I secured a second cab for Holmes eventually, but the damage was done. He turned silent on me and I dozed, and all I'm really clear about is that he thinks his client should have lent him a dog-cart if she was going to expect personal progress reports from him on a daily basis. Oh yes, and I have "a grand gift for silence" when I'm sleeping.

It goes against the grain with me to apologize to him for this, but I suppose I'll have to. At least I can be sure of one thing. "Send the sot home, Watson. We don't need him." Nobody could ever mistake Holmes for a married man.

* * *

Success! Holmes has approved 'The Red-headed League' (not without argument, as you shall hear, but I got the better of him at last) and —you boon, you!—there is no impediment to my telling the story of 'The Man with the Twisted Lip', always providing I disguise his client sufficiently "to preclude identification by my public." Ha! I have disguised more than that in my time, and so I told him. Not that he should have needed the reminder. Hadn't he just finished reading 'The Red-headed League'?

"It is extraordinary, Watson. Quite the most extraordinary thing you've done. And I do not make an exception of that last adventure of yours, that ridiculous 'Scandal in Bohemia'—which was not set in Bohemia at all, as you'll recall, but right here in London, divided approximately evenly between the venues of St. John's Wood and Baker Street. I hardly recognized myself in that one. I do in fact recognize myself in this one, but that's about all I recognize."

I spoke soothingly. "The deductive chain, Holmes, is entirely your own. You must have recognized it."

"Yes, yes, I have already admitted I recognized my own part. The dialogue, the deductive chain, the *dénouement*. It is the rest of it I'm having trouble with. This Jabez Wilson, this John Clay—I suppose you got his name from the deposits on his trouser knees? I thought so. But why, Watson? You take an ordinary case"—hardly ordinary in my opinion, involving as it did an insatiable shopkeeper, a shop assistant happily working for half wages, a fortune in gold, a bank half a street away behind a vegetarian restaurant, and a tunnel connecting their two cellars—"and then you complicate it. You introduce the most fantastic elements and you expect your readers to believe you. You do recall Dr Mortimer's observation about the incidence of red hair in *Homo sapiens*? You must, you couldn't possibly have missed the import of his remarks, your adventure is by way of being an answer to the good doctor. But what if someone notices the sheer impossibility of the thing? Won't you feel embarrassed if one of your readers challenges your veracity?"

It was time to introduce a note of reality into the conversation. That is the trouble with all of this scientific accuracy we hear so much about these days—it takes no account of reality.

"One of my readers, challenge my veracity regarding Jabez Wilson's red hair? I am surprised at you, Holmes. You forget, most of my readers will not have met any of us. Whom do you think the average reader will find it harder to believe in, a red-haired pawnbroker named Jabez Wilson or a consulting detective named Sherlock Holmes?"

His grin—not very practiced—won my point for me. In no time, we were both grinning from ear to ear. Good, I thought. If Holmes could be brought to understand the magnitude of the task I have set myself with these adventures of his, then he might be persuaded to moderate his literary expectations to a more normal level.

"I liked the part about the encyclopaedia," he offered.

"I thought you might," I said. I endeavoured to hide my satisfaction. This was not the time to ask him whether he had also enjoyed the scene in the bank or my description of Mr Wilson.

"Do you send a copy to Dr Mortimer?" he asked.

"Of the published version, I think, Holmes." (I was not about to incorporate Dr Mortimer into my pre-publication gauntlet.) "The *Strand* is a popular magazine, but unlikely to come his way in the Canary Islands without my assistance."

"If Dr Mortimer has a fault," Holmes said thoughtfully, "It is that he is a little limited in his conversation—inclined to be dogmatic in his opinions."

So much understanding was a heady experience for me. "I will let you know if anyone objects to Jabez Wilson's red hair or my Red-headed League," I promised.

"But you do not anticipate it?" he asked. It was still bothering him.

"No, Holmes, I do not anticipate it. I anticipate nothing but praise, this side of the Canary Islands."

And I gave myself up to the sweet contemplation of its arrival in the Canaries. "You see, Sir Henry, England has not forgotten us." Indeed we haven't.

* * *

December marked the appearance of the Mary Sutherland

adventure, 'A Case of Identity' (which was no adventure for her, poor girl), February, the publication of the Irene Adler story, 'A Scandal in Bohemia'. Did I tell you what Fitsch did about that? He actually sent me a note congratulating me on the quality of my last-minute replacement for 'The Adventure of the Blue Carbuncle'. He didn't know I had it in me, 'A Scandal in Bohemia' was a gem, an absolute gem. It had style, it had grace, it had pathos, it had breadth (whatever that is). Maybe he should always reject my first effort just to see what I can come up with when I put my mind to it, ha ha.

I hope he is going to be similarly enthusiastic when he receives 'The Red-headed League'—and writes to say so. I am worried about Holmes. I don't think he was completely convinced by my argument last night. Why must he make everything so difficult? Personally, I don't think I'm taking any risk with this adventure at all. Dr Mortimer is out of the country, isn't he? Well, then. I don't anticipate a single objection this side of the Canary Islands. In fact, I'll go further and admit *(mea culpa)* that I am looking forward to the day when Dr Mortimer is riding his hobby-horse hell for leather and is shot down by someone in his audience citing my very own adventure of 'The Red-headed League'. It could happen. It could!

Memorandum: Never send anything to Mr Fitsch until the last possible moment. And try to keep at least one adventure in reserve in case of unforeseen difficulties such as those which prevented the publication of 'The Adventure of the Blue Carbuncle' last month.

I can't tell you how good it feels to be in a position where I can finally take my own advice. At the present moment, I actually have not one, not two, but three adventures ready and at hand, marked with the seal of Holmes's reluctant approval. For April, 'The Red-headed League'. (There is no point in letting Holmes's permission to publish grow cold and stale in a case like this.) For June, 'The Boscombe Valley Mystery', whose introduction I have just rewritten for the fourth time, hoping to manage an allusion to 'The Sign of Four' that will survive Mr Fitsch's editorial attentions.

The trick is to weave the allusion so tightly into the narrative fabric that Fitsch will find the attempt to excise it to be more trouble than it's worth. This is not an easy thing to do, as anyone who's ever made the attempt can tell you. Alternatively, I suppose I could try to make my reference so off-hand and by-the-way that friend Fitsch will miss it altogether. The problem with that approach being that any reference as well hidden as all that is apt to amuse Mr Fitsch no end while it calmly sails past the rest of my readers. But enough about 'The Boscombe Valley Mystery'. Either I will see The Sign of Four mentioned in the June issue of the *Strand* or I won't, and there's an end to it. After all, when you come right down to it, there's nothing I can plant he can't remove. And nothing on earth I can do about it.

I owe my fifth adventure, like my second, to Sir Henry Baskerville. If he hadn't broken his heart over Beryl Stapleton, I doubt that Holmes would ever have permitted 'A Scandal in Bohemia'. As it is, Holmes's gracious capitulation in the matter of Irene Adler has simplified the situation enormously. I didn't have to throw myself on his mercy over the February issue, which means our original agreement still stands: 'The Five Orange Pips' will be my fifth adventure, appearing in August. Assuming all goes well, October will then see the adventure of Hugh Boone, 'The Man with the Twisted Lip' in print.

It has just occurred to me. My present contract with the *Strand* expires with the October issue. If I want to see my Christmas story, 'The Adventure of the Blue Carbuncle' in print, I shall have to commit myself to writing six more adventures.

Fitsch, you devil!

Chapter 23

If I didn't mind loose ends and blighted expectations, I would end this diary right here—"Fitsch, you devil!" certainly seems to strike the proper note. Then again, if I didn't mind loose ends and blighted expectations, I wouldn't be in this line of work in the first place, turning history into fiction. I owe it all to Mary Sutherland, remember. To Mary Sutherland and a heart that's easily moved to indignation on behalf of the unsuspecting.

It is a great comfort to me, seeing how well that's turned out—Mary is in absolute alt over Miss Morrison's happy ending. "Isn't it romantic, John? And you thought Dr Stamford was a certified bachelor!" " Actually, I thought Mr Holmes was the certified bachelor—I thought Stamford was three parts gone and no help for it. I'm glad I was right. Young Stamford is the best of good fellows and Miss Morrison—you may say what you like about Miss Morrison, but I say she deserves her chance at happiness. It cannot be easy playing the lovesick daughter for the sake of a man you no longer love, especially when you know that he is already married, to your mother.

Unlike Hosmer Angel, young Stamford has no interest in Mary Sutherland's small inheritance. He is smitten with her air of abstraction, her sense of style (did I tell you about her butter-coloured boots?), her "innate delicacy." Many a happy marriage has begun with less. She in turn is taken with his candour, his courage, his manly devotion. Why are women so much better than we are at focussing on the essentials? It was a stroke of genius on his part, introducing her to his Great-Aunt Gertrude. Nothing could have been in greater contrast to the courtship of Hosmer Angel.

'The Man with the Twisted Lip' is going splendidly, but whether that is a happy accident (as I suspect) or a sign that I am finally learning how to manage the adventure writing process (as I hope) is anybody's guess. My attention-getting opening practically wrote itself, and that in spite of the fact that almost none of it could be presented the way it actually happened. Every name, every incident, every telling bit of description had to be reupholstered in the fabric of my imagination before I could use it.

My first duty was to find a new name and create a new family background for the Hucknells. Claire Hucknell is a modern-day saint and I won't have her embarrassed by my adventure. Abel, too, deserves better of me than that. It will not hurt my story to have me encounter him between pipes in a state bordering on sobriety, able to appreciate his wife's concern and to cooperate in his own rescue. Should 'The Man with the Twisted Lip' ever come Abel Hucknell's way, I want him to read it and feel a stiffening of his backbone, not a blow to his pride. Unless I miss my guess, he is going to need all the pride he can lay his hands on if he is to survive his hunger for the smoke.

It actually worked out rather well. By giving him a clergyman for a brother, I was able to speak out about this pernicious habit without sounding at all preachy.

A new name and a small portion of social prominence brought the Hucknells off safely, but it took several tries to achieve the geographical obfuscation of the Silver Bowl. I don't mind my readers strolling down Baker Street, checking to see whether there is a Number 221, but I'll be dammed if I'm sending anyone to Upper Thames Street looking for "my" opium den. The trick is to be specific but contradictory as to distance and direction, all the while referring to landmarks which don't exist. Geographical permutations must be made. Then, of course, I had to go back to Upper Thames Street to make sure I had not inadvertently described the location of some other den of iniquity.

For once, I've had no problems with the plot. Of course, when you come right down to it, plot problems are inevitably moral problems. Is this a suitable resolution of that conflict? Can I live with this as one of my stories?

I believe that I have felt morally justified in my approach from the beginning, but there's no denying I went through a bad patch after Mary Sutherland's unexpected visit. I still remember the horror I felt as I struggled to remember her name—Sarah Morrison, soon to be Mrs Clive Stamford.

In 'The Man with the Twisted Lip', we have one of those rare but welcome situations where telling the story can only do good in the world. Hugh Boone (not his real name) may have promised the magistrate that he would refrain from his fraudulent if lucrative activities, but there's no doubt in my mind that exposing his fraud and chicanery in the *Strand* will go a long way towards assuring that he keeps that promise.

Chapter 24

I don't know when I am any more. Between backdating my adventures to create the impression of Holmes as a man well established in business and projecting them into the future to create a sense of "presentness" when they are due to appear in print, I have actually published two adventures as having happened at a date that is still in the future.

Holmes thinks it is a great joke. "God help anyone who tries to create a chronology of my career from your adventures, Watson! 'The Sign of Four' isn't even internally consistent. You give the date as July 7th of an indeterminate year and describe December of 1878 as being nearly ten years ago, which any fool can tell you makes the year 1888. May 4th, 1882 is then 'about six years ago'—so far, so good, Watson—but that date inaugurates an annual pearl inheritance for your Miss Morstan, who has received six pearls by that 7th of July. How is it possible? 1882, 1883, 1884, 1885, 1886, 1887, 1888—she must have seven pearls if the year is 1888. The year must be 1887. 1888. 1887. 1888. That missing pearl is going to cause more headaches to more people…"

Oddly enough, he is not at all disturbed by the 1890 date in 'The Red-headed League' and 'The Five Orange Pips'. No, there he prefers to take the long view: "A hundred years from now, no one will notice the inconsistency, Watson."

I shall be very surprised if a hundred years from now, anyone is noticing anything. Or if anyone besides Holmes and his brother ever notices the "missing" pearl.

I'm just happy my strategy worked. Mr Fitsch was so certain he didn't want 'The Sign of Four' that I had no qualms about placing it in Lippincott's magazine, where I was stunned to find that the usual rate was nearly twice that for the *Strand*. Mr Fitsch and I are going to have to have a little talk before I sign my next contract.

1891

Chapter 25

His name is Moriarty.

Holmes was in that state of feverish excitement that allows of no impediment, a state that in his case is uniformly accompanied by a crystalline purity of vision, wholly focussed on ways, means, and devices. There is no reasoning with him at such times, and I find myself committed to an early morning trip to the Continent for some dark purpose that sounds remarkably like a duel, as difficult as that may be to believe in this day and age. I am to bring my Eley's No. 2, as usual, and the precautions that must be taken in preparation to my securing a cab for the first part of my journey will occupy a full twenty minutes in what I devoutly hope will be the half-light of a very foggy morning. I have already drafted my note for Jackson, who will be pleased enough at the chance to steal another patient or two.

Mary is another matter.

As is perhaps inevitable at this juncture of our married life, there is not at this time that perfect unanimity of spirit between us that would allow me simply to say that I was with Holmes. Not, at any rate, when we won't be found firmly ensconced in his rooms in Baker Street, under the watchful eye of Mrs Hudson. The second thing Mary will do is to discover that I have taken the Eley's or, as Holmes would correct me, "that the Eley's is missing from its usual place."

Ten minutes with Holmes and I am unable to have a normal conversation with myself.

One would have to be totally unaware of the hazards of the married state not to realize that what little information I do possess is hardly of the sort to reassure a woman, either of her husband's truthfulness or of his good sense. Holmes in the gravest danger from a mathematics coach? Holmes involved in two preposterous street accidents in one afternoon,

Holmes set upon by bludgeonmen in the evening, Holmes fastening our shutters against air-guns, Holmes fleeing our home by way of the back door, scrambling over our garden wall to vanish into the night? No wife can be expected to understand why this is the time for a little Continental holiday—why this is not a matter for the police. "Be careful, John" hardly seems to cover the situation.

Holmes is such a bachelor. "Mrs Watson is away? Then there will be no difficulty about joining me."

No difficulty indeed. Holmes seems to think that all you have to do is present a woman with a *fait accompli* and you will be spared the debate. On the contrary, my dear Holmes! Nothing inspires a woman to greater heights of eloquence than a situation that cannot be remedied.

For my part, I confess I am relieved that Mary is visiting her cousin, although not for the sake of avoiding any objections she would have voiced about our expedition, which objections are in any event not so much forestalled by her absence as they will be magnified and enhanced by my own. At the moment, it is her safety which concerns me most.

It has forcibly occurred to me, writing this by the very inadequate light of the single lamp Holmes was willing to risk, that if any of Moriarty's henchmen saw Holmes arrive and yet missed his precipitate exit out of our kitchen door, then they undoubtedly believe that he is spending the night here, with me. It is a moot point whether it is better to throw open the shutters as a sign of good faith or to try to think of them as a species of protection, however slight. I shall get no sleep tonight in any event. From what Holmes tells me, Moriarty is perfectly capable of bringing the house down around my ears in order to unearth his quarry. Now that Holmes has made his escape, air-guns are the least of my worries. Not even a blind man could mistake me for Sherlock Holmes, and I doubt that Moriarty uses blind men as his marksmen.

Moriarty. I could wish that Holmes had some facility for (or at least a passing interest in) describing the ordinary details of human existence, for I find that I have no least idea of how old this James Moriarty is, where he comes from, what he looks like—who his people are. Holmes passed over these petty points completely.

His name is Moriarty and once upon a time he held a chair in mathematics at one of our more obscure universities, and I do not even know which one. Today he makes his home in London, where he is ostensibly employed as an Army coach. He published a paper as a young man on the binomial theorem, of all things. That is what Holmes had to say of him. I have no sense of the man's voice or walk, accent or demeanour. He could come to my surgery door right now and unless he introduced himself as Professor Moriarty or condescended to start a conversation about the intricacies of the binomial theorem, I should have no way of recognizing him.

Moriarty has much the same sort of mind as my friend Holmes, thus earning his complete respect, and a veritable army of minions where Holmes has only his four ragged street urchins, myself, and (where no physical exertion is required) his brother Mycroft. Small wonder that Paris beckons to Holmes. Faced with the Napoleon of crime, you do well to select a battlefield where you will not be outflanked.

The Continent it is.

* * *

I have sent my things on to Victoria Station, unmarked as per Holmes's instructions. My revolver is at my side, Mary has been told as little as was husbandly possible, and I have raided the housekeeping money against the necessities of travel. Once again I see before me the curious incident of the dog in the night-time—Moriarty has made no move against me and I might have spared myself a sleepless night.

I will say, however, that it's been a productive one. If I can persuade Fitsch to publish 'The Naval Treaty' in two instalments, as two of the twelve monthly adventures I am contracted to provide (as seems only fair—it is twice the length of the others and the first part ends on a very suspenseful note), then I will be eleven adventures to the good and need write only one more to complete my obligation for this year. I will also have set the stage very nicely for next year, when I should like to do 'The Hound of the Baskervilles' as a serial with perhaps half a dozen instalments. I've been over my notes again and again—I know I can do it.

Let's see. There's 'The Musgrave Ritual' coming out in next month's issue, 'The Reigate Puzzle' for June, 'The Crooked Man' for July, 'The Resident Patient' for August, 'The Greek Interpreter' for September (I do like this one!), and then for October and (I hope) November, 'The Naval Treaty.' Perhaps the Moriarty case will provide the final problem. If not, there's always 'The Cardboard Box.' Fitsch doesn't care for it and neither do I (Susan Cushing is a poor substitute for Hermia Marie Cathcart), but it will do in a pinch.

What time is it? A quarter past eight! I have just time enough to shave before I begin rejecting hansom cabs, barreling through the Lowther Arcade, hurling myself into the brougham Holmes will have waiting for me, and then, on to Victoria Station and our reserved carriage on the Continental express.

I have rather a lot of questions for Mr Holmes this morning.

Chapter 26

It is no use—the more I learn about Moriarty from Holmes, the more he seems to have sprung fully formed from the brow of Athena. At least, I think it is Athena. Holmes, of course, would know immediately who it was. For all his twaddle about being above the niceties of a general education, he is quite likely to know more about whatever it is that you are trying to say than you do. I learned to appreciate it years ago as one of his more restful qualities.

I arrived at the end of Lowther's Arcade at very nearly exactly the hour specified by Holmes, and took my seat in his brougham with no more to complain of than a shin barked on its top step and the momentary queasiness that is entailed by a driver who is something of a madman. At one point, I remember, I entertained the unworthy thought that my driver might be Holmes in disguise, but dismissed it from my mind. Holmes may be many things but he is not obese, and the shift and play of the brougham testified to the impressive weight of this man, who was every bit as massive as he looked. I spent the short journey to Victoria rubbing my shin to restore the circulation and congratulating myself both for having remembered to instruct the cabman not to throw away the piece of paper with the Lowther Arcade address on it, and for having the wisdom to tip him handsomely enough to indulge me in this way.

These were Holmes's instructions and therefore not to be trifled with, but I wonder now why I could not simply have asked him for the paper back again. I must ask Holmes.

Once arrived at the station, I had of course to locate our carriage and wait for Holmes. There was no great difficulty in locating the carriage, which happened to be the only one reserved on that train, but waiting for Holmes tried me to the utmost. I was naturally preoccupied with thoughts for his safety, trying to take what comfort I could from the fact that the brougham had been there as expected. If, however, he had made those arrangements before seeing me last night, as seemed only too likely, then there was no knowing what might not have befallen him since he scrambled over my back wall. The curious incident of the dog in the night-time began to take on an ominous significance. My heart kept chiding me that I should have insisted that he spend the night with me, while my head kept reminding me that in all the years I've known him, I have never once succeeded in persuading him to do anything at all that he had not already decided to do.

All the while I was engaged in this mental debate, counting the minutes until I should have to decide whether to remain on board should Holmes fail to appear, I was simultaneously occupied in fending off a barrage of highly intrusive gesticulation directed at me, as the sole occupant of the carriage, by a wizened prune of an Italian priest who simply could not be made to understand that this carriage was reserved, dammit, reserved. I was still trying to make him understand the situation when the train gave a jolt and began to move. I had one hand on my hat and the other on the door preparatory to a hasty descent, when I was hauled practically off my feet by my octogenarian Italian friend.

"Holmes!"

I cannot conceive what pleasure there is for Holmes in these encounters.

"Glad you were able to join me, Watson, but you should have more faith in me. Look, there's Moriarty on the platform—ah, he's missed the train!"

And I had missed my chance for a good look at the Professor, who was simply an angry man above medium height receding into the distance by the time I reached the window. In fact, if I am to be precise, he was not even that, but rather one of two angry men above medium height receding into the distance. Either he was in company or there were two men both very angry indeed at having missed the train, but for different reasons. I decided to chance it.

"Who is that with him, Holmes?"

"Why, was there anyone with him? I did not observe it," was his reply.

Holmes was entirely himself again, rolling up his clerical garb and tossing it into his hand-bag in one easy motion. It did not surprise me to learn that it was to be my fault that Moriarty had tracked us to Victoria Station. It was inevitable. Holmes accepted my assurances that I had carried out his instructions to the letter, somehow managing to prove from that, to his own satisfaction if not my own, that they had been keeping a watch on my movements and that I had led them here. How plausible that is in view of his having arrived on my doorstep undisguised and unmolested last night, I hope someday to be able to leave it to my readers to decide.

The critical piece of the argument, as I recall, was that someone had set fire to his rooms in Baker Street during the night, thus showing that...

"Mrs Hudson?" I interrupted.

"Your concern does you credit, Watson," he said, as if the thought had never entered his head. "As it happens, no great damage was done to the interior or to the structure, and no one was injured. According to this morning's *Telegraph*, the alarm was given in good time by a Mr Charles Hilton, who is almost certainly Cheese Stilton. I believe he had the watch last night."

I could appreciate his amusement. "Cheese" is the newest addition to the Baker Street Irregulars and cannot be much above ten years old. There was satisfaction in foiling Moriarty so neatly.

The incident itself supposedly showed that they had completely lost sight of Holmes and were reduced to watching me. It seemed to me to be equally likely that this was a gesture of spite and contempt, done in full knowledge of Holmes's absence, and I no longer regretted the sleepless night spent in defense of my home, although I knew better than to mention it to Holmes. It would only have confirmed him in his supposition that Moriarty had followed me here, to learn that I had had a lamp burning all night.

"Your timetable, Watson." The practical details are ever my responsibility. "We leave the train at Canterbury."

My immediate reaction was that we might have gone to Canterbury last night, with far less trouble and at far less expense than by reserving a first class carriage on the Continental express.

"Moriarty, Watson! By now, he has hired a special—it is what I should do myself in his place."

I could not help reflecting that if Holmes could predict Moriarty's actions by reference to his own inclinations, then Moriarty might be able to predict my friend's actions in the same way. Holmes meanwhile was in a state of happy excitement I was hard-pressed to account for under the circumstances, which struck me as fairly grim, I must say.

Those few people at Canterbury on a Saturday morning were all waiting for the Continental, and I eyed the barren platform with considerable misgiving. This was not the place that I would choose to meet a potentially murderous attack and yet I had small hope of persuading Holmes to leave until he had verified his hypothesis. Regardless of the risk, he would always rather be right than be safe. Someday this preference of his is going to get him killed. The only cover in sight was a small mountain of luggage, which reminded me...

"Our luggage, Holmes!"

I watched the train pull out of the station, bearing our bags off to Paris.

"It can't be helped, Watson," he said cheerfully. "With any luck at all, they will be met by Moriarty." Then, almost as an afterthought: "I trust the passenger list does not include any bona fide Italian prelates of advanced years."

With that, he tucked his black hand-bag firmly under his arm and ducked behind the baggage, leaving me as always to bring up the rear. I remember thinking with some bitterness that it probably contained his shaving tackle as well as his cassock and his Italian eyebrows. I found out later that he also had a missal in there, with a ribbon marking the Mass for the Dead. His sense of humour would do justice to Edgar Allan Poe.

Moriarty came and Moriarty went, and I for one found his passage something of an anticlimax. I wish him joy of our luggage.

Chapter 27

We lunched in Newhaven. Fried plaice and a bottle of stout "to celebrate our escape in Canterbury."

Holmes talked about a variety of things over lunch: the mating habits of the common or lesser plaice, the new bottling techniques for alcoholic beverages, the advantages of Brussels as compared to Paris (here, I must admit, he lost me), some flowering shrub he looked forward to seeing in Switzerland with a peculiar name, and Flemish art. I cannot imagine where he got his information about the plaice, but it was fascinating and almost made up for the nonsense he was spouting about the Flemish school. It is absurd to think that Rembrandt and Vermeer will be remembered when our own Turner and Constable are forgotten. Holmes rarely requires my spoken agreement, however, so I smiled and nodded, biding my time. It came with the coffee.

"So, Watson, what do you make of the Professor now that you have had a look at him?" he asked.

I choked on a mouthful of coffee, grateful I had done with the fish. "Hardly that, Holmes. I have been within hailing distance of him twice but so far I have not laid eyes on him except at a distance of fifty yards and growing. He may have a first-class brain, I will take your word for that, but I would feel better if he also had a face."

"If he also had a face! Watson, you are good for me! Do you have any idea how hard it was for me to get my first glimpse of that face? I was weeks upon his trail before I was able to effect an approach and in my role as a blind beggar, I could not allow myself to stare. I have had but one good look at him myself and that was in my rooms in Baker Street yesterday, when my attention was, understandably I think, divided between our conversation and the gun in the top drawer of my desk. He is—an academic. A slight stoop, a hunching of the shoulders, a forward thrust to the head, which tends to wobble slightly from side to side in times of stress. A low, hissing voice that a roomful of boys would have to strain to hear. A tall man who would be taller if he carried himself better."

The impulse was uncontrollable. I straightened my spine, squared my shoulders, raised my chin. I shot a look at Holmes, but his thoughts were elsewhere and no wonder. It was a curiously repulsive picture I sought to assemble.

"He sounds almost reptilian," I ventured finally.

"Yes, Watson, 'reptilian' is the very word. Puckered eyes, hooded eyes, a malignant mind. He is… reptilian." His knuckles showed white where he gripped the table.

It was all vivid enough for me to be able to quote verbatim should this adventure ever come before the public, but it did not actually go very far toward giving me the picture I wanted. What did I know about Moriarty the man? Only that he had a scholar's posture, a soft voice, some slight trouble with his sibilants, and a guarded expression. My own expression is particularly transparent, I am afraid. At least, Holmes finds it so.

"Tell me, Watson, did you happen to recognize the driver of your brougham this morning?"

His own voice had a rather reptilian quality today, I thought, as I bent my mind to the problem. As far as I knew, not even Holmes could be in two places at the same time, but there had been some little delay between my leaving the brougham and meeting Holmes the Italian cleric. How much delay, I really couldn't say. Once again I had seen but had not observed. (Observation always seems to involve more arithmetic than I am likely to have bothered doing.) I had got to the point of wondering whether a hundredweight of potatoes under the coachman's seat, properly manipulated with his boots, would give the same effect as the equivalent weight on the coachman, and had virtually impaled myself on the horns of this bizarre dilemma, when Holmes rescued me with a word.

205

"Mycroft," he said solemnly.

"Mycroft?"

"Mycroft."

So much for my notion that our safety was compromised by my ignorance of Moriarty's physical appearance. It is several years now since Holmes surprised me by having an older brother, Mycroft. To have failed to recognize both Holmes brothers in the space of perhaps twenty minutes, the one my coachman, the other my only fellow passenger in a railway carriage reserved for two, hardly strengthened my position. I thanked heaven I had not told him my suspicion that it was Sherlock Holmes, suitably padded, who drove the brougham while manipulating a sack of potatoes with his feet. Things were awkward enough without that.

"It is not your fault, Watson," he remarked kindly as we made our way from the chop house to the quay. Since I had never supposed it was, I was able to maintain a dignified silence.

I should confess at once that I am unable to be precise about the conversational details attached to the crossing. Our little celebration in Newhaven sealed my fate while we were still in the harbour, leaving Holmes to hope that Moriarty was only half as poor a sailor as his old friend Watson.

Holmes himself is as comfortable at sea as he is at home, and equally knowledgeable in either setting. As I saw when he set out to entertain me with an impromptu lecture on the art of navigation in the sixteenth century, with particular application to the voyages of Vasco da Gama. He was bent on explaining the differences between the early sextant and the astrolabe when I begged him to stop. I suppose I am as interested in the topic as the next man, but there is a time and a place for everything, and that was not it. He took my objections in good part, I remember, and presumably repaired to drier quarters at about that time, although I could not swear to it. I remained glued to the railing for the duration and we did not meet again until we docked, at which point I was for obvious reasons better able to support the company of a man with Holmes's taste in tobacco.

I remind the reader that I never wanted to be a travel writer.

Dieppe. A brief argument with Holmes on the quay, which sick as I was, I yet won. The sun was going down, tomorrow was Sunday, and we should present a very odd appearance if we were to arrive at our hotel with one small clerical bag between us. What about shaving tackle? Toothpowder? Travel guides? Braving the local shops, I managed to outfit a couple of carpetbags against our simple needs. When I saw the quantity of maps Holmes judged essential to our progress, I knew I had done well. Besides, I had a great need at that point to spend half an hour with the ground steady beneath my feet.

Our flight to the Continent came to an abrupt halt a little later, in Brussels, where I watched us register in the obvious hotel under our own names and drew my own conclusions. He has courage, my friend Holmes. Or a fine sense of his own immortality. He certainly stands by his deductions in a way that interferes with *my* sleep.

I suppose it is up to the Yard now. All our hopes are for Monday—that is, tomorrow. Monday is the day fixed for the arrest of Professor Moriarty and his gang. The first thing Holmes did after watching Moriarty's special steam past the station in Canterbury was to send word to Inspector Patterson at the Yard: Moriarty was gone to Paris in pursuit of our luggage, which was ticketed for the Hôtel du Louvre. Holmes was (for Holmes) positively jubilant. Let them only arrest Moriarty and his minions on Monday and he would engage to connect the Professor to a range of criminal activity that would have all London howling for his blood. It will be the apotheosis of his career.

I don't know. Speaking only for myself and only in this diary, I must admit I feel both too young and too old for this particular adventure—too old to revel in the excitement of the chase, and too young to wish for anything remotely resembling an apotheosis. What do you do with yourself after you've had an apotheosis?

Holmes hasn't said anything to me, but my guess is that we will remain in Brussels tonight and reassess the situation tomorrow. All of our activity since our arrival has been cerebral, and most of that was Holmes's. Knowing that no good comes of interrupting him at these times, I left him smoking and thinking in our room and took myself off to the hotel lobby, where I have been amusing myself (as Holmes would put it) with my journal. For once the verb is reasonably accurate. What I should be doing, I know, is writing a letter to my wife, who is going to be very upset when she returns home to find my note. Considering that I wrote it in a state of siege and had to take into account the possibility that it might fall into the hands of Moriarty's men, I think I did very well, but I can't expect Mary to see it that way.

2 a.m. Saturday, 25 April, 1891

Dear Mary,

I am called away on an emergency—one whose nature makes it absolutely impossible that I should give you my direction even if I knew it, which I assure you I don't. Do please try not to worry.

Dr Jackson takes my rounds.

Leave the shutters up! I will explain when I see you.

JOHN

P.S. I took the housekeeping money.

Mary is not, thank God, of a nervous disposition, but when I add to this very connubial communication a newspaper report, however garbled, of a mysterious fire at 221B Baker Street on that same night, I can't help feeling I owe her something more in the way of explanation.

I wish I hadn't told her to leave the shutters up.

I know what this reminds me of—it reminds me of my last holiday, the one I spent on Dartmoor, alternately hunched over the Baskerville family stationery and my diary, waiting for the Hound to appear. I have just been writing to Mary, advising her from my heart never to be caught in Brussels on a Sunday. Will this day never end?

Moriarty. It is easy enough to hold myself absolved from having to struggle with the intellectual problem of Moriarty, given the distinctly marginal quality of the information at my disposal. The difficulty comes in accepting this absolution. Try as I may, I cannot keep my thoughts from straying in his direction. Moriarty has assumed epic proportions in my mind. He is an elemental figure, an archetype of evil, an atavistic force. He draws my thoughts as a magnet draws iron filings and it is useless to remind myself that he could hardly fail to disappoint in the flesh. Professor James Moriarty—his very name has the taste of evil in my mouth.

I have a much clearer picture of Inspector Patterson. "Inspector Patterson? In a word, ambitious, Watson. A man with an instinctive understanding of hierarchy. He knows who it is he has to please at the Yard, make no mistake about that. He finds me—useful. And so have I found him."

I have known many men like Ivor Patterson in my day, but none like Professor James Moriarty.

* * *

"So, Watson, how are you enjoying Brussels?"

Holmes materialized at my elbow in good time for dinner, apparently none the worse for his long vigil.

"Very much indeed." The platitude was out before I had time to think; I hastened to retrieve my position. "I rarely get the opportunity to spend this much time in a hotel lobby at home. If you just wait long enough, the entire population of the city will pass by your window. I have not seen Moriarty yet, but perhaps tomorrow…"

His response was more of a grimace than a grin, but it told me what I wanted to know. He believed Moriarty would discover us if we stayed. We were no longer safe in Brussels. By unspoken agreement, further conversation was postponed until we should have had something to eat. The situation was grave, but not yet so grave that Holmes should have to end his forty-eight hour fast by missing dinner. We repaired to the *salle à manger* and made a very good meal of oxtail soup and a kind of beef ragout (*Note*: I must tell Mary about truffles), of which Holmes, normally the most moderate of men, rashly had two portions. He has no regard for his digestive system and no respect for mine. He actually asked me whether I was quite recovered from the crossing—did I feel able to go on? I told him tartly that as far as I knew, one usually travelled from Brussels to Geneva by land, not by sea.

* * *

Two mortal days in Brussels, but it is Monday at last and it promises to be a day of activity. Holmes has wired Inspector Patterson at the Yard for the arrest particulars, providing addresses in Copenhagen, Amsterdam, Strasbourg, and Lyons for the confusion of the Professor, should he still be at large. I *think* we are going to Strasbourg, but nothing is certain. Holmes asked me whether I wanted to send Mary a wire ("It may be some days before we can risk another communication, Watson—you understand"), but if I understand anything about the situation in which I find myself, it is that a telegram from Brussels saying ARRIVED SAFELY LEAVING SHORTLY would do little to allay her anxiety. Mary may not know where I am now, but at least she imagines me lost in my own country. The note I left said nothing about the Continent. That's why I spent yesterday writing that letter. Mary is going to want to know who proposed we go to the Continent, why I agreed to go, how we evaded Moriarty, why Holmes can't go to the police, what we're eating, how I'm sleeping, and a thousand other things I couldn't possibly cover in a telegram.

I told Holmes that I would prefer to post the letter which I had written. I assured him that it was a simple catalogue of the events of the past few days, that it made no mention of [whispered] Switzerland—I even offered to let him read it. It was an offer I knew he'd decline.

"What, all that?" he said. "We only left London on Saturday, Watson. What will you have written in a week or so?"

If he thinks my letter is long, he should take a look at my diary.

Chapter 28

In the past five days we have been to Canterbury, Newhaven, Dieppe, Brussels, Strasbourg, Geneva, and half a dozen points northwest too small to mention. No part of this expedition has unfolded as I anticipated it would. At every point I have been taken by surprise, lately as much by Holmes's attitude as by external events. Something is wrong, something more than he has told me, which is bad enough, God knows: Moriarty free, presumably furious, bent on vengeance, and as Holmes thinks, stalking us.

It feels like years since Holmes burst into my study with his talk of air-guns and erupted over my garden wall, years since I even thought I understood the situation. We alternate between bouts of frantic haste—first in our mad escape from England and now in our scramble southward along the Rhone—and brief periods of inexplicable idleness. We were two days in Brussels, where we kept to our hotel, and I understand that we will be some days in Meiringen next week, assuming the Reichenbach Fall lives up to its reputation.

I don't understand it. We take no precautions, don no disguises, use no false names. Holmes remains in a state of excitement bordering on elation. He is preternaturally alert, every nerve on the stretch. Every conversation we have takes place against a background of Holmes looking for Moriarty, Holmes listening for Moriarty, Holmes waiting for Moriarty. A week of this and I will be in a state of nervous collapse myself. It is as if our only defense against this, this mathematics tutor is to stay one step ahead of him, to keep moving all the time.

Holmes's conversational code is a simple one: if he wants you to know, he will tell you. Nine times out of ten, he will then explain why you did not need him to tell you that—you should have deduced it from the hat he wore on the 14th inst., from the uneven distribution of the blacking on his boots, from the unusual ink stain decorating the second phalanx of the index finger of his left hand. I have sometimes thought that it is only the mounting pressure of these mute witnesses, these tiny clues that only he can read, that finally induces him to confide in me. However that may be, it is clear to me that our friendship has endured these ten years partly because I will permit him to dole out his revelations in this way, little by little, in his own good time, while I myself am an open book, a primer if you will. Under ordinary conditions I am content that it should be so—he takes nothing from me that he does not take from everyone else, after all, and he does make some return, in time—but current conditions are not ordinary. Something has gone wrong, badly wrong, and I have no conversational right to broach the subject with my friend. I am condemned instead to play detective, a role in which I have little interest and less aptitude, to sift each hour of the past few days, to try and wrest from their inconsequent doings a larger pattern of cause and effect. I have no alternative. Holmes can not or will not let me help him.

I wish Holmes had more faith in me.

* * *

The truth is, Holmes on holiday is even more unnerving than Holmes at work.

If anyone had told me that I would find Holmes's Continental dress disturbing, I would have laughed in his face. Holmes in mufti, Holmes in a burnoose, Holmes banging the drum for the Salvation Army, Holmes in a dhoti, these I could support with equanimity. Holmes in Hessians, Holmes in sandals, Holmes in snowshoes even. The demands of disguise can be brutal, as I know to my cost. However, for reasons which I cannot begin to imagine, we are not in fact travelling in disguise and in consequence, I find the sight of Holmes taking his ease in *lederhosen* and short pants, waving an Alpine-stock at each new discovery, difficult to take in my stride. He has gone native in Switzerland, just two days after crossing the border.

I suppose I must be grateful that he is still speaking English to me. He insists on speaking German to everyone else.

Always before, when I have managed to tear him away from London (on medical grounds, needless to say), he has been just as restive as the impaired state of his health would permit him to be, scarcely able to endure the fresh air and rural pursuits long enough for them to have their promised effect. No matter how brief a stay I have agreed to, always we have had to cut it short. Now that we are stranded on foreign soil with an evil genius intent on tracking us down, Holmes is disposed to be pleased by everything, happily discovering an appetite for natural science. At least half of his conversation is given over to rhapsodies about Nature's palette, the pine forests that make our own British woodlands seem tame, the glory of the heights, the reliability of the sunshine, and the charming variety of songbirds on the Continent. We travel miles to see a curious waterfall or an unusual geological formation. It is unnatural.

Today he suddenly became convinced that there is some mystery attached to the foraging behaviour of the honey-bee relative to the solar azimuth and spent three interminable hours moving a dish of scented sugar-water across a meadow on his knees, counting the visitors at each station along the way. I must confess, I find all of this distinctly trying. When he said he thought we had time for a little experiment this afternoon, this is not at all what I thought he meant. From now on, my journal accompanies me everywhere.

When I think how I have tried to persuade him to take some interest in life beyond the confines of his work! I can hardly blame myself for never having presented him with a bowl of sugar-water, but the irony is complete. Horses, dogs, fishing, racing, hiking, rowing, shooting, and what I should have suggested was bee-farming.

The day ended on a particularly contentious note when Holmes tried to persuade me to abandon him and return to England, on the puerile grounds that from here on, our journey would become increasingly dangerous. This is not the first time he has insulted me in this way, languidly pointing out the danger in what is palpably, patently, unmistakably a dangerous situation. I defy anyone to read 'The Adventure of the Speckled Band' without recognizing Dr Grimesby Roylott as a dangerous character well in advance of Holmes's congenial warning to me on the outskirts of Stoke Moran. Why, the man caught up a steel poker, bent it into a horseshoe, and waved it in our faces within minutes of introducing himself to us in our own home. In my own phlegmatic way, I am prepared to recognize the threat in that.

It would doubtless come as a surprise to Mr Holmes to learn that a physician routinely exposes himself to death and disease. I have seen typhus, I have seen diphtheria, I have seen smallpox. In my military days, I saw diseases I had no name for. At least in my casework with Sherlock Holmes, I know that I won't be bringing the risk home to Mary with me on my return. My wife is safe from Moriarty, if out of my reach, and I am a free agent. I told Holmes that I had not come all the way to Interleuken merely to buy him a change of linen and a supply of shag in Dieppe.

I may not have his degree of courage, few men have, but neither am I made of the kind of stuff that would abandon an old friend to his fate in desperate circumstances. He should know me better than that by now. How often do we have to have the same conversation?

Chapter 29

So this is what it's like to be in shock.

I seem to be doing everything that is required, but very slowly and deliberately, as if from a great distance. I watch my hand move across the page and I recognize the handwriting, but that is my only connection to this activity. I am writing this because that is what I do, but I no longer remember very clearly why I do it.

It felt so strange to have the gendarme ask me about Holmes and write my answers down. That's what I do, I wanted to say. I ask the questions, I write down the answers.

This tea is cold and the cup has a slight crack near the lip on the side with the handle on it. Why have I never noticed before how fragile everything is? It never occurred to me that Holmes might die in the course of this adventure. All the while Holmes was telling me how willing he was to trade his life for Professor Moriarty's, he must have been serious. I thought he was planning to put some great plan into effect. I have become so used to watching him pull a rabbit out of his hat that it never occurred to me that he might not have a plan this time. I kept waiting for him to let me in on the secret. How could I know that there was no secret? God forgive me, I was impatient with him. I could not understand why were spending our time collecting "views" and listening to birdsong. How could I have been so blind? I am glad Holmes had this week, glad we climbed the Gemmi Pass, glad he found his honey-bees. No man goes to his grave regretting the time he spent marvelling at the beauty of this world. I thank God he had this week.

They tell me the telegraph office is closed now until morning. One of the little disadvantages, Holmes would say, of life in the country. I don't mind. I find that some telegrams are much harder to write than others.

To Inspector Patterson at Scotland Yard: HOLMES MORI-ARTY BOTH DEAD SECURE ADDITIONAL EVIDENCE BLUE ENVELOPE PIGEONHOLE M BAKER STREET DESK INVESTIGATION CONTINUES—DOCTOR WATSON. It was his last request of me, that I should tell Inspector Patterson about the blue envelope marked "Moriarty." Holmes never did have much respect for the ingenuity of the Yard.

To my bank, for funds. I should have liked to have wired my bank earlier, but Holmes wouldn't hear of it. "It doesn't matter, Watson," he said. "You can pay for the accommodations on our return journey." There will be no return journey, for Holmes.

To my wife, Mary. I hate sending Mary a wire like this, but there simply isn't anyone else I can call upon in this instance. Holmes was far too jealous of his privacy to admit many people into his circle. He had clients and he had colleagues (of a sort), but he did not have friends. Stamford would do it if I asked him to, but it would take so much explanation! He hasn't seen Holmes in years, not since Holmes failed to attend his wedding. Mary has at least heard of Mycroft, which puts her one step ahead of everyone else, as far as I know. If my letter has arrived from Brussels, she will even have heard of Professor Moriarty. What is more to the point is that Mycroft will have heard of Mary or if not, will imme-diately deduce the connection from her name. Dr Stamford's sudden appearance could only introduce an additional note of confusion at this most confusing time. And Mary will say all that is kind, as much for Holmes's sake as for mine. I can't help it that she is a woman. She is still infinitely more suit-able than Lestrade, for example. If the Holmes boys wanted to avoid women, then they should have peopled their lives with men.

To Mary, then: BRACE YOURSELF HOLMES PRESUMED DEAD IN MUTUALLY FATAL MEETING WITH MORIAR-TY AT REICHENBACH FALL ONLY WITNESS MISSING NOTIFY BROTHER MYCROFT PALL MALL DIOGENES

CLUB BEST COME SOONEST WILL WAIT ENGLISCHER HOF MEIRINGEN—JOHN.

I have now done all I can do until tomorrow.

I can't take it in. My friend Holmes—dead.

At three o'clock this afternoon, Monday, 4 May, 1891, Professor James Moriarty kept his appointment with Sherlock Holmes at the Reichenbach Fall, with apparently fatal results on both sides. The River Aare keeps their bodies.

May God have mercy on their souls.

* * *

Holmes is not known in Switzerland, or this would be receiving far more attention than it is. The authorities appear to have dismissed it from their minds and it falls to me to see that some small portion of the physical evidence is preserved against the arrival of Holmes's brother Mycroft. I am not doing very well.

I was up early this morning, thinking about the crowds of curiosity seekers that would be drawn to the Reichenbach Fall once the dramatic story of the Holmes-Moriarty debate gained currency in the village. At my insistence, we had been very careful yesterday not to spoil the two sets of footmarks leading up to the Fall. The fact that wherever the two sets of footmarks overlapped, it was always the broader imprint that was superimposed, told me that the two men had walked to the Fall in single file, the man with the narrow boots (Holmes, I'm sure—Holmes has, had very lean, scraggy feet) leading the way. Those same footmarks might tell an expert like Mycroft even more, I reasoned. Holmes had the greatest respect for his brother's deductive abilities and any stray thoughts I might have had to the effect that this was a case of brotherly hyperbole—sibling rivalry gone awry—were laid to rest long ago. I have met Mycroft Holmes and he is everything his brother said he was.

And so I returned to the Reichenbach Fall this afternoon,

218

carrying with me a bucket, a collection of cardboard collars, an outsize wooden spoon, and five kilos of plaster of Paris (and a devil of a time I had, trying to buy plaster of Paris in sleepy little Meiringen, let me tell you). It felt good to have a plan of action. I would fill my bucket at the Fall and I would use my sturdy umbrella, in service *en route* as a makeshift walking stick, to screen my casts from the Fall's spray while they set. I congratulated myself: I had thought of everything.

It took me well over two hours to reach the path at the top, encumbered as I was, and when I did, puffing a bit from the exertion (those five kilos weighed a lot less at the bottom in Meiringen, than they did at the top by the Fall), I found that the surface of the path was perfectly smooth and untroubled. There wasn't a footmark in sight—not one. I was staggered. Had this all been a dream? Was I dreaming now? Even the area directly behind the Fall, the part where their great struggle had taken place, chewing up the ground and the surrounding vegetation, was in pristine condition. It finally hit me—the spray from the Fall. The reason the path had taken such good footmarks in the first place was the spray from the Fall. That gentle mist keeps the path perpetually impressionable.

Hannibal and all his elephants could have visited the Fall last night, and left no more trace upon the surface of the path than this. In my frustration, I stamped a set of footmarks of my own into the earth and sat down to time their disappearance. It was necessary in any case for me to rest my leg before beginning the descent.

* * *

I don't seem to be able to rub two thoughts together to make a third, no matter how hard I try. Today was nothing but wasted motion, and the worst of it is that the telegraph office is now closed for the day and that means I won't hear from Mycroft or Mary until tomorrow.

They have put Holmes's things in storage here at the Englischer Hof and given me a new room—two examples of what I have come to see as innkeeper Peter Steiler's uncommon kindness and consideration toward his guests. No doubt it helps that he, of all the Swiss hoteliers we've met, recognized the name of Sherlock Holmes when we registered. That's what comes of having served as head waiter at the Grosvenor Hotel in the late eighties. He particularly admires 'The Red-headed League', although he immediately added that he hasn't seen any of my recent work, Meiringen being so far out of the way. So thoughtful of him, because of course the last thing any author wants to hear is that he hit his peak the third time out and hasn't said anything worth hearing since.

I must send him a copy of *The Adventures of Sherlock Holmes* when I return home.

* * *

I can no longer hide it from myself: the Swiss messenger is the key to the mystery. He must have been one of Moriarty's minor mercenaries, or why hasn't he come forward to tell what he knows? He delivered the forged message which drew me off at the critical moment. He remained with Holmes while I hurried off to Meiringen. He must have witnessed Holmes's meeting with Moriarty. He was the reason I was willing to leave Holmes alone and unprotected in the first place! I blame myself. Oh, how I blame myself! I could pass him in the village tomorrow and not even recognize his face.

I should have suspected him. I can forgive myself for having accepted the note as genuine—Holmes doubted the note at once, but I am not good with physical evidence and this the whole world knows—but why did I not suspect the messenger? I am usually good with people.

I looked at the boy, saw a likely lad of about my height

whose voice was probably still cracking this time last year, and accepted him as my substitute without a moment's hesitation. Holmes said a few words in German, of which I recognized one, *"Rosenlaui,"* they haggled a bit (I know numbers when I hear them), and the matter was settled to Holmes's satisfaction: the young Swiss had agreed to serve as his guide to Rosenlaui, I agreed to meet him there when I could, and there I was, rushing back to the Englischer Hof at Moriarty's behest. The irony of it! To be drawn off to comfort a dying woman who did not exist, when it was my friend Holmes who was in danger of death. My friend Holmes, dwindling into the distance behind me, waiting for Professor Moriarty.

I didn't give the boy another thought until they asked me for his description. "Young, well-grown, Swiss, about my height, German-speaking, loden cloak" is about as useless a description in rural Switzerland as one can well imagine.

I wonder—I will always wonder—what Holmes was thinking of, to let me go like that. He suspected the note right away, he said. He must have suspected the messenger. Why would he choose to face Moriarty and his young confederate alone in a mountain gorge, armed only with an Alpine-stock? Did he want to die? No, that I can't believe. I won't believe it! He had courage, that's all. He had courage and he was so sure that he would die in the course of this encounter that he took no thought of the legal position. Duels have seconds and wars have correspondents, for a reason. It is so that the concept of a fair contest can be defended, as appropriate.

How could Holmes have decided to dispense with my company under circumstances like these?

*   *   *

I have nothing to show Mycroft Holmes when he comes. The footmarks have dissolved in the mist, I can't describe Moriarty's messenger, and now Inspector Grillot tells me that Holmes's farewell letter and Moriarty's tissue of lies were sent to Geneva on Monday, for analysis. What does he mean, analysis? I just wanted to make a copy for Mycroft. I can't think why they kept Holmes's letter, anyway—it was addressed to me.

I wish my French were better. I should have brought Peter Steiler with me, to translate. Another opportunity lost.

* * *

Today's *Journal de Genève* had the story—a couple of paragraphs at the bottom of page six, describing the accidental death of two British tourists at the Reichenbach Fall and deploring the absence of a guardrail along the path. I begin to understand what Inspector Grillot meant when he assured me that they do not have murderous attacks on innocent people in Switzerland. My translation follows.

"The eminent Professor James Moriarty and his compatriot, Monsieur S. Hoelms [misspelled—and the reporter obviously balked at 'Sherlock'], plunged to their deaths at the Reichenbach Fall late Monday afternoon, the disturbed state of the meagre vegetation suggesting that first one and then the other lost his feeble hold on life. [How can they write such stuff?] This reporter can only wonder—again—why there is no guardrail at the overlook. How many lives must be claimed by the Reichenbach Fall before the honest citizens of Meiringen will admit the necessity of 'spoiling the view'? The 'natural traction of the path' was insufficient protection for these visitors to the Reichenbach Fall, as it was insufficient protection for the good Anne-Marie Fleisch earlier this year.

"Search teams composed of local volunteers have been combing the lower banks of the Aare River since yesterday morning, sadly without result. Suicide is not suspected."

I should not have thought that Switzerland was Catholic enough for suicide to be the issue, but perhaps it retains its fascination in a country where murder is unknown.

I keep telling myself that Mycroft will know what to do.

222

One small mercy is that when Reuter's picks up this story—and they will—there is every chance that the London newspapers which decide to feature it will fail to connect an obviously elderly and unremarkable S. Hoelms [sic] doddering on the brink of the Reichenbach Fall in the wake of the similarly doddering and superannuated but still "eminent" Professor Moriarty, with the vigorous, sure-footed, and very remarkable detective, Sherlock Holmes of Baker Street.

* * *

No word from Mycroft (or Mary), but Inspector Grillot stopped by to tell me that I am free to leave Meirengen whenever I like, a permission all the more confusing in that I cannot recall having been asked to stay. I thought this was my idea.

I wish Mycroft were here. I want to take him up to the Reichenbach Fall, lay the existing evidence before him, and listen to his reconstruction of the tragedy. Until then, I am going to feel all frozen inside, wondering what exactly happened up there, how I killed my friend, where I went wrong.

I need to rub elbows with some of the other people whose lives he touched, to remind myself that I am not the only one Holmes held at a distance. I don't think anyone really knew Sherlock Holmes.

Not even Mycroft.

Chapter 30

If Mycroft won't leave London, he won't, and there's nothing Mary or I can do about it. It's hard, though—hard that he didn't think my friendship was worth a single word of guidance or sympathy from him. If it hadn't been for me, Holmes would have died alone and unmourned in a foreign country, with no one to protect his memory.

Mary arrived in Meiringen about an hour before sunset on Thursday, in half-mourning, bless her feeling heart, with a black arm-band for me. I should have thought of this mark of respect myself, I know, and if it had been anyone else but Holmes, I would have. But with Holmes dead in mysterious circumstances in Switzerland and Mycroft out of reach in England, someone had to take on the role of the dispassionate investigator. I couldn't be both the grief-stricken friend and the impassive observer, I had to choose. I told myself that I would be the grief-stricken friend—later. I was so sure Mycroft would come.

Mary tells me that there was no question of her breaking the news to him—Mycroft Holmes knew all about it. He was in contact with both Scotland Yard and the Swiss embassy, and he was treating the incident as an exercise in diplomatic relations. I feel sorry for Mycroft. Mary says she doesn't think there will be a memorial service. Every time she tried to raise the topic with him, he brushed it aside saying that there would be time enough to discuss that when they had recovered the body from the river. He understands everything else, he must know that there is very little chance of that, with the river swollen to a torrent with the spring run-off. What is surrendered to the River Aare in the spring, the river keeps.

I don't know what to think, how to feel. Mary says Mycroft mostly seemed to feel embarrassed by his brother's death. I don't feel embarrassed, I feel angry. I am angry with Holmes for accepting the necessity of a meeting with Moriarty. Is war inevitable then? Must we accept war and destruction as long as there is one enemy who is willing to fight? Is that all it takes for war—one side willing to attack, the other willing to defend? Must we lie down and be trampled for peace?

I seem to have handled this whole thing very badly. If I couldn't prevent their meeting—and I accept that, they were grown men, responsible for their own actions—still, I might have handled its aftermath better than I did. I was so sure Mycroft would come and yet I had practically nothing to show him. I wish I hadn't climbed the Gemmi Pass with Holmes last week! I might have known how it would be. Every time I push myself beyond what I can comfortably do, I pay for it with a week's lameness. If I hadn't been having so much pain, I might have seen through Moriarty's ruse, at least to the extent of insisting Holmes accompany me back to Meiringen so I could tend to my patient. As it was, I was so grateful to be spared the long, hard tramp to Rosenlaui that I accepted the letter as genuine without a moment's hesitation. You don't look a gift horse in the mouth. There was the pain in my leg. There was my summons on behalf of the dying. There was the Swiss messenger to keep Holmes company. No doctor can ignore a cry for help. I don't think I exchanged ten words with Holmes before I was hurrying down the slope to Meiringen.

I didn't look twice at Moriarty's messenger because I was thinking about my patient—and my hip. I was still thinking about my patient (and my hip) when I spotted a middle-aged Englishman striding over the uneven ground toward the Fall. He's in fine fettle for an academic type, I thought approvingly, and promptly forgot all about him.

There was no dying patient at the Englischer Hof. The letter wasn't from Peter Steiler. It must have been written by that tall Englishman who was there earlier… It was too late then to wish for another look at Professor Moriarty and his messenger. I had had my chance to be of service to my friend and I had missed it. I have to find a way to live with the memory of that failure, as with so many other failures, imputed and conceded.

All the way back up the Fall, I was haunted by the possibility that Holmes had been set upon by Moriarty and his messenger and who knows how many others, everywhere at once in that undefended place. I kept asking Peter Steiler about the messenger—he must know him, the lad was Swiss. I couldn't seem to take in the fact that I was the only one who had seen the boy. It was as if my brain were frozen. I kept urging myself to hurry, without being able to increase my pace in the slightest. I kept questioning Peter Steiler, without being able to take in his answers. I could feel myself verbally going round and round in circles. And still we weren't at the top. It was like one of those dreams where everything is forever out of reach, across a divide. It was like the dream I had last night, where I was on my hands and knees on the soft loamy path right by the Fall.

I don't know how I got there. It's very dark, so dark I can't see anything at all. I can feel the sun's warmth on the back of my neck, on my shoulders through my coat. It's a strong sun, so I know it's not really dark. But I still can't see anything. This isn't a dream about being blindfolded or struck blind—there are no bandages on my eyes and I am not concerned about my lack of vision. I accept the conditions of my dream. I can't hear anything, either. I know the Fall is there—I can feel the spray on my face, I even know where it's coming from (the direction, I mean)—but I can't hear it roaring. The Reichenbach Fall is silent and I accept that, too.

I can feel the soft loam of the path taking the impression of my hands and knees. The Fall is on my left, the cliff is on my right. Ah, I am facing the end of the path, at the top. Yes, my hands are ever so slightly higher than my knees. I must be climbing the rise to the Fall. I take a tentative half-step forward, feeling my way. Another. A hand grabs my wrist and I react instantly, collapsing onto my stomach, arms outstretched. Holmes takes my other wrist now, too. He is hanging over the edge. I clutch his wrists convulsively, bearing his weight, digging the toes of my boots into the softness of the soil. I can feel his boots thudding into the side, scrambling for purchase, finding it, losing it. The pull on my arms fluctuates wildly, but I am not drawn forward. I can do this, I think exultantly. I have him! And then—I don't. A soundless scream fills my head to bursting and I don't know which of us is screaming. I don't know which of us opened his hands. I only know that I am alone. And awake. And alone.

I thought nightmares were the province of children. Perhaps we are all children when we are faced with the death of someone we love. A death like this—sudden, violent, and with no body to bury—is so difficult to bear. I want the ritual of a funeral and if Mary is right, there won't even be a memorial service. I want to tell Holmes I'm sorry. I'm sorry I wasn't the friend he wanted me to be. I'm sorry I failed him.

I don't know how I failed him and I don't know when I failed him, but I must have failed him at the last or why should he have let me go like that, without a word? Why would he have preferred to face Moriarty and all his minions alone at the Reichenbach Fall, the Swiss messenger and God knows how many others with him, when he could have secured my presence with a word? A casual "Have you ever seen Peter Steiler's handwriting, Watson?" would have stopped me in my tracks, I promise you. We could have faced Moriarty together, on the stony road to Meiringen, away from the Fall, two against two, and avoided the romance of single combat. What would have happened then, I wonder? I will always wonder what would have happened then. And why it was not acceptable to Holmes.

This whole thing is tearing me up inside. I should have grieved when I could, decently, in private, instead of taking on the role of the detective and waiting for Mycroft to arrive. Mycroft isn't coming. And this isn't fair to Mary. It must feel as if I don't care about her all. I am so far away—it's hard for her to get my attention. I can sit here and write in this stupid diary for hours on end rather than talk to her. It must be terribly painful. Why can't I feel her pain?

If Mycroft thinks he can postpone his grief, he is no better than a fool. A grief deferred doesn't withdraw politely from the room. It sits in your favourite chair, helps itself to your pipe and slippers, and clamours for a bigger fire and something to read. You are cut off from all your comforts and still, in spite of that, it is always at your elbow, tugging at your sleeve: "Now? Now?" Give way to anger and your anger will give way to grief. Your only hope is to look past your grief and practice being far-sighted, all the while keeping yourself very busy with something very near at hand—a diary, for instance.

No one could have worked harder than I did to preserve what little evidence there was, but to what end? The Swiss are satisfied that Holmes could have been saved by a handrail, Mycroft won't leave London, and I can't describe the missing witness any better than I have done. I'm not suddenly going to remember a scar on his cheek or a gold tooth in his head. He was young. He looked happy. He spoke German, we were in Switzerland, I assume he was Swiss. Someone should probably be investigating whether Professor Moriarty coached any Swiss students this year, but again, to what end? Nothing brings back the dead and nothing less than that will satisfy me.

I don't know why I decided it was more important to play detective than to mourn my friend, but I know that I have paid a heavy price for my decision. All week long, I have felt the inexorable pressure of my determination driving a wedge between me and my world. Colours were less distinct. Sounds were duller. Furniture was harder to avoid. My shins are a mass of bruises, none of which has had time to turn yellow in the middle. If someone had pointed out to me (but no one did) a charming Alpine scene or a tasty local dish, I could have labelled its ingredients with my usual efficiency, but now nothing was piquant enough to warrant that attention on its own. I needed someone else to say, "Look at that!" and, as I say, no one did. If this is how life was for Sherlock Holmes, all flat and tasteless, it is small wonder that he experimented with cocaine. The life of the mind is vastly overrated.

And what do I have to show for all my efforts? Practically speaking, nothing at all. My statement and the two letters have returned from Geneva, where Swiss graphology experts have no doubt confirmed that my statement of the events in question was written by me, Holmes's farewell letter by Holmes, and Moriarty's lying decoy by Moriarty—or failing that, that these three writing samples were written by three different men. The authorities here insist on keeping the originals but with their permission, I have made a copy of the letter Holmes wrote to me. Mycroft has his sources, as he told Mary. If he wants to read Moriarty's missive, let him seek his sources out once more. My days as a detective are done. I do not want to see that letter, much less copy it out in my own hand.

It's funny—Mary tells me that when she read my telegram, she understood my "BEST COME SOONEST" line as a plea to Mycroft Holmes, as indeed it was. But that wasn't Mycroft's understanding. He was impervious to my plea, did not even recognize it for what it was. "When do you go?" he asked politely, handing it back to her. It was as if his brother's death had nothing to do with him: he parts company with us here, there's nothing he can do about this situation.

The one completely reliable characteristic of the brothers Holmes has been their ability to confuse the Watsons in their inmost hearts. When he added that to the best of his knowledge, I was merely helping the police with their inquiries and had not been taken in charge, Mary's confusion was complete. She told me that by the end of her conversation with Mycroft Holmes, she was so worried about me that she had completely lost sight of the fact that Holmes was dead and she was supposed to be comforting his brother.

Mycroft may be fixed in London, but he had a clearer picture of my overall situation than I did. If Peter Steiler hadn't sent his grandson running for that gendarme, if he hadn't accompanied me back up the mountain, I might have found myself seriously suspected of murdering my friend Holmes. Why not? Two foreigners (how odd it is to have to think of oneself as a foreigner!) go up to the Reichenbach Fall and one comes back. Comes back, moreover, with a strange tale about a murderous mathematics tutor (who is also foreign) and a Swiss messenger lad he can't describe and no one else has seen. The sun is setting and it is now too late to visit the scene of the crime. By morning, I'm in a Swiss gaol and the footmarks have disappeared in the mist. Then they discover that I am a writer—of detective fiction. I am too much the realist to suppose that the testimony of a couple of graphologists in Geneva would have precipitated my release under those conditions. No, once incarcerated, I would have had to produce more than a couple of letters to win my freedom.

When I look at the situation from a purely selfish point of view, I suppose I would have to say that I have been remarkably lucky. I actually arrived on the scene behind the police. Between my bad leg and Mr Steiler's age (he wears it well but they don't call him Peter Steiler the elder for nothing), we were easy to overtake and the gendarme caught us up before we were in shouting distance of the top. He saw for himself how heartsick I was, how glad I was to see a member of the local constabulary, how badly I was limping. I felt like a horse that has been ridden too far too fast. I was trembling with muscle fatigue. He saw the footmarks, he measured their stride. I didn't have to tell him I hadn't made those impressions any more than I had to tell him I had to rest before I could begin the descent. He could see that for himself. Thanks to Peter Steiler, who is as fluent in French as he is in English, there was no language problem, no frantic fumblings for the translation for "murderous" or "decoy" or "forgery." The words they teach you in school are never the words you need in an emergency. I owe Peter Steiler far more than a copy of *The Adventures of Sherlock Holmes*.

I am so tired. How odd to think that within the space of a few days, I shall have no reason to pick up my pen. Fitsch is going to have to take 'The Cardboard Box', after all, adultery or no adultery. I won't be writing any more adventures of Sherlock Holmes. I have brought my second contract to a successful conclusion, which is something to be proud of and grateful for in this uncertain world. I won't be signing a third. How could it be otherwise? Without Holmes, I will have no subject.

Finally, I have nothing to say.

1893

Chapter 31

We'll call him John Sherlock Watson—in memory of our friend. And he will give shape to our dreams, fullness to our days, and immediacy to all our fears. Our future will have his face. We will become our parents and he will be our child and those we have lost will be found again, in the curve of his cheek and the sound of his sigh. If I didn't know better, I'd swear I was writing this under the influence.

What stories we have saved for him! All of the Morstan family stories, all of the Watson family stories (we are, we were, the last of our lines), and all of the adventures of Sherlock Holmes I never had the heart to tell the world. He alone will thrill to the slavering Hound of the Baskervilles. He alone will feel the spray from the Reichenbach Fall as a chill in his bones and shrink from the touch of Professor Moriarty.

When Mary and I were first married, I often pictured her with a baby in her arms and a child at her knee—I think I was trying to accustom myself to this unnerving idea in advance, by degrees. Then as the years went by and the Stamford family took on dynastic dimensions and Mary's friend Celia delivered twin girls, I suppose I must have stopped picturing this. I know that when we sold the practice on Mortimer Street and moved to Kensington, I was secretly rather pleased that the late Dr Adams had been a bachelor—no nursery, you see. Mary was airing cupboards and disposing of motheaten relics for months, but at least there was no box-room painted a sensible green, with a broken hobby-horse in the corner and a cache of childish drawings tucked away in one of the window-seats, the way there was in our last house. We were able to put every room in the house to good use and just look how well it's turned out! I should have bought a house with no nursery years ago—we might have had an absolute houseful of children underfoot by now.

How I shall enjoy painting the spare bedroom a sensible green!

* * *

I hope Mary is carrying a boy because otherwise this child is going to have to go through life as Wanda Wilhelmina Watson, which strikes my ear as a wanton abuse of parental authority. I know I shouldn't let this hideous thought dampen my enthusiasm for the child in any way, but "Wanda Wilhelmina"? That's a bit thick, isn't it?

I didn't know Mary's middle name was Martha or that her Aunt Mae was originally Maida Margaret Morstan. It seems a fairly pointless custom to me in view of the fact that Mary became Mary Martha Watson when we married, but a family tradition is a family tradition and this one is obviously very important to Mary, who describes it as a way of welcoming a daughter into the family, affirming that she will always be our little girl. So I told her: "Mary," I said, "'Wanda Wilhelmina' it is." And I hope the child appreciates what we've done for her.

The best way to handle this, I think, is to suppress the child's middle name as too grand for everyday use. Mary should be amenable to this, I think—after all, I didn't know her middle name was Martha until last night. She even signed our marriage lines as Mary Morstan. If my wife Mary can be happy without a middle name in daily use, it seems to me our daughter Wanda can, too.

"Wanda Watson"—I can get used to that. It's Wanda's little sisters Wallis Whitney and Wilona Winter, I feel sorry for.

"Wallis Whitney Watson" is terribly reminiscent of Wee Willie Winkie.

* * *

Ever since Mary told me she was expecting, I have been walking around smiling at nothing. They say that expectant mothers glow like brides, but I think that's because they don't want them to feel jealous of the expectant fathers, their husbands. I feel like I have been unexpectedly released from prison and led blinking into the light of a perfect summer day, without a cloud in the sky.

We are going to have a baby.

Life is full of possibilities again, as has not been the case for years. I am enjoying the writing. I haven't forgotten why I stopped—it had become a fruitless exercise, an excuse for wallowing in pointless self-recriminations—but now that the future finally means more to me again than an empty extension of the past through the tedious medium of the present, I can see how much I've missed this. As usual, what I needed was a story to tell. I am left wondering whether the difference between those who recover from a loss and those who remain bowed down with grief is less a matter of temperament than it is of circumstance.

A great grief may require the corrective of a great joy—or such a preponderance of little joys as can be equally difficult to arrange. When it comes, the shift is unmistakable—like finding yourself on level ground again after a long, arduous climb up a treacherous incline covered with scree.

I will admit to a slight feeling of disorientation now that I don't have to worry about my emotional footing. It seems like such a long time since I had leisure to observe the scenery! The most ordinary sights and sounds catch me by the throat and gladden my heart. As I write these words, the smoothness of the paper beneath the heel of my hand is a poignant source of physical pleasure, as is the rhythmic regularity of the words that flow from my pen.

I was teasing Mary this afternoon, thinking about that Morstan family tradition. She must have been madly in love with me, to have been able to overlook the handicap of a name like Watson.

It may be five years since Jack the Ripper claimed his first victim, but he's still current enough to sell newspapers. Today's lead story: a "retrospective" of the crimes which shocked the nation, raising the question of how the police can have acted so expeditiously in ridding the metropolis of the Moriarty gang and yet have failed even to have identified the madman who once roamed the streets of Whitechapel, slaying at will. I could answer that question for them in one word: Sherlock Holmes. All right, two words—it's still the right answer.

Holmes was excluded from the Ripper investigation, but the Moriarty case was all his. It was Holmes who accumulated the evidence against the Professor, Holmes who orchestrated the mass arrest that Monday, to the everlasting credit of Scotland Yard's own Inspector Patterson. And it was Holmes who bore the brunt of the Professor's wrath and paid for the success of that investigation with his life.

In a way it's a pity that I was never able to bring myself to tell the Moriarty story. It doesn't seem right that the investigative success of our time should remain permanently associated with Inspector Patterson's name. Or that the last time Holmes's name ever appeared in print, it should have been misspelled in a garbled account of his "accident" along the path to the Reichenbach Fall. For want of a handrail, the great detective was lost—it's insulting, that's what it is.

I'm not the only one who has had difficulty accepting Holmes's death. I know for a fact that his brother Mycroft is still paying the rent at 221B Baker Street two years later and that Mrs Hudson is still giving the old rooms a good turn-out once a week. She told Mary the other day that it wouldn't be "respectful" to let the dust take hold.

Anyone would think that Holmes had been a house-proud man.

* * *

Letters in all the most popular newspapers, from a Colonel
James Moriarty (Retired), objecting to the use of the term "the
Moriarty gang," which he understands to be an outgrowth of
the vicious persecution(!) visited upon his innocent brother,
the late Professor James Moriarty, who was blameless in all
things, by that "infernal hothead" *(The Standard)*, that "curst
encroaching busybody" *(Daily Chronicle)*, that "officious
humbug" *(Daily Telegraph)*, that "self-appointed avenger of
the downtrodden" *(The Times)*, Sherlock Holmes. God knows
what new forms of invective will have occurred to him in
time for the evening papers. Colonel Moriarty must have
been stationed abroad when the story first hit the newspapers, two years ago. Every paper in town carried a running
account of the arrest and conviction of the Moriarty gang.

I notice that Colonel Moriarty doesn't say that any of the
men who were arrested as part of the Moriarty gang were
unfairly tried or unjustly convicted. I guess that "curst
encroaching busybody," Sherlock Holmes, accumulated
enough evidence against the individual members of the gang
to satisfy Colonel Moriarty's exacting judicial standards—it is
only the identification of the gang with the name of its leader,
his brother, which offends his sense of propriety.

Family pride is a laudable quality when not taken to
extremes. This is an extreme. Colonel Moriarty has blinded
himself to the truth and that is his privilege, but when it
comes to besmirching the reputation of my friend Holmes, he
has overstepped his bounds.

* * *

Mary is right. I can try to cover the evidence linking Professor
James Moriarty to the death of Sherlock Holmes in one hope-
lessly detailed paragraph that will be too long for anyone to
publish, or I can send each and every Editor on Colonel

239

Moriarty's list a brief but dignified note to the effect that a full, unvarnished account of the facts surrounding the final, fatal encounter between Professor Moriarty and Sherlock Holmes will be found in a forthcoming issue of the *Strand Magazine* under the title 'The Final Problem', and say that I would be obliged if Colonel Moriarty would refrain from further out-bursts of misguided loyalty until he is in possession of those facts.

Whether or not they publish my letter, I know what I have to do. And I know that it won't be easy. For two years and more, I have spent every waking minute trying not to think about the events of that time. They may trouble my dreams, I told myself, but they will not absorb my waking hours. But that's of no consequence now.

I owe this to Holmes. That's all that should concern me.

I owe this to Holmes.

1894

Chapter 32

First the child and then the mother. How shall I bear it? I am forty-three years old and everyone I have ever loved is dead.

Celia and I chose the dress together: her dark blue. I haven't seen Mary in that dress since she told me about the baby. My son, John Sherlock. He was mine for such a little breath of time. A week, what's a week? And now they are laying out his mother. They say trouble always comes in threes, but that doesn't frighten me today. What is there left for me to lose, now that I've lost my Mary? No lilies—I must remember to tell Celia, no lilies. Mary doesn't like lilies.

They're calling me.

* * *

The things people say, to try and ease a grief! You have to wonder, really, whether they can hear themselves at all or have simply learned deafness in order to preserve their good opinion of themselves. "What do I think Mary would want me to do with myself now that she's gone?"

I think Mary would want me to mourn her as she would have mourned me had our roles been reversed. And I think that Mary would want me eventually to cease my mourning, to grow past my grief over my loss and into a fuller consciousness of the sweetness of life for however many years remain to me.

But how I am to do that, she herself could not have told me. We could neither of us long endure the imagining of that long loneliness. And now it is become a dream from which I will not wake.

Chapter 33

If I ever wondered how I would know when my diary had run its course, my curiosity has now been satisfied: Holmes has conquered death and whatever I may decide to do about his miraculous return, I shall have no need for this journal after this afternoon.

It has been three *years* since we parted at the base of the path to the Reichenbach Fall.

I will write down what happened, everything that happened. If I write it down, then I will understand it. By writing it down, step by step, I will make it my own and come to an understanding of what has happened to me. Holmes is alive. Holmes is alive and Mary is dead. I was with her when she died. I closed her eyes. I kissed her cheek, grown cold in death. I threw the first clod of earth on her coffin. I buried her, I know that, in the grave that holds our son. But if I know that, why do I start at every little noise, expecting it to be my Mary, come to turn up the lamp or to ask me whether I would like another cup of tea?

The grave has opened and Holmes has come forth, and all I can think about is that I would give anything, *anything* for it to have been Mary instead of Holmes.

* * *

I fainted when I saw him. I actually fainted. I don't know that I would recommend the experience exactly, but it had definite points of interest. One moment I was expostulating with Holmes in his guise as a superannuated bibliophile of the querulous type and the next moment the old man had collapsed into my friend Holmes, long since lost to me but now receding into the perfect blackness of the tunnel that had opened up behind him. The darkness was edged with a disturbance that was almost light, halfway between a tingle and a shimmer. My mouth was dry, the sound of the surf was pounding in my ears, and when I licked my lips, I lost my hearing altogether. The next thing I knew, I was horizontal and Holmes was forcing brandy between my teeth under the mistaken impression that this was the medically approved course of treatment—revival by intoxication.

Where do these myths come from? If people who know nothing about medicine would only stand back and do nothing in case of a medical emergency, the world would be an infinitely safer place. I smell like a distillery.

The walls insisted on tipping around Holmes as he apologized for his dramatic intrusion into my study, explained that he had not intended to reveal himself to me today, and assured me that he would not have done so at all but for the coincidence of finding me among the curious congregated outside the residence of the late Honourable Ronald Adair. The Honourable Ronald Adair? I did not recognize the name. There was a headache waiting for me in the distance like a squall on the horizon.

I remember thinking, quite clearly: Holmes has come back from the dead in order to talk to me about a stranger. Then I realized that he had come back from the dead in order to talk to me about a case, and I surrendered to the inevitable. Time enough to pay attention when we were talking about something that interested me. I concentrated on maintaining my sensory hold on our surroundings and was gratified to see the room assume a less lively demeanour. Meanwhile, Holmes had fixed on a new topic, 'The Final Problem', my account of his fatal confrontation with Professor Moriarty at the Reichenbach Fall.

"Do you know, Watson, I quite liked 'The Final Problem'? That picture of me, locked in Moriarty's arms, the two of us hurtling through space to the rocks below—it was most affecting. Your interpretation of events was sadly flawed, as you can see,"—and here he gestured at himself, obviously alive and well—"but the effect on the reader was everything I could have wished. I, myself, reading it in Aix-en-Provence, was most sincerely touched. It is a talent, you know, Watson, to be able to evoke an emotional response in your readers. I have rarely been so moved by a piece of prose. Mrs Hudson tells me that the story of my demise hasn't hurt the business one bit, either. Of all the unexpected developments that have attended my life in recent years, that has been the most unexpected."

"You have seen Mrs Hudson?"

"This afternoon. It has been quite a welcome home, taking it all in all," he said, preening a little. "At least you fainted quietly, Watson! Mrs Hudson had hysterics all over the parlour, running from pillar to post and back again before collapsing in a damp heap in front of the piano, to weep on the keys. Upon my word, I don't know whether she was pleased to see me or merely sorry to lose the extra money Mycroft has been paying her to leave my shingle up and handle my callers in my absence."

"You are unfair," I cried.

"You think so? Well, perhaps. But you can have no idea how tiresome she was, Watson! She wanted to know whether you were aware that I had survived my meeting with Professor Moriarty and when I told her that I had yet to see you, my entire morning having been given over to Inspector Lestrade, she threw her apron over her face and began rocking and keening. 'Dr Watson will be so pleased, Dr Watson will be so pleased,' I thought she said. 'Dr Watson will be so pleased?' I asked, a jigger of brandy at the ready. She dropped her apron, dabbed at her eyes and said fiercely, 'Dr Watson will be so *grieved*.' But you aren't grieved, are you, Watson? Of course not. Really, she was completely irrational—wouldn't touch the brandy. I did my best, but I'm not at all sure she understood my instructions about this evening and her role is critical.

"The practice itself is in fine shape, I'm happy to say. Mrs

Hudson tells me that she thinks there has actually been an increase in traffic while I was away. The effect of your adventures, no doubt, Watson. Credit where credit is due! There was a slight dip at the end of the year when 'The Final Problem' first came out, but within a couple of months they were knocking at my door once more, many of them wearing a black armband in my memory.

"On Mycroft's advice, she has been telling all and sundry that Mr Holmes has been called away for the foreseeable future and would they care to leave a message? The strange thing is, many of them do. She said they seem to find it *soothing* to contribute to her book of messages for Sherlock Holmes. Can you imagine the kinds of minds they must have, Watson? They have heard about my death and therefore they are coming to consult me about their problems. When we die, Mycroft and I, all pretense to logical thought will die with us. What a world it is, eh, Watson?"

An inch of brandy, a splash of soda. It would be best not to drink it, I realized, and offered it to Holmes, who accepted it with a nod.

"You're not having any?" he asked.

"Not just yet," I said, silently promising myself a double when he had gone. "Tell me about Moriarty."

I don't know why I bothered. Certainly, I was not interested in the mechanics of his escape—his knowledge of baritsu, Moriarty's unwarranted confidence in his own physical prowess, the way he deceived me over the footmarks on the path. I knew by then that it was to be my fault entirely. He had to do what he did, I gave him no choice. He never intended to deceive me, but I am so easily deceived! (A shake of the head, expressive of wonder.) Many times he wanted to contact me, to explain, but always Something held him back. If I have a fault as a friend (and the reader of these words will readily perceive that I do), that fault is the perfect transparency of my good nature. Anyone can see right through me, just by looking. How could he trust me with his secret when I have never concealed anything from him? Trust has to be earned and by trusting him, I had earned his contempt.

It was interesting to see how closely his telling of the story matched my emotional reconstruction. It has been an education for me, writing these adventures of his. I wonder if he realizes how illogical it all is.

Think about it—he can trust only those people who are able to deceive him. Isn't that another way of saying that there is no one he can bring himself to trust? But I am forgetting about his brother Mycroft. Mycroft has known the truth from the beginning, "about this and about other things," he said vaguely, suggesting that additional revelations await me this evening. And so we go adventuring. "Until nine-thirty, then, Watson. Do you still have your old service revolver? Good, we may need it." And he was gone.

It's not that Mycroft is more trustworthy than I am—it is that Mycroft is his brother, another member of the Holmes clan. He should have married, should my friend Holmes. It is not good for man to be alone. Holmes has been too much alone. It has changed him.

The one thing he kept repeating was that his farewell note was completely genuine—he'd never lied to me. It wasn't lying to refer to the enemy by his code name; that was routine practice with espionage cases. The Swiss messenger now, he was surprised I hadn't taken more notice of the Swiss messenger.

"A member of Moriarty's gang?" I ventured.

"A reasonable hypothesis when you thought me dead, Watson, but you forget: I survived the battle of the Reichenbach Fall. No, young Hans was all that he appeared to be—young, Swiss, and very obliging. He is, in fact, the reason I am not wanted by the Swiss police today. When you tell this story, Watson, and you will (we can't leave all London under the impression that I am dead!), you must be sure to emphasize the part he played. I don't want your readers imagining that I deliberately dispatched some inoffensive soul on my

Continental holiday. It was a piece of advice I'd had from Mycroft, Watson: whenever possible, stage your bit of by-play before the eyes of a witness drawn from the local population. That way, your witness will have instant credibility with the local police, who are thereby spared the awful responsibility of having to trust in the word of a foreigner. Mycroft may not have much personal experience of foreign travel, but he is eminently practical.

"When you set off for Meiringen that last day, Watson, I knew that the crisis was near at hand. The letter was an obvious forgery. Moriarty was on his way to meet me and there was murder in his heart. Now that it had come to the point, I was not nearly so pleased by the prospect of trading my life for his as I had been in London, with all of his followers bent on following me, nipping at my heels. Most of them had been arrested while we were in Brussels, after all, and while I knew I had other enemies, still, we had had a very pleasant holiday together, you and I, and life was sweet once more. The sun was shining, the birds were singing, and the world lay waiting at my feet. There is something about standing on a height, Watson—I felt that it behooved me to take thought for the future.

"For the first time, I considered the possibility that I might survive my encounter with Professor Moriarty. What if our struggle were to conclude with his death at my hands? How could I hope to prove it wasn't murder? Moriarty had been the instigator of the violence from the beginning, but where were the witnesses to that? Not even you, Watson, could have testified to that. All you knew, of your own knowledge, was that I had evinced a certain amount of uneasiness on the subject of a certain Professor Moriarty and that our fitful progress across the Continent appeared to be a reflection of that uneasiness. 'Might it not have been the case, Dr Watson, that your friend Holmes was *pretending* to flee this man, all the while he was luring him to Switzerland?' You see, Watson? How could you have argued the point?

250

"I knew from my study of the terrain between Rosenlaui and Meiringen that the Fall could also be viewed from above the path, at two different elevations. Hans Schmidt was young and active. He made nothing of circling round and climbing up to the first lookout. He'd often done it; it would take him about a quarter of an hour. My instructions were simple: I told him to stay hidden, to expect to see violence on the path below, and to observe everything as best he could from his hiding place without compromising his own safety. If I survived the encounter and he was satisfied that I had acted in self-defense, within the confines of the law, then there was the further request that he delay sharing his testimony with the police for the space of a week while I did what I could to ensure my personal safety: my attacker had his friends.

"You could not have done this for me, Watson. Setting aside the handicap of your nationality, you could not, with your leg, have managed the climb. Besides, the good Professor was expecting to see you hurrying down the path to Meiringen. I had to use young Schmidt. I had to let you go."

* * *

Holmes fails to confide in me and then he blames me for being uninformed. He isolates me, wanting to control the view his biographer takes of him, and then he resents the fact that I have not come to share his conclusions for my own independent reasons.

What he said was true—my information, such as it was, had all come from my friend Holmes. Had he been charged with Moriarty's murder, I should have had no way of proving his innocence. I know as well as he does that I am no substitute for him as a detective. Deprived at the last of so much as a good look at Professor Moriarty, hustled off to Meiringen as a child is hustled off to bed, I should have had nothing to offer him but my faith in his innocence. The question still remains: was this worth nothing to him?

Had I discovered Holmes still prostrate at the edge of the Fall, accused of voluntary manslaughter, I should have worked tirelessly for him (as in fact I did in his absence), interpreting footmarks, wiring Mycroft and the Yard, defending him with all the words at my command. It was painful for me, writing 'The Final Problem', but I did it. I did it because I could not allow Colonel James Moriarty to impugn my friend's reputation, even if it was out of misguided loyalty to his own dead brother.

It was typical of Holmes, imagining that I might be jealous of Hans Schmidt, the young Swiss messenger. How could I possibly object to his inclusion? I'm glad Holmes thought of it. I know my limitations and I know that no part of me has ever wanted to see Holmes suffer on their account. But what does the inclusion of young Schmidt as a witness on that occasion have to do with my exclusion as his friend and confidant for three long years?

I have to get ready. Holmes will be here shortly and he will expect me to be well-versed in the facts of the case as they have been reported in the press. How odd that our paths should have crossed outside the residence of London's latest murder victim. I assume Ronald Adair was murdered—I can't see Holmes interesting himself in a suicide. And he was extremely interested—he went on and on about how pleased he was to find that I had not lost my taste for criminal investigation. He did not scruple to say that he had timed his resurrection perfectly. The trap was baited, the blind prepared. It only remained for us to wait for it to spring and retrieve our prey.

I didn't have the heart to tell him I didn't know anything about his precious case, but it's true—a death in the family does tend to take one's mind off the rubbish in the newspapers. I have never even heard of Ronald Adair, as far as I know. I was tramping through the streets as I have done every day since Mary died, hoping to win the grace of a good night's sleep through the penance of physical exertion. (I have to do it. It's what I have always told my patients to do when they have trouble sleeping.) I saw the crowd, I was grateful for the distraction (these days I am grateful for any distraction), and so I stopped and gazed at the upstairs windows with the rest of them. I didn't have to know all of the details. It was enough for me to find myself emotionally in tune with someone again, if only for a few minutes. How could I know Holmes was watching me, measuring my grief with his eyes?

All he cares about is that I am a bachelor again, free to go adventuring with him. But I am not a bachelor, I am a widower, and all I can think about is Mary. The way I am now, I am like a question without an answer. I unnerve people. I unnerve *myself*. The only one I don't unnerve is Holmes, and I find that unnerving.

Holmes wants me to bring my service revolver with me and I will, but I'll be damned if I'll take any ammunition. I still have to shave and eat a couple of sandwiches. Change my shirt, which smells of spirits.

One last thing. I don't know whether he was trying to tell me something with this, or if he simply hasn't looked at it since he thrust it into his notebook in Florence three years ago, but I have the scrap of paper he used to compose his wire to Mycroft after legging it over the rise at the Reichenbach Fall into Italy. He saved it for me, he said, in case I wanted to use it in my next adventure. The date is 5 May, 1891, and it is addressed to Mycroft Sigerson at Whitehall.

VENI, VIDI, VICI AND WATSON HAS HIS FINAL PROBLEM AFTER ALL

RELYING ON YOU TO MAINTAIN STATUS QUO ANTE

PRESENT SITUATION SUITS ME

R I P SHERLOCK HOLMES

WILL RESOLVE LEGAL TANGLE BEFORE LEAVING
SWITZERLAND

SEND FUNDS ROSENLAUI

YOUR LOVING BROTHER
ALTAMONT SIGERSON

"Sigerson" is an interesting choice. If "Siegfried" means victorious peace and "Sigismund" means victorious protector, then what do you suppose "Sigerson" means? And am I to suppose it is a coincidence that my name is Watson?

Nine o'clock, time to have done. I mustn't keep Holmes waiting.

Chapter 34

"Why are you telling me this?" I asked. I meant, *Why didn't you tell me this earlier—this afternoon, three years ago, any time during the past three years?* but that's not how he heard it. You can know someone for years and years, and then find out you don't know them at all.

He spoke slowly, as if he were speaking to a child. "Because Lestrade may be with us this evening and I would not have you at a disadvantage, Watson." Of course. He was ever considerate of my feelings. "Must we talk about this now, Watson?"

I waited then, letting the chill darkness of the empty house fill up my soul. There was a strong smell of cat in the air, emanating from the ground floor, manifesting itself in a sharp ammoniated pricking in the back of my throat. It was important that we keep the windows closed. Holmes peered down into the street: nothing yet.

"Lestrade was in on the joke?" I asked softly.

"There was no 'joke,' as you put it, Watson. You make it sound as though I'd *planned* to deceive you. How can I make you understand? There was no planning to this at all. One thing led to another and at each point, I made the decision that maximized my advantage. That's all. You would have done the same in my position." I wondered briefly whether he actually believed that, then dismissed the question as irrelevant.

"I thought you'd see through it yourself, Watson! Aren't you the one who coined the name 'Lestrade'? What could be more obvious than the name 'Moriarty'? Less trade, more art—that's what I wanted. I kept waiting for you to ask me about it."

"But why—"

"Watson, try to understand. For the first time in my career, I had come up against a worthy opponent. 'Know thyself' is considered to be one of the most reliable maxims for a well-spent life, but I say 'Know thy enemy' is a better, because knowledge of an enemy's history, habits, and henchmen is the surest route to knowledge of how to protect yourself against him. Moriarty's history was and is largely a matter for conjecture, his henchmen were legion, and I was forced to rely almost entirely upon my understanding of his habits. I knew Moriarty prided himself on his ability to move undetected among his victims, gathering information and lining his pockets. His men didn't rely on sticks of dynamite to effect their entrances. They opened locked doors and oiled their hinges, removed what was most valuable (and could most easily be sold), and locked up the rest before they left. Often it was weeks before the Yard was called in, so sure were the owners that the thief had to be a member of the household or (in the case of a business theft) the company. Many a happy family or commercial partnership foundered in the wake of a visit from the Professor's men. I could not fail to anticipate the visit they would make to my consulting rooms, their careful search among my notes. I actually coined the name 'Moriarty' before I knew to whom it might refer. That's right, Watson! I deduced the nature and existence of the spider from the extent of his web, and I named him accordingly.

"I got the idea from you, Watson, and it answered beautifully. My rooms were searched four times that I know of and on no occasion were any of my notes removed or tampered with. Moriarty knew that I was aware of his activities, but what proofs I had, the extent of my knowledge—that, he was never able to discover. I was able to put a name to him at last and that is the name I shared with Inspector Patterson, but still I called him Moriarty to myself; the only difference was, now I called him *Professor* Moriarty. I knew something of his history now, you see. I knew the tale of his public accomplishments, his University appointment, how he appeared to make his living.

"When I sat down at the foot of the path to the Reichenbach Fall to compose my farewell note, I had no thought of deceiving you. You were the least of my worries, believe me! I thought about the Professor, waiting impatiently for me to finish my letter—how long would he allow me for this task? I thought about the Swiss messenger, Hans Schmidt—was he in position? Would he be a reliable witness? And I thought about Inspector Patterson, whose case against Moriarty's men would be incomplete without the contents of the blue envelope in my desk, the one marked 'Moriarty,' filed under M. Without explicit instructions from me, through you, he would search my rooms in vain for that information, as had Moriarty's men before him. My farewell note was absolutely genuine. I expected to die, remember. I expected to die and I was determined to do everything in my power to ensure that I should not die in vain."

Most people, I thought sourly, would be content to think they had not *lived* in vain.

"Say something, Watson," he demanded. I remember telling myself that it was a good sign that he wanted my reaction. It meant that he knew my wits might not be totally overwhelmed by his explanation.

"It was your idea to give everyone a different name, Watson," he added. And I knew that unless I could pinpoint the source of my discomfort within a matter of seconds, he would expand upon this theme until it became apparent even to me that it was in tribute to his old friend Watson that he had called him Moriarty.

"The newspapers!" I gasped. I had him now. "They talked about the trial and conviction of the Moriarty gang. How could that be if 'Moriarty' were a code name?"

"How could that be if 'Moriarty' had been his real name?" he said, amused. "Watson, you aren't thinking! Moriarty was as I described him to you: an Army coach, a former professor, a respected member of society who died an untimely death in an unfortunate accident abroad. He was never charged with a crime. How could the Yard link his name to a band of murdering thieves? I think Patterson did very well by me. He honoured my memory in the only way open to him. If you check the records, Watson, you will find that 'the Moriarty gang' gained its name only after Inspector Patterson received your telegram about the blue envelope in my desk in Baker Street."

"And the letters?" I asked, my heart sinking along with my voice. (Say it isn't so, I pleaded with him in my heart of hearts.) "The letters from Colonel James Moriarty, the Professor's brother, attacking you in *The Times* and *The Standard* and…?"

"Written by me," he confessed, and I could hear the smile in his voice. He wasn't half pleased with himself. "Watson, you should have known. You should have guessed! Colonel *James* Moriarty, Retired, brother of Professor *James* Moriarty? Really, Watson! What mother ever named her two boys James?"

* * *

How often, I wonder, does a friendship die all in a moment? Surely this cannot be a common occurrence, I tell myself. Surely, I would have heard about the phenomenon, if it were. There would be some account of it—in Shakespeare. Or the Bible.

I would have trusted Sherlock Holmes with my life. And the irony of it is, I should have been perfectly safe in doing so. What I could not trust him with was my pride.

We had been in competition with each other from the beginning, and I didn't even know it.

Chapter 35

Holmes has proposed that I should sell my practice, put the furniture (Mary's furniture) in storage, and move back to Baker Street with him, and I have promised to think it over. "Don't say anything now, there's a good chap. Go home and sleep on it, Watson. It was like the old days tonight, wasn't it?"

But the old days were never like this. Not for me.

* * *

I remember how it felt, waiting with him in the empty house, how dark it was. How damp! There was a strong odour of cat drifting up at us from the ground floor, but it was on the first floor—our footsteps sounded very loud as we climbed the stair—that Holmes told me that "Moriarty" was a code name of his own invention, known to everyone but me. Useless to tell him that he could have given Moriarty's mother a dozen sons named James and it would not have sufficed to make me doubt him.

He had played me perfectly, from first to last, even to the timing of those revelations. Impossible for me to leave him there in the empty house to await his doom alone. What should I do, take my empty revolver with me or give it to him for his protection? It was impossible. It was all of it impossible, I decided. Holmes, Mary, the child—it was more than I could bear. I *refused* to bear it.

We waited for our quarry in the dark of the empty house for over two hours. Holmes was restless at first, alternately haunting the window and abusing Lestrade. "You don't have to worry about Lestrade, Watson." And: "Lestrade is used to your little fictions, Watson. He probably thought Moriarty's alias was your idea." And still later: "I don't actually know whether Lestrade knew about the code name or not, Watson. He was not on that case but the Yard knew, certainly, and Lestrade works for the Yard, so I think we must accept the possibility that Lestrade knows what Patterson knew. The capture of the Moriarty gang was the success of 1891. I have no doubt they talked about it among themselves." I wanted to laugh. It wasn't *Lestrade's* opinion of me I cared about.

Towards midnight, Holmes grew restless again. "Not asleep, are you, Watson?" he whispered.

"Not yet," I admitted wryly, whispering in my turn.

"It seems I owe you an apology," he said in a more normal tone of voice, and for a moment, I allowed myself to hope. (If he could bring himself to apologize to me...) "I appear to have led you and the good Lestrade on a bit of a wild goose chase. If you will bear with me for another quarter of an hour—What is that? Quiet, Watson!"

If I were still in the business of recording the adventures of Sherlock Holmes, the next few minutes would have been worth a thousand words, at least. As it is, suffice it to say that I, Dr John H. Watson, laid low one Sebastian Moran, in Holmes's own words, "the second most dangerous man in London," using a gun that wasn't even loaded. On the strength of his unique weaponry and highly original *modus operandi*, this Sebastian Moran is to be charged with the murder of his one-time gambling partner, the Honourable Ronald Adair, who was a shade too honourable (compared to Sebastian Moran) for his own good. It was another feather in the cap of Sherlock Holmes, consulting detective.

How very odd. It didn't occur to me last night (truthfully, I found his croaking cries of "Watson, you saved my life!" a trifle melodramatic under the circumstances), but if Colonel Moran was the second most dangerous man in London because Moriarty was the first, and if that same Professor Moriarty (whatever his real name was) has been dead for almost three years, doesn't that mean I felled The Most Dangerous Man in London with my empty gun? Blast that

Holmes! Am I never to be able to take what he says to me at face value?

For all I know, he staged my triumph over Moran in order that I might appear to advantage in front of Lestrade.

Is that possible? Yes, I am convinced that it is. He was very worried about what Lestrade might say to me. And it certainly seemed to me to be unnecessary for Holmes to tackle Moran in that ill-advised way. Where was Holmes's knowledge of baritsu last night? In a matter of seconds, Moran had him pinned to the wall and was throttling the life out of him. From where I was standing, fumbling for my revolver, the outcome of the conflict was never in any doubt. Ignorant of my presence and intent on strangling Holmes, Moran was an easy target. One good blow behind the ear with my gun butt and Moran was down for the count.

"Watson, you saved my life!" croaked Holmes.

"Not at all, Holmes," I replied, prying up my victim's eyelids and wishing I could see his pupils. Good, he was beginning to stir.

"What have we here?" asked Lestrade, shining his dark lantern in our direction. "Dr Watson, as I live and breathe. Good to see you again, Doctor! I was sorry to hear about your wife. And who's this?"

There was no awkwardness between me and Inspector Lestrade. How could there be when we have both been cast in supporting roles in the continuing drama of Holmes's career? I venture to say that Lestrade and I understood each other better last night than we have ever done before.

* * *

I know his name is Sebastian Moran because that was the name Holmes gave him, to me and to Lestrade, and Moran made no effort to deny the appellation. Oh, it is impossible! If I have to ask myself after every one of Holmes's remarks how it is that I know that he is speaking the truth, I might as well give up the association at once. Is that what I want? I've lost everyone else—my wife, my child, my brother, my parents. Do I really want to lose Holmes now, for the second time?

I don't know. I can't think. Nothing makes sense to me any more. I mourned the loss of my friend Holmes for three years and he was content that I should do so. My grief suited his purposes, not that he has been able to articulate those purposes very well. His story is a mass of contradictions, and that in itself is strange. For when has it ever been the case that I observed a contradiction that was hidden from my friend Holmes?

"4 May, 1891. Meiringen, Switzerland. Sherlock Holmes narrowly escaped death today at the hands of Professor James Moriarty [sic], a fellow Englishman, in an unprovoked attack at the brink of the Reichenbach Fall. Mr Holmes, a consulting detective whose activities on behalf of Scotland Yard have made him a general favourite with our readers, reported that he owed his escape to his knowledge of baritsu, an Oriental system of self-defense. 'The true disciple of baritsu allows his enemy to defeat himself. He rushed at me, I abandoned my resistance, and his own momentum sent him plunging to the depths below. There was nothing I could do.' Hans Friedrich Schmidt, age 15, who saw the entire incident while searching for birds' nests in the vicinity of the Fall [I have to make some excuse for his presence], confirmed Mr Holmes's account in every particular. No motive has been given for the attack."

When Holmes appeared in my study yesterday afternoon (really, it is a good thing I don't have a weak heart), he told me that the reason he had climbed the overhang, abandoning me to my false conclusions, was that he wanted to lull his enemies—his London enemies—into a false sense of security, to shake off any further pursuit. My blood ran cold when I thought of him climbing that cliff, searching for handholds and footholds, coming to rest on what he described as "a mossy ledge" about twenty feet above the Fall. I remember that cliff and when I described it as a sheer wall in 'The Final Problem', I was not conscious of any element of exaggeration.

Over and over again he assured me that only his loving brother Mycroft (and the Swiss messenger and the Swiss police) knew of his escape. Perhaps he thought that if he said it often enough, he could make it true. Perhaps he thought that with enough repetitions, he could hypnotize me into believing it. I don't know.

His rationale was the usual one, long familiar to me. I was known to be his friend. "They" would be watching me. He could not confide in me lest I inadvertently give the game away. It was best I know nothing. It was necessary I know nothing.

I don't know why I didn't believe him, but I know I didn't: it was an empty revolver I brought with me to the empty house. I remember thinking how appropriate that was. Truth to tell, I felt strangely empty myself, drained equally of every last vestige of pity and grief. I didn't know what to believe, what to think.

Last night heaped revelation on revelation. More art, less trade. I was the least of his worries. I should have known. Those scurrilous letters he planted in *The Times* from "Colonel James Moriarty" last year? Merely a way of testing my intelligence while gently urging me to tell the story of his death. I should be proud of that adventure. 'The Final Problem' was a literary triumph, far and away the best thing I've done.

Then, back in Baker Street, more revelations. *Voilà!* Direct from Paris, France, the wax bust of Holmes which had served as his decoy, taking the bullet Sebastian Moran had meant for the back of my friend's head. The capture of Sebastian Moran, Moriarty's ablest lieutenant, had settled an old score for Holmes: Moran was the very man who had accompanied Moriarty to Switzerland three years ago and tried to pick Holmes off his mossy ledge by tossing boulders down on him. Moran's men had probably been watching the windows at 221B Baker Street for signs of his return for years!

263

It makes no sense. Once Sebastian Moran began heaving boulders at him, Holmes must have known that the secret of his survival was out. Hans Schmidt knew it, Sebastian Moran knew it, Mycroft Holmes knew it, eventually even Inspector Grillot knew it. The only one who didn't know it was his old friend Watson. As I was the only one kept ignorant of the fictional state of Professor Moriarty's name.

I should have walked out when he told me about his previous acquaintance with Sebastian Moran, "Moriarty's ablest lieutenant." Why did I wait, smiling and nodding as if I agreed with his assessment of the situation when I didn't agree with him, at all, about any of it?

I don't know. I can't think. It is the effect of piling one shock upon another until nothing feels safe and secure. Mary and the child are dead, and with them all of my comfort and most of my hope. Holmes is alive and eager for me to lend him my countenance. "What you need now is work," he told me, clapping me on the back—and that was the closest he came to mentioning Mary's name all evening.

Chapter 36

I can't eat, I can't sleep, and my mind *will* go round in circles. I have tried giving myself designated times to mourn ("Watson, you may have an hour"), but the heart doesn't work that way. My plans, my needs do not impress it, and why should they? I gave my heart to Mary a long time ago.

What I don't understand is why all thoughts of Mary lead directly to Holmes. It is as if all my grief for Mary had at its center my grief for Holmes, and I know that's not true. I loved Mary. What does Holmes have to do with it?

When I think of all of that misplaced agony when I thought Holmes was dead! The guilt, the despair, the marvelling at Mycroft's bizarre behaviour, which isn't nearly so bizarre now that I know the truth. How he must have squirmed when Mary arrived to break the news to him! He handled it well, though. He had her out of there and on her way to Meiringen in a matter of minutes. But then the Holmes boys always do handle things well. When your only concern is how to maintain your advantage, it's easy to handle things well.

No. It's not fair to blame Mycroft for this. It's no more his fault Holmes chose to hide from me than it was my fault I never suspected the deception. Always, always, it comes down to this for me. How could he do it? Why would he do it? Mycroft merely protected his brother's secret, as I would have done myself. For all he knew, Holmes's life was still in danger, the general belief in his destruction his only protection. It was not for Mycroft to enlighten Mary, and by the time I had returned to England, the deception was firmly established. Mrs Hudson had her instructions and I, I was of no more consequence than Mrs Hudson.

At the moment, Holmes appears to be keeping his distance, waiting for me to call upon him in Baker Street. When I do, he will probably expect me to bring 'The Adventure of the Empty House' with me. It is my move and at another time, with Mary by my side, I might have managed it, but now? I doubt I have the emotional dexterity for this. It is not in me to be sorry that Holmes survived his meeting with Moriarty, but I have never felt less like celebrating a victory in my life. I am so tired of rising to the occasion. Sleeping, eating, shaving, listening to my patients describe their symptoms—everything seems to take so much concentration now. So much effort. And now I have 'The Adventure of the Empty House' to write.

All week long I have been wrestling with the circumstances of his return, trying to make a start on 'The Empty House', but to no avail. Part of the problem is that I can't decide how much of the story I have to tell. Must I tell everyone that "Moriarty" was a code name and that Holmes forced my hand with those letters in *The Times*? Or is it enough to admit that I was the reason he decided to play dead these three years past? However much (or little) I decide to tell, it is bound to be humiliating.

I even toyed with the idea of telling the story as if I believed that rigmarole of his about how he left me to mourn his death in order to keep his survival a secret from the forces of evil— when all the while it was no secret to the premiere representative of those forces of evil, Sebastian Moran, who has twice used Holmes for target practice.

Oh, why did I write 'The Red-headed League'? It is impossible for me to imagine my readers seeing through anything at this point.

* * *

I tell myself that it is important to write 'The Empty House' even if I am the only one who ever reads it, and that makes sense to me (if only because I have to do something to lay this memory to rest before it becomes an obsession with me), but it doesn't move the writing forward. The fact of the matter is,

266

it is extraordinarily difficult to construct anything like a finished piece of prose for what you have been assured will be no audience. Holmes, you see, has decided that we are better off without it. You have to admire his technique. It is because my last adventure was so successful that he wants no more adventures from me now.

"'The Final Problem' has established me as London's court of last resort far more effectively than anything you could possibly find to say about me in the future, Watson. Will you look at this Message Book? Twenty-two entries in the past three days! Mrs Hudson tells me that roughly half of my callers do in fact decide to leave a message for me. Do you realize what this means? Even if half of these are mere bids for attention from curiosity seekers with nothing of a curious nature to offer us in return" (a social possibility he obviously considered the height of rudeness), "there will still be plenty for us to do. And, of course, now that Scotland Yard knows I have returned to London, we may count on the odd bone from Lestrade, as well.

"The last thing we need is an 'adventure' of the empty house, Watson. Why, the volume of business that would be generated by the announcement that I am alive and well would be absolutely crushing. I should have to close my office and retire to the Sussex Downs to keep bees."

The flippant tone might have deceived someone else, but I knew he was serious. Holmes is always serious. Holmes always means what he says. But why should an adventure of mine drive him into retirement? He must know that any sudden rise in traffic would be a temporary aberration.

"I believe I shall make it a condition of accepting a case," he went on, "that my clients tell no one of my return. Yes, that will be best. I have no doubt that it will be an advantage to me to be strictly anonymous."

I gather it is to be my part to see that Holmes continues to have his cake and eat it too, at least in this regard. He is to be both the most famous and the strictly anonymous private detective, as he is to be both my friend and utterly free of any least obligation toward me. And yet I know—in a way that has nothing to do with logic and is as inarguable as the apprehension of beauty (or of death)—that Sherlock Holmes continues to count himself my friend as he has not counted himself the friend of any other human being in all the years I've known him.

Chapter 37

I went through all my old notes about Holmes last night and it was as I remembered it: I never published one word about Holmes while he was alive, without his express permission. After his "death," I vowed to stop writing altogether rather than profit from our friendship.

There were many tales I might have told—some I had already written. I have a manuscript with the working title 'The Birlstone Tragedy' that is not only as long (and potentially as valuable) as 'The Sign of Four', but virtually complete. All it lacks are a few opening and closing remarks linking the death of Eddie Birdwoods to Professor Moriarty. Did I publish that story? No, I did not. And what about the Hound of the Baskervilles? The hours I'd spent studying my notes relative to the Hound had me itching to try my hand at a serial. As for shorter tales, real "adventures" such as delighted the heart of my old friend Fitsch, there were the adventures of the second stain and Charles Augustus Milverton and I don't know how many others. What about that stockbroker's clerk, Paul Kyle Croft? I could have done something with that, but I didn't.

In the three years since my friend's death, I have written only one adventure of Sherlock Holmes and that adventure, 'The Final Problem', was written in defence of his memory and as I now know, at his instigation. He put those words in my mouth and now that I know how false they were, I also know that any attempt on my part to set the record straight will be construed as an attack on his career.

How could he do this to me? What did I do to deserve this? He must know that his friendship meant more to me than the writing did.

Writing my two questions down, I am dimly aware that these are not equivalent questions for my friend Holmes, as they are for me, but the realization is so far removed from my usual style of thinking that I am unable to do more than marvel at it. I wish Mary were here, that I might discuss it with her! There was very little about human nature that was hidden from my Mary.

I do miss her so.

Chapter 38

The only time I really feel free to think of Mary is when I am with Holmes. Perhaps I *should* sell my practice and move back to Baker Street with him. This certainly isn't working.

I thought at first that if I could find the words to describe his return, I might be able to encompass that experience and lay it to rest, but I know now that I don't have it in me to write 'The Adventure of the Empty House' at present. Someday maybe, but not now—not today. I have to get some distance from these events before I can do that. I have to decide how to think about them first. And yet, it seems to me that all I do these days is think about them. I'll be changing the dressing on someone's leg or listening for a tell-tale gurgling in some-one else's lungs when all of a sudden I am back on the path to the Reichenbach Fall or adrift in the empty house, searching for I don't know what. Everyone has been very kind, very patient with me, but that is because they think it is the loss of my wife that is responsible for my air of abstraction, and then I feel guilty because I haven't been thinking about Mary at all, but about Holmes. I loved my wife and I want to grieve for her, but there seems to be some kind of mental law to the effect that one can only obsess about one person at a time and right now, all roads lead to Holmes.

I have felt this way before.

Of course, I remember now! This remind me of the time I found myself standing at the edge of the path to the Reichenbach Fall with a bucket and ten pounds of plaster of Paris, utterly confounded by the absence of yesterday's foot-marks—how could they be gone? This feels as impossible to me as that did and yet I know now as I did then, that some-how the present state of affairs could have been predicted.

There are no contradictions in this world. There are only misunderstandings leading to disappointments which a proper interpretation of earlier events would have enabled one to foresee. I believe that absolutely. It is why I have always so admired Holmes—he can pick out the chain of cause and effects better than anyone I've ever known. And so I am condemned to sift through my memories of my friend, searching for the tone of voice, the facial expression, and the turn of phrase that will explain it to me.

* * *

Very interesting conversation with Mrs Hudson, whose niece Mrs Minnick is a patient of mine. I suspect that it was a deliberate attempt on Mrs Hudson's part at a casual meeting with me—her niece is well past the calves' foot jelly stage, thank goodness. It doesn't do for a physician to say so, but Mrs Minnick has the constitution of a horse. Would that all my patients had her recuperative powers.

Mrs Hudson tells me that Holmes has resumed his practice and has hired a page boy "with brass buttons on his jacket" to handle the flow of traffic and run messages for him. She obviously feels that the tone of the establishment at Number 221 is much improved in consequence. She also said (raising one eyebrow to make sure I appreciated the significance of her remark) that while half of Holmes's callers eventually accept her invitation to leave a message for the absent Mr Holmes, she wanted me to know that "almost all of them, without exception" (Mrs Hudson is not known for her logical gifts) ask to see his good friend Dr Watson first.

I thanked her, of course, but I can't help wondering why the devil she went to all this trouble to tell me this. She'd have done better, surely, to have saved this bit of information for Sherlock Holmes.

* * *

It was the first New Year's Eve of our marriage and Mary

wanted us to make New Year resolutions. We would write them down and then exchange lists, so that we wouldn't "inadvertently sabotage each other's most cherished dreams next year." I remember wondering which of Mary's many friends and acquaintances was responsible for that suggestion—I hadn't made a New Year resolution since I was at school.

I hemmed and hawed, I watched my pipe go out, I lit it again. I wondered what kind of resolutions most people make. I crumpled my current list and tossed it into the fire—writers have to learn to hold paper cheap, it doesn't come naturally. Finally, I admitted to a resolution to meet my obligations to the good gentlemen of the *Strand*, to establish a professional relationship with Holmes, and to replace the missing slates on the roof—the part over the linen closet.

I was so touched. Every one of Mary's resolutions mentioned my name.

* * *

Not a word from Holmes these ten days past. If I want to see him, I shall have to go to Baker Street and that as soon as may be because if I wait much longer, I am going to be unable to muster the necessary strength of character.

Once upon a time, I did what I could to help him establish himself as a consulting detective by bearing witness to his very considerable abilities in that regard in the public press. That is not what he wants from me now. But where is the advantage to him in securing a silent witness?

* * *

Holmes was glad to see me, I think. I remind him of his beginnings, the long years of occasional clients—of clients who had heard of him at second, third or even fourth hand, clients who were expecting "something rather different," who had to be coaxed before they could bring themselves to discuss the painful circumstances which had brought them to a stranger's door. There was none of that today—none. Holmes has more work than any one man can handle. His clients pass each other on the stair and telegraph their congratulations shyly, with their eyes. "You, too? I hear he's excellent!"

Every client is made happy by the sight of the others and now that he knows this, Holmes is taking special care not to solve anyone's problem in one visit. I think he found it soothing to have me at his side, taking the detailed notes this method of working requires. Knowing that I am there to handle the more mundane aspects of the business frees him, as he said himself, to concentrate upon the deductive aspects of each case. And there's another mystery solved. When is a witness not a witness? Answer: when he is a secretary.

* * *

Holmes is going to have to understand: I play billiards with Thurston every Thursday evening, have done for years. If Holmes cares to join us, well and good (no danger of that, I know! Thurston keeps whatever minor intellectual gifts he may have well hidden), but I will not abandon Thurston now simply because Sherlock Holmes chooses to crook a finger. I, too, have my obligations.

* * *

The question of my remuneration was raised today. My loyalty, my secretarial skills, my ability with firearms, and my "reliability" were all mentioned. My secretarial services alone were worth—I cut him off with a gesture before he could insult me with a figure.

"All I want is your friendship," I said, letting my hand fall to my side.

I doubt he was able to appreciate the irony.

Chapter 39

After nearly getting ourselves killed aboard the *Friesland* at the beginning of the summer due to a major mis-communication, Holmes and I have recovered enough of our old ease together to have chalked up an impressive number of cases solved. The important (and practically impossible) thing for me to remember is that Holmes expects me to take his instructions and explanations literally, as I quite naturally used to do. He is not speaking in metaphoric terms, and he seems genuinely puzzled by my persistent efforts at interpretation.

After toasting my first volume of case notes last night, a massive manuscript volume ("The first, I hope, of many—to a productive association!"), Holmes again proposed that I should resume my old residence in Baker Street.

"What do you say, Watson? I should be very glad to have you and so, I make no doubt, would Mrs Hudson. She seems to think you have a moderating influence on me. Absurd, isn't it? You can see how much you are needed. I could not possibly have brought all of these cases to a successful conclusion without your assistance—and your notes! Soon it will be 'flu season again. Will you tell me that you find your own cases more interesting than you do mine?"

"I wouldn't say that, Holmes." (I would never be so rude.)

"Well, then! Will you tell me that you can be happy in Kensington?"

I was stricken to the heart. It is only because I know that Holmes did not know what he was saying that I managed to keep from striking him. He doesn't understand. How could he, as isolated as he is?

"Watson, you are wary now of coming to any permanent conclusion—I can understand that. But he who hesitates is lost, and I do not choose to lose my Boswell. I have taken the liberty of drafting an advertisement for the *Lancet*, offering your practice for sale. Won't you let me send it in?"

"Let me see that," I said.

It was inept to the point of foolishness, I thought, and automatically began to edit it. Not "a modest little practice," but "a comfortable living." Not "general practice, " but "family practice with emphasis on midwifery and minor surgery." Many doctors prefer a younger patient base, as I do myself. Never use the word "death" in an advertisement about a medical practice! (Is he mad?) Finally, the thing was done.

"For sale. Small Kensington practice, near Notting Hill, by ex-Army surgeon seeking early retirement for personal reasons. Family practice, with emphasis on midwifery and minor surgery. Modern consulting rooms, with gas and electricity. A comfortable living, a comfortable home. We were happy here. Apply in person at— etc."

"Shall I send it to the *Lancet* for you?" he asked gently. "To run until further notice?"

"You may send it in," I compromised, "but tell them it is not to run more than once." If I am meant to sell my practice, once will be enough.

Holmes doesn't know it, but I intend to ask £10,000 for my modest little practice—not a penny less. If I meet anyone who is willing to part with that sum for that practice, I will know that the sale was meant.

It's not worth half that amount.

And in Conclusion

So ends Dr Watson's diary, rather more abruptly than it began. Readers who are familiar with Conan Doyle's later adventures, especially 'The Norwood Builder', will be able to confirm this brief sketch of subsequent events.

Dr Watson was, as always, as good as his word. He put his "small Kensington practice" up for sale, and as luck—or as Fate—would have it, he found a buyer almost immediately: one Dr Verner, who met Watson's asking price ("the highest price that I ventured to ask") with, writes Watson, "astonishingly little demur."

At another time, in another place, Watson might have looked this particular gift horse in the mouth. Although never what we would call a suspicious man, neither was he so attracted by the idea of besting an opponent (or by the prospect of financial gain) as to simply take the money and run. It was Holmes who saw all men as his natural enemies, not Watson. The problem, however, was this: having chosen to leave this decision in the hands of Fate, Watson had to play the game. He could stack the deck, setting a price on his practice so high that no sane man would meet it, but if Fate sent him the purchase price, then he would have to sell. Watson accepted Dr Verner's very obliging offer and returned to Baker Street in August of that same year (1894), as Holmes's secretary.

Much of the astonishment Watson felt at the time may have been astonishment at his own bad luck rather than at Dr Verner's peculiar behaviour. Then again, Watson may not have felt much of anything at that time. Newly bereft of his wife and child, sideswiped by grief, unable to absorb his new knowledge of Holmes, about to lose his practice, the very home he'd made with Mary, Watson may have been in that state of transcendent numbness where you only know that your shoe is pinching you when you see the blister. Watson may have known, intellectually, at some level, that there was something odd about that transaction without having been able to feel anything at all. Be that as it may, it was, Watson tells us, "an incident which only explained itself some years later, when I found that Verner was a distant relation of Holmes, and that it was my friend who had really found the money." Once again, Watson had failed to see it coming.

It is significant that whereas the three-year lacuna in Holmes's career in the wake of the Fall is known as the Great Hiatus, no term has been proposed for the much longer lacuna in Watson's career as a writer. The fact remains, however, that Watson's inaccurate account of the events at the Reichenbach Fall, 'The Final Problem', published in 1893, was for many, many years the last words his readers had from him.

When Watson finally managed to fight his way free of the paralysis which gripped him, it was to put the final touches on a project begun long ago, 'The Hound of the Baskervilles', arguably the most popular adventure of them all. This nostalgic look back at the early days of his collaboration with Holmes ran as a serial in the *Strand* from August 1901 to April of the following year. The final instalment of "The Hound" thus appeared in print eleven years after the Fall, and still there was no public acknowledgment of Holmes's survival.

The pressure on Watson must have been severe, from all directions. As Holmes's secretary and general factotum, Watson would have been treated on an almost hourly basis to the sight of desperate people, turning to the risen Holmes with their eyes shining with hope, then turning to Watson in confusion, wondering why he had lied to them.

How did they handle it? Did Holmes say that it would all be in Watson's next adventure? Did Watson say that they would have been equally deceived? Or was it Mrs Hudson's job to impress upon prospective clients the need for tact, the great importance of avoiding any awkward questions? The only thing we know is that the two partners did not under-take to explain the situation. Had they done so, had they agreed together on what to tell and how to tell it, Watson's tale of Holmes's return after the Fall would have appeared in print much sooner than it did.

Setting aside 'The Hound of the Baskervilles', Watson's "Great Hiatus" was to last nearly ten years. Imagine: ten years of silence on the subject which if not nearest to his heart (his life with Mary must have been that) must have been nearest to his lips a dozen times a day. Certainly it was the subject near-est to his integrity.

'The Adventure of the Empty House' did not make its appearance in the *Strand* until October, 1903. Just as Watson finally found the words to tell the story of Holmes's "return from the dead," Holmes retired from active practice, fleeing London for the Sussex Downs and a life devoted to the study of philosophy and a little light bee-farming. The timing was almost exact, as we know from 'The Adventure of the Creeping Man', one of the last cases Holmes ever handled, in September of 1903.

Coincidence? Fear of a sudden, unmanageable rise in the demand for his services? Or something else?

I leave it to you to say.

The End